Praise for Nightingale

★ "This tale of a reluctant orphan forced to play the hero offers numerous feats of derring-do as well as insight into the importance of making and having friends. . . ."

—*Booklist*, **starred review**

"Lark's journey from thief to reluctant hero to champion is a joy to witness. . . . From its unique magic system to its diverse cast of engaging characters, this adventure is a worthwhile read."

—*School Library Journal*

"A solid if unexpected blend of *She-Ra and the Princesses of Power* and story of the birth of labor unions, this novel works well with its unique premise. . . . Kids new to workers' rights and how they function have a great fictionalized example here tied into this 'chosen one' hero story."

—*Bulletin of the Center for Children's Books*

"Fagan's novel is well paced and will hold readers' attention from the get-go. Lark has gumption and, despite her initial reluctance to assume the role and responsibilities thrust upon her, proves the perfect vessel for sympathetic character growth. . . . An entertaining, organic, action-packed combination of adventure, science fiction, and fantasy."

—*Kirkus Reviews*

Also by Deva Fagan

The Mirrorwood
Rival Magic

NIGHTINGALE

DEVA FAGAN

Atheneum Books for Young Readers

New York   London   Toronto   Sydney   New Delhi

ATHENEUM BOOKS FOR YOUNG READERS
An imprint of Simon & Schuster Children's Publishing Division
1230 Avenue of the Americas, New York, New York 10020
This book is a work of fiction. Any references to historical events, real people, or real places are used fictitiously. Other names, characters, places, and events are products of the author's imagination, and any resemblance to actual events or places or persons, living or dead, is entirely coincidental.
Text © 2021 by Deva Fagan
Cover illustration © 2021 by Marion Bordeyne
Cover image of feathers by VikiVector/Essentials Collection/iStock
Cover design by Rebecca Syracuse © 2021 by Simon & Schuster, Inc.
All rights reserved, including the right of reproduction in whole or in part in any form.
ATHENEUM BOOKS FOR YOUNG READERS is a registered trademark of Simon & Schuster, Inc. Atheneum logo is a trademark of Simon & Schuster, Inc.
For information about special discounts for bulk purchases, please contact Simon & Schuster Special Sales at 1-866-506-1949 or business@simonandschuster.com.
The Simon & Schuster Speakers Bureau can bring authors to your live event. For more information or to book an event, contact the Simon & Schuster Speakers Bureau at 1-866-248-3049 or visit our website at www.simonspeakers.com.
Also available in an Atheneum Books for Young Readers hardcover edition
Interior design by Rebecca Syracuse
The text for this book was set in Adobe Caslon Pro.
Manufactured in the United States of America
0322 OFF
First Atheneum Books for Young Readers paperback edition April 2022
2 4 6 8 10 9 7 5 3 1
The Library of Congress has cataloged the hardcover edition as follows:
Names: Fagan, Deva, author.
Title: Nightingale / Deva Fagan.
Description: First edition. | New York : Atheneum Books for Young Readers, [2021] | Audience: Ages 8–12. | Audience: Grades 4–6. | Summary: After twelve-year-old Lark, determined to escape her squalid life, steals a magical sword from the Royal Museum, she reluctantly becomes the next Nightingale, destined to vanquish an ancient evil.
Identifiers: LCCN 2020026200 | ISBN 9781534465787 (hardcover) | ISBN 9781534465763 (pbk) | ISBN 9781534465770 (ebook)
Subjects: CYAC: Magic—Fiction. | Swords—Fiction. | Boardinghouses—Fiction. | Orphans—Fiction. | Fantasy.
Classification: LCC PZ7.F136 Nig 2021 | DDC [Fic]—dc23
LC record available at https://lccn.loc.gov/2020026200

For Charlie

CHAPTER ONE

Maybe it was because my name was Lark, but I had always loved heights. The way everything small fell away, leaving me with the thrill of possibility. Even now, when I was about to do the most dangerous thing I'd ever done.

Perched on the roof of the Royal Museum, I could almost convince myself that the world was full of opportunity. The city of Lamlyle spread in glittering splendor around me like the spangled skirts of a fine lady's gown. Aether lamps sparkled their otherworldly light, tracing the patterns of streets and outlining the dark mystery that was Prospect Park. If I squinted, I could even make out the lights of the great barges on the river. Barges that could carry me away to grand and faraway lands, to find adventure, to be free.

But the truth was, I wasn't free. My debt to Miss Starvenger bound me tight and heavy as iron, and just as unbreakable. If I didn't escape it soon, I'd be trapped forever in a life I hated. A life my mother had died fighting to save me from.

That was why I was here. All I needed was to make this last leap over to the museum's west wing, then drop down to pick the lock on the window. A wiggle inside, and I was golden. Literally. There were enough treasures in the Royal Museum to pay off a thousand debts.

I probably should have felt guilty, but really, all I felt were nerves. Guilt could wait. No, guilt could go stuff it. Guilt was for people who had other options.

I breathed in cool night air dashed with the scent of smoke and sugarcakes from the nightmarket in the next square. The gap before me seemed wider now than it had a few minutes ago. But it was the only way to reach the west wing, to get inside and claim my prize. The great glass dome of the central observatory was too slick, and there was no convenient wisteria vine on which to climb.

Just jump, I told myself. I'd practiced it a dozen times. But my feet remained rooted to the roof.

A quaver of voices sent me hunching down, wary of being spotted by the patrolling watch below. Peering over the edge of the roof, I saw two girls on their way to the nightmarket. Girls like me, from the looks of it. Ragged around the edges, underfed, underloved. As they passed out from under the glow of the lantern, I blinked. Because the light seemed to chase after them. It wrapped around them, a faint luminous gleam that bloomed from their skin, their patched and faded smocks, even the long braids slipping down their spines.

Factory girls. People called the folk who worked in the

aether shops "haunts" for a good reason: they looked like living ghosts. The luminous aether dust seeped into their clothing, their hair, their flesh. Beautiful and terrible. The magical stuff might power marvelous works of artifice, but it was dangerous. Too much of it, and you truly did become a ghost. You couldn't touch things. Couldn't eat. Couldn't speak. Eventually, your body faded completely away.

Not that anyone seemed to care. The factories kept right on hiring, and there were always folk desperate enough for coin to answer.

A swell of fury rose in my chest, ember-hot and useless. If I could, I'd stick Mr. Pinshaw, the factory owner, at one of his own grinding benches to see how he felt after breathing in poison all day. But I was only twelve. An orphan. It took every scrap of my strength just to stay alive and whole. Wishing to do more was like wishing for a star to fall into my pocket. My mother had tried to change things, and she'd died because of it. I wasn't going to make the same mistake.

One of the girls below stumbled, coughing. Soundless gasps shook her frail limbs, nearly bending her double. Her friend tried to reach for her, but her hand slid right through the sickly girl's arm. My own body tensed in useless sympathy. Maybe it was just a momentary flicker. Please, let it just be a flicker.

Finally, the girl straightened, catching her breath. I sagged in relief as they walked on, slipping away like gleams of moonlight lost in the clouds.

That sad scene was my fate if I didn't find the gumption to make this leap and seize fortune by the scruff of its neck. Plenty of Miss Starvenger's other girls were already answering the whistle, trotting down every morning to grind raw aether ore into dust, coming home gleaming and flickering. That was Miss Starvenger's idea of "charity." Take in a clutch of young girls from the orphanage, then squeeze every scrap of copper and silver out of us that she could. Even if it meant sending us to the haunt-shops. We owed it to her, she said, for all the care she'd invested in us.

Not me. *Never.* The factories had killed my mother, but they weren't taking me. Even if I had to risk death and dishonor.

I tugged a bit of black cloth from my pocket and tied the makeshift mask across my eyes. Five paces back along the roof. A turn. My legs coiled tight and strong. I ran, straight toward the edge. Launched myself into the air.

Flew.

My feet slammed into the roof of the western wing. I stood, shaky but victorious, shoulders back, feeling the air fresh and triumphant in my lungs.

I would make my own fate, starting tonight.

I didn't belong here. Everything in the posh halls of the Royal Museum made that utterly clear. No matter how carefully I stepped, my footfalls rang like warning bells through the dim corridors. The displays full of lush velvet robes mocked my threadbare breeches and coat. But none of that was going to stop me. I needed coin, and no one was going to notice a few missing trinkets.

My pulse buzzed with anticipation as I crouched before a glass-fronted cabinet. A bevy of small gold trinkets lay within: a handful of rings, a toothpick, a thimble. Because of course when you already ruled an entire country, you couldn't possibly use a *brass* thimble. Or pick your teeth with slivers of wood like the rest of us.

Then my gaze caught on something even better: a set of silver hair combs shaped like songbirds. Larks! And silver was easier to fence than gold.

I tugged a thin bit of metal from my cuff. The lock didn't look bad. The moonlight filtering down from the skylights above revealed no protective runemarks, either. A moment of careful fiddling and the lock gave a satisfying click. I was about to pull open the doors and claim my prize when a distant scuffing made me freeze.

My breath burned in my chest as I held it, listening.

There it was again. Something, somewhere behind me in the hall with all the swords and armor, also known as my escape route. Wonderful.

I could leave the loot and run for it. I could take off my mask and make up some story about getting lost as the museum closed. If they caught me, I'd only be guilty of trespass.

Given my age, it was likely I'd escape serious punishment.

But if I gave up, this entire escapade was a waste. All the planning. All the time I'd spent watching the guards, plotting my route to the roof. That final, perilous leap.

And, worst of all, if I didn't make my weekly payment to Miss Starvenger, she'd order me to the factories to work off the rest of my debt. Turn me into a haunt, like those girls I'd seen, coughing and fading away.

The silver combs glittered, taunting me. Stuff it, I hadn't come this far to give up now. I snatched them from the shelf and shoved them into my coat pocket, then added the golden thimble and a few other baubles. If I was going to dabble my toes in the water, I might as well jump into the sea.

I crept back past a collection of marble statues, then sidled behind a large display of spears. There was *definitely* someone else in the museum. A cool blue light spilled from somewhere on the far side of the room. A boy was speaking.

And he was blocking my way out.

He stood in front of a low, wide pedestal bearing a single artifact: a sword. His spindly body was bent nearly double, as he traced something—runemarks?—in an oval around the blade.

In spite of myself, I let out a low breath of wonder. I'd never seen someone doing aethercraft. The practice of artifice was rare these days. My housemate Sophie said that, in theory, anyone could do it—it was like cooking, you just needed to follow a recipe. But so many of the cookbooks had been lost during the Dark Days, and now only folks with coin could afford the proper ingredients. Which they only had thanks to folk without coin working themselves into haunts in the factories.

The boy shuffled along the pedestal, still intent on his work. What *was* he doing? Maybe he was a very young museum guard, working late to add new wards on a prize display?

He wasn't *dressed* like a guard. He wore dark blue breeches and a pale linen shirt. There was a matching blue jacket slung onto the shoulder of a nearby suit of armor.

Curiosity tugged at me, but I couldn't afford to linger. What mattered was getting past him unnoticed, to the windows that filled the wall behind him. In particular, the one on the far left, which I had left cracked open after scrambling down from the roof earlier.

His back was to me. It was my best chance. I adjusted my mask to make sure my face was covered. Then I scuttled forward, ducking behind a gruesome display of armored mannequins playing out some ancient battle, complete with splatters of gore.

But the blasted boy must have heard something. He straightened abruptly.

I froze as he searched the shadows, a slight frown on his narrow, pale face. He didn't look much older than I was. Maybe thirteen, at most. And he definitely wasn't a guard, not with that glimmer of gold around his neck, a medallion with an insignia I couldn't make out from this distance.

But the tight set of his shoulders and gleam of sweat on his brow seemed proof enough he wasn't supposed to be here any more than I was. He stared into the shadows near my feet for a few seconds longer before returning to his work. That's right. I was just a breeze. A creaky old floor settling. Nothing to worry about.

I should have made another go for the window then, but the mystery of the boy and the sword gnawed at me, tempting as a fat purse. He'd begun to intone some sort of invocation. I could make out only a few phrases.

". . . nightingale return . . ."

". . . new champion arise . . ."

". . . defend the land . . ."

I thought of all the stories I'd heard of the marvels of the Architect, who first taught the sorcerous craft of artifice. The wonders of the Golden Age, when all of Gallant glittered with enchantment, when diamond-bright airships raced across the sky, aetheric threshers harvested grain so that no one was hungry, and magical devices cured any injury.

My housemate Sophie didn't think it could really have been all that grand, or it wouldn't have fallen apart so easily. You couldn't fix the world with artifice, she said, because no artifice could turn human cruelty to kindness, or greed to generosity. That was why she was so fired up about making new laws to protect workers. She said that was the only way to actually change anything.

And she was probably right. It was foolish for me to linger here. What did I care about some rich boy enchanting a sword? It had nothing to do with me. It wasn't going to change my life. Only the trinkets in my pocket could do that.

Then I saw something that knocked every bit of breath from my chest: a vial of glowing blue liquid. The boy held it in his hand, brandishing it above the sword.

I gaped at it, my chest swelling with wonder. Aether was the most valuable substance in the entire world. A single drop could power a streetlight for days. That was why the factories churned on, eating up desperate folk to crush the poisonous ore into dust, then boil it into stable, harmless liquid aether.

The boy didn't seem to care that he held a king's ransom in one hand. He leaned out and poured the entire bottle's worth over the sword. There was a fierce intensity in his expression. It reminded me of Sophie when she was caught up explaining some bit of philosophy. Whatever he was doing, it was vitally important to him.

I crept forward in between two of the armored figures. I had to see what he was doing. How had a boy—even a rich one—gotten his hands on so much aether? And why? A buzz of excitement rippled over my skin, driving away all sensible thoughts. Hundreds of factory workers had turned themselves into haunts to fill that vial. What was worth such a price?

The gleaming blue liquid ran into a groove along the length of the blade, then into more runes etched into the steel itself. For a moment, the entire weapon seemed to glow, the runes blazing into my eyes, even when I blinked. The light flared, suddenly brighter than noon.

I gasped, jerking back, wary of being spotted.

And caught my pocket on the knee of the armor beside me. Cloth tore. Metal crashed down, an iron fist driving me to the floor and setting a horrendous clatter echoing through the air.

Ears ringing, bones jangling, I struggled to free myself. Finally, I slithered forward, escaping the armor's embrace, only to find the boy staring at me with a mixture of amazement and outrage.

"Who are you? Who sent you?" he demanded. "If you're here to stop me, you're too late!"

I held up my hands as I stepped to the side, putting the pedestal and the sword between us. It had stopped glowing, though its runes still held a faint blue gleam. "I'm not here to stop you. In fact, I'll just be going now, if that's all right with you."

"No," he snapped. "You need to explain yourself. You're not allowed to be here."

"Neither are you!" I spat back.

For one brief moment he looked uncertain. Guilty, even. Then he tossed back his floppy black hair and said, airily, "Of course I'm allowed to be here. It's my museum."

I blinked at him. "Aren't you a little young to be a museum director?"

"I'm the *prince*," he blurted out, sounding irritated. "This is the *Royal* Museum."

I cocked my head, looking him up and down. "You're not the prince."

"Yes I am!"

"Prince Gideon is seventeen. And blond."

"I didn't say I was Gideon," snapped the boy. "I'm Jasper. His younger brother."

"Oh." I squinted, trying to find the resemblance.

To be honest, I'd almost forgotten there *was* a second prince. Heir apparent Gideon was a constant feature in the ephemera-boards, his dashing smile beaming down from the sides of buildings and factories throughout the city. He always seemed to be winning a horse race, or saving a drowning kitten, or attending a charity gala. He'd been only sixteen during the last war, but he'd still managed to lead a small unit of the Bright Brigade to win a key victory over the neighboring country of Saventry. The whole city of Lamlyle was in a swivet over his birthday next week, when he would finally be crowned king.

All I recalled of Jasper was a hazy image from Queen Jessamine's funeral procession. A small, skinny boy blurring into the background.

But the person standing before me now was definitely not blurring away. He was vibrantly, distressingly present, his intent blue eyes taking in every detail of the scene.

He glanced at the floor a few paces away from where I stood. Something glittered there. Silver combs. I stifled a curse, slapping one hand to my pocket, only to find the cloth ragged, hanging empty and torn. Rust that rotting armor!

"Though I hardly need to justify myself to a thief," said Jasper.

Ugh. Why had I let myself get distracted? Now I was deep in the pot and the water was starting to boil. I tried to lift my chin to feign nonchalance under his accusing gaze. "I'm no thief. Those just got knocked out of their displays."

"And, what, you're just wearing that mask because you're shy?"

Oops. I had forgotten about the mask. Rust it. Well, at least he wouldn't be able to recognize me. You know, next time I got invited to tea at the palace.

He held up a glittering palm-size box. "You'd best surrender now."

"Or you're going to throw a snuffbox at me?"

He gritted his teeth. "It's not a snuffbox. It's an aethercom. All I have to do is trigger it and there'll be a dozen soldiers from the Bright Brigade here before you can blink."

I smirked at him, even though my heart was battering my chest. "Why are you skulking alone around here if you're the prince? What are you up to that's so secret?"

A rich flush burned into his pale cheeks at my words. "Nothing that a thief need worry about," he snapped back. "Now are you going to surrender, or do I need to summon the Bright Brigade?"

I drew in a steadying breath. There was no way I was surrendering. And I saw only one source of leverage in the room. So I grabbed for it.

The moment my fingertips closed around the hilt of the sword, everything shifted. A brilliant light fell over me, sharp and bright as diamonds. I heard something like music being played in a room very far away, but so beautiful it made me want to cry. Even the air smelled different, blown in from some faraway meadow full of flowers I had no names for.

A hum ran through me, starting in the hand that held the sword, arcing up my arm and into my chest, then spreading out to every other limb. What was happening? I tried to let go of the weapon, but my fingers only spasmed, clutching it tighter. A voice—or maybe it was several voices, speaking in unison— said, *Greetings, Nightingale*.

Then, suddenly, it was over. The light was gone, the air smelled musty, and I was standing across an empty pedestal from an angry prince, clutching a sword that might have just spoken to me.

CHAPTER TWO

I shook myself, trying to clear the odd, tingling sensation that clung to me. I still had an angry prince to worry about. And he looked more furious than ever.

"Give me that sword!" demanded Jasper. "You don't deserve to even be touching that, thief!"

I'd already started backing up toward the windows.

"I'll give it back if you let me leave," I said. "Put down that aethercom thingy." If he really could summon the Bright Brigade, I couldn't risk just making a run for it. Not when they could chase me down on their flying velocipedes.

The prince gritted his teeth. "You have no idea what you're doing. The fate of all Gallant is at stake!"

"The fate of the entire kingdom depends on you doing some sort of secret aethercraft on an old sword?" I snorted. "*Someone* has a mighty big opinion of himself."

"Have you been watching the ephemera-boards?" Jasper demanded. "We could be at war again any day now."

"Plenty of folk are miserable with or without a war."

Jasper gave a strangled groan. "Of course you don't understand. You're just some guttersnipe."

My breath burst out as the word jabbed into my chest. It was true, but that didn't mean it didn't hurt. "Oh? Really? What I don't understand is why this museum is full of gold and jewels when there are people burning themselves into haunts in the factories just to put a lousy pot of carrot soup on the table for dinner. Why folks in the Scrag have to decide between starvation that will kill them quick, or work that will kill them slow, while the folk in the Cutlet only have to decide whether to wear the mauve taffeta or peacock brocade to the next gala. If you really care about the fate of Gallant, why don't you do something about *that*?"

I finished the speech with a fierce glare, but I was actually rather pleased with myself. I'd remembered most of my housemate Sophie's last tirade against the factories almost word for word, though her delivery had been better. Also, I was pretty sure I'd mispronounced "taffeta."

Jasper gaped at me. Good. I backed up another step toward the windows. I was almost close enough to make a break for it.

"Stop!" Jasper called, starting to move around the pedestal.

"Freeze!" I swung the sword toward him, meaning to ward him off.

And it exploded.

A silvery light burst from the tip of the blade, arcing

out toward the prince. He yelped, diving behind the empty pedestal. Chilly air gusted over my cheeks, the recoil sending me stumbling.

I blinked through a hazy mist to see Prince Jasper, staring at the pedestal between us with a look of mixed awe and horror. It was encased in a shimmering prison of ice. Frozen solid.

"It worked," he said in a hollow voice.

"What worked?"

"The Nightingale," he said. "She answered!" His eyes fixed hungrily on the blade. "I reawakened the sword of the champion!" Then he seemed to remember who he was talking to. "Look," he said, clearly struggling to keep an even tone, "that sword is dangerous. It belongs to the Nightingale."

"The Nightingale?" I repeated dully.

"The hero of Gallant who fought the Crimson Knight?" Jasper drawled. "Maybe you've heard of her?"

"Everyone's heard of the Nightingale," I spat back. "And everyone *also* knows the Nightingale died two hundred years ago when she stopped the knight from destroying the realm."

Because of course she died. That was the price of heroism, even back then.

"Exactly. And she stopped him with that sword. So you need to put it down. You don't have any idea what you're doing."

I stared at the frozen pedestal. A shudder rippled through me. Prince Jasper was right. I didn't want anything to do with a magic sword that might accidentally turn me into an ice cube. "Fine! You can have the stupid thing!"

I tossed the weapon away from me, sending it skittering across the marble floor toward the prince's boots.

An odd feeling gripped me the moment the weapon left my hand. Like I wanted to snatch it back. The empty ping in my chest felt like the first night Mum wasn't there to tuck me into my bed, to tell me stories of the glorious life she had planned for us.

I shook off the useless feeling. This wasn't the time to go all foggy-eyed. I had to make my escape, now, while the prince was distracted!

I hooked a leg up onto the window casement, pushed the glass panel open, and prepared to swing out onto the ledge to make my way back to the roof. I glanced inside to see Jasper bending to reach for the sword where it lay.

The sword twitched. Jasper yelped. The blade shivered, a glitter racing over the etched runes, before it suddenly flew up into the air, racing toward me.

I gasped as the hilt caught me smack in the gut and tore my grip from the casement. I flew backward into the empty dark air.

A shriek ripped from my throat as I fell. I twisted and turned, scrabbling for something, anything to halt my deadly plunge to the ruthless stone pavement far below. My fingers brushed the hilt of the sword, still—somehow—nudging into my chest.

And then, suddenly, I wasn't falling anymore. I was hanging in midair, the sword now clutched tightly in my hand.

My breath caught in a great gulp. My pulse thundered. Carefully, I looked down.

Far, *far* down. My feet floated well above the tops of the aether lamps.

"Wh-what?" I could barely force the word through my lips. A part of me was still falling, still convinced I was about to be cracked open like an egg on the street.

The sword wiggled in my hand. "Are you doing this?" It felt ridiculous to be talking to a sword. But it also felt ridiculous to be floating twenty feet above the street.

"Hey, you! Thief!" Prince Jasper's voice echoed from above. Looking up, I could see him leaning out the window. "Come back! That sword belongs to the Nightingale!"

But the sword, apparently, had other plans. The next moment I was whizzing away, flying across the street toward the Royal Library. I yelped as the weapon gently lowered me onto the rooftop. My feet settled onto solid stone and I sagged in relief, bracing myself against the gargoyle that glowered out from the cornice.

The prince shouted, but I could no longer make out the words. He brandished something that glittered ominously. The aethercom!

I glowered at the sword in my hand. "Look, I appreciate you saving me from a cracked skull, but I can't just steal a magic sword from the prince of the realm! I'm going to leave you here, and he can come get you back. All right?"

I uncurled my fingers from the hilt, trying to place the weapon on the rooftop. But the cursed thing spun back up, waggling at me like a reproachful finger. When I tried to back away, it chased after me, nudging itself into my hand again.

I blew out a breath of frustration. "Fine! Fine, I get it. You want to come with me. But the prince wants you back, and I'm sure he's already got soldiers on the way."

The sword tilted rakishly, its edges glittering.

"No! We're not fighting the Bright Brigade!" They were the best of the best, and specially trained to use artifice in battle. I pinched the bridge of my nose with my sword-free hand, trying to think. "All right, we need to get out of here. We need to get somewhere safe. Can you do that flying trick again?"

In response, the sword zoomed up into the air, taking me with it, but leaving my stomach behind. A strange, wild glee filled my chest as the world filled with glorious possibilities.

"I guess that's a yes!" I called as we sailed off into the night.

The city of Lamlyle wasn't actually shaped like a sheep, but tradition chopped it into pieces as sharply as any butcher's cleaver. Not that everyone used the names. The nobs surely never said they lived in the Cutlet, but that was what it was: a choice cut of serene, tree-shaded avenues crowded with fancy town houses and aether lamps in a glittering diamond rope to light the night. And on a slight rise, overlooking the river Rhee, the brightest gem of all: the palace itself.

On the north bank lay the Shank, home to the markets and guildhalls, and the folk who worked them, solid and dependable. Then the Rump, a bit more run-down, with crumbling brickwork and folk still reputable enough to have a bit of finery for feast days. And, last of all, farthest downriver, bony and abandoned, was the Scrag, home to the poorest of the poor, who couldn't afford to live anywhere but the slums in the shadows of the aether factories.

Folk like me, with nowhere else to go.

"Down there," I told the sword, and it dipped obligingly toward a crumbling brick town house near the middle of the Scrag.

I stumbled as my feet touched the rooftop. If it weren't for the sword hilt smooth and warm in my hand, I might have thought I'd just woken up from a strange and terrifying dream. But it was real. It had happened. I'd stolen a magic sword from the prince. Well, I suppose you could say it had stolen itself. Though I didn't think the prince would see it that way.

I held the sword aloft, frowning into the shimmering surface of the blade. "So what am I supposed to do with you now?"

The sword gave a shiver, sending a faint glimmer of aether-light along its blade, highlighting the metalwork of the hilt. I could see now that the grip was modeled in the shape of a bird; its outstretched wings formed the cross guard, its flared tail the pommel. The head and beak curved out along the base of the blade, glittering with two deep blue sapphire eyes.

I tried to remember what the prince had said, back in the museum. Something about the fate of the kingdom of Gallant, the sword of the champion, and the Nightingale. I'd heard of the Nightingale, of course. She'd been a great hero, back in the time of the Architect, famous for defeating the terrible Crimson Knight. Before the Nightingale stopped him, the artificed metal warrior had murdered the Architect and nearly destroyed Gallant, driven by some unfathomable rage.

And, like all heroes, she'd paid for that victory with her life. Why anyone would choose such a path was beyond me. I certainly knew better.

"If you really are the sword of the Nightingale, I don't know what you're doing tagging after me," I told the blade, gesturing to my mask. "You heard the prince. I'm a gutter-snipe. A thief!"

The sword wiggled its cross guard as if shrugging.

"It's all well and good for you," I said, "but I'm the one who'll end up with her hand chopped off if they catch me."

This time the sword made a slashing motion, as if slicing at unseen enemies.

"Oh? So you mean to take on the entire Bright Brigade? No, I think we'd better find you a place to hide for now."

I glanced around the rooftop. Piles of broken clay filled one corner, the remains of what had once been giant urns and planters back during the Golden Age, when all Lamlyle glittered with artifice and this town house had been home to some rich sods who needed a rooftop garden for their crystal teas. That would have to do.

I slid the sword behind one of the heaps of rubble. "You need to stay here, all right? I'll come back in the morning."

And hopefully by then whatever Prince Jasper had done to the weapon would have worn off. With luck, it would be just a hunk of steel. It would be a risk to fence it, but it was my only chance at redeeming this entire mess. The sword had already cost me my loot, it was only fair it got me something back.

"Good . . . er . . . sword," I said cautiously. The sword gave a twitch but remained where I'd placed it, even as I padded away.

I let out a sigh as I retreated into the stairway that led down into the town house. It had worked. The sword had obeyed me, for now. And I could worry about what to do with it tomorrow. I tore off my mask and shoved it into my remaining pocket, feeling a surge of frustration that I hadn't divided my booty between them. If I had, I'd still have something to show for all tonight's fuss.

I set my feet carefully as I made my way down, pausing every few steps to listen for the sounds of someone stirring below. It was late. Surely Miss Starvenger must be asleep.

The third-floor hallway welcomed me with faded, threadbare carpet and tattered wallpaper covered in sagging posies and sickly-looking violets. The door to the dormitory was cracked open at the far end. Right now my lumpy mattress and thin blanket sounded like paradise. Tomorrow would be a new day. One where I could get things right, finally. I just needed to avoid Miss Starvenger until I had the coin I needed for this week's payment.

My shoes scuffed lightly along the patchy carpet. I hoped Sophie was asleep. I didn't want to deal with all her inevitable questions, and I *especially* didn't want to have to explain the sword. Sophie *loved* laws, and I was pretty sure there was a law somewhere that said you weren't supposed to steal magic swords from princes. If it were anyone else, I wouldn't let it bother me. But Sophie was the one person in the world who still made me wish I were a better person.

I was just reaching for the dormitory doorknob when a voice spoke behind me. "Well, well, Miss Granby. I hope you have a very good reason for breaking curfew."

Icy dread rushed into me. I stood for a moment, bracing myself, then turned to face the voice.

When I first came to the boardinghouse, I thought Miss Starvenger was the most beautiful person I'd ever seen. A roses-and-honey complexion, rich waves of glossy nut-brown hair, eyes like a summer sky. Clothes so lovely and stylish she might have stepped out of one of the colorful fashion plates I used to ogle on the ephemera-boards.

Even now she was wearing a lavender dressing gown, lace running in a creamy cascade down the front and along the wide cuffs. Fluffy violet slippers peeked out from beneath the long skirt. Her hair was loose, spilling in ringlets down her back. But there was a sharp glint in her smile that terrified me. I knew now that beautiful people could hurt you just as easily as plain ones. And Miss Starvenger had the power to wound me worse than any other.

I swallowed, trying to find the words that would save me.

"Perhaps you were securing your next payment?" She checked the watch pinned to her lapel. "It's after midnight. You know what that means." She held out one hand, brows arching expectantly.

"I don't have it," I said, straightening my shoulders, trying my best to look confident and assured. "But I will. Tomorrow. I mean, today."

She sighed. "Dear Lark, do you know how many nights you've spent under my roof?"

"Seven hundred and thirty-seven," I said. Just over two years ago, after my previous placement failed so miserably.

"Indeed," she said. "Seven hundred and thirty-seven days of three square meals, clothing, and lodging."

I had to clamp down on the snort that was trying to leap out of my throat. Miss Starvenger's cook set a miserable table. Sure, there were three meals a day, if you considered watery porridge and dry toast a meal.

"Perhaps you don't realize just how costly it is," she continued, "keeping you and the other girls here. You don't understand the sacrifices I've made in order to teach you children the skills you need to survive in this world."

"Yes," I said, unable to help myself. "It must be terribly hard for you. You do look so dreadfully worn down."

Miss Starvenger's blue eyes sharpened, sensing my sarcasm. Even so, my words must have pricked some doubt. She lifted one hand to pat her hair, then smoothed her dressing gown, glowering at me.

"You owe me a considerable debt, Lark," she said. "I would be doing you a disservice to ignore that. This is not a kind and generous world, and you need to learn to take responsibility for yourself. Now, Mr. Pinshaw was just asking if I had any more likely young ladies who might be able to help out. He has some new royal contracts that involve significant additional—"

"I'm not working in a haunt-shop!" Fear crackled in my words, harsh and sharp. I thought of those girls I'd seen in the street earlier and felt my chest tighten, imagining that gleaming dust drifting into my lungs to fade me away. I remembered my mum's voice. *I'm doing this for you, Lark. I didn't have any other choice. But you will.*

Miss Starvenger's lip curled, as if my fear disgusted her. "In that case, I have no other option but to send you back to the orphanage. But you understand I still need to recoup my losses." Carefully, precisely as a carver boning a fish, she lifted one finger to stroke the gold chain around her neck. It was just enough to make the locket at the end slide out from her lacy collar.

I stared at it, my fear burning into a sharper desperation.

My mother's locket. The only thing in the entire world I had left of her. The locket bound us together, mother and daughter, even when she wasn't there.

That was what she'd told me the night she'd slipped it over my head. There was a meeting of the Aether Workers' Union that night, but I hadn't wanted her to go out. I'd been having nightmares, ever since the big man had banged on our door a few weeks earlier, growling at her to keep her mouth shut. But Mum said she had to go out. It was an important meeting. She and the other workers were going to make Mr. Pinshaw listen, and if he didn't, they were going to go on strike.

He can't run a factory with no workers, she said. *We have power, Lark. Even the smallest of us. And when we put that power together, we can do great things. Everything is going to change.*

She was right about one thing. Everything had changed that night. Because the next morning Mum was gone and all I had left were eight years of memories and that locket.

Which was why seeing it around Starvenger's neck filled my mouth with such a bitter poison. The witch had taken it from me the first day I came to board with her, and I'd spent the last 736 days plotting how to get it back.

I hated this. Hated how small and powerless she made me feel. Hated that she'd taken something I loved and turned it into a weapon to beat me back into the little cage she kept me in. I could feel the bars pinching closer, even now. But I refused to stop fighting. I had to believe I could break them.

"That locket is *mine,*" I said. "It belongs to me."

Her lips twitched. "Dear Lark, don't you understand? You have nothing. You owe everything to me." She jingled the locket. "This trinket isn't worth much, but I suppose I can have it melted down. The gold will cover some of the expenses for your upkeep."

"No!"

Miss Starvenger's eyes narrowed. She knew she had me in her power now, curse her. "Is that all? Haven't I taught you better manners than that, Lark?"

She wanted me to beg. To ask her *nicely* not to destroy the only thing in the world that meant anything to me. My insides cracked at the realization.

Then I saw something that scattered every other thought into a chaotic whirl: something silvery and sharp, slicing through the air from the direction of the stairs to the roof. The sword, aimed right at Miss Starvenger.

CHAPTER THREE

*I*f I didn't do something, the blasted sword was going to murder Miss Starvenger right in front of me. I flung up both hands, crying, "Stop!"

Miss Starvenger blinked. It obviously wasn't the reaction she'd been expecting.

But my command had worked. The sword hung frozen in midair, the sharp point quivering barely a handspan behind Starvenger's unsuspecting shoulders.

"That's not necessary," I said carefully, fighting to keep my voice level.

Miss Starvenger frowned at me, probably trying to make sense of my odd behavior. Behind her, the sword made a similar motion, cross guard rotating in confusion. It gave a wiggle, gesturing toward Starvenger.

"There's no need to destroy her—it, I mean," I said. "We can find some other answer, can't we?"

The sword made a shrugging motion, then gave another hopeful stab toward Starvenger.

Oblivious to the bloodthirsty magical sword behind her, Miss Starvenger pursed her lips, then said, "Very well. What do you have to offer as an alternative?"

"Put it away," I said, glaring past her at the sword, hoping it would get the message. "I'll come back for it when the time is right."

Miss Starvenger sniffed, but did slip the locket back under her collar. Meanwhile the sword gave a sulky sort of wiggle, then retreated, sliding into an old urn filled with decrepit umbrellas that sat in the corner of the hall. The hilt gleamed among the darker handles, but it would do for now.

"So then," Miss Starvenger said sweetly, "I trust this means you're prepared to do your part? You can report with the other girls to Mr. Pinshaw tomorrow at the eight o'clock whistle. If not . . ."

She let the words trail off, arching one delicate brow as she touched her collar again, just where my locket was hidden.

Rust and dross. I was trapped. There was no way out. Panic buzzed in my chest, as if an entire swarm of bees had lodged there, ready to sting.

And then I had the most terrible thought of all.

There *was* a way out. I could let the locket go. Maybe I was a sentimental fool for even caring about it. My heart rattled, loud in my ears, and it felt like the whole world was waiting.

No. Foolish or not, that locket was more than just a bit of gold. It was my connection to Mum; it was my soul. Or as much of it as I had left. And I couldn't let Starvenger take it from me. Not even to escape the factory.

"I'll do it," I said, "I'll go—"

"Will this cover it?" asked a voice behind me.

I spun around to see a short, sturdy girl standing in the hallway just outside the dormitory. Her thin nightgown only reached her knees, revealing the one clubfoot that turned slightly inward. Her hands were on her hips, her chin jutting up. Sophie always looked poised to deliver a speech.

She limped forward, ignoring my agonized look, holding out a small purse that jingled as she dropped it into Starvenger's hand. Rust it, she was going to help me whether I wanted her to or not.

Miss Starvenger hefted the purse, then spilled two silver coins into her palm and sniffed. "I suppose this will do for today's payment. But I will expect the next one on time, Miss Granby. There will be no more indulgences."

She marched away, heading down to the second floor and her own suite of rooms.

I stood for a moment, watching Miss Starvenger until she disappeared down the stairs, before I turned back to Sophie. Wonderful, clever, infuriatingly noble Sophie. A part of me wished I could throw myself at her, hug her tight, thank her for saving me. It was probably what Sophie expected. That was what friends did. And, in spite of everything I'd done, Sophie still thought I was her friend. That I deserved kindness and loyalty.

Really, it was my own fault.

When I arrived at Miss Starvenger's, Sophie had been the first of the other girls to greet me, and honestly, I was horrible to her. Didn't laugh at her jokes, didn't return her smiles, didn't even offer to swap her chore rotations when she was sick with the grippe. Life so far had taught me all too well that caring about anyone or anything was dangerous. Besides, I didn't intend to stay any longer than necessary. I just needed to figure out where Miss Starvenger was keeping my locket, and I'd be gone. I'd make my own way in the world.

I thought I'd struck gold—literally—when I found a padlocked trunk in Miss Starvenger's study. It took me five nights to crack it, and when the heavy iron clasp finally clicked open, I could feel my soul practically lift out of my body on wings. I was going to be free!

Except that my locket wasn't there. There was *nothing* in the trunk except a couple of musty old books. So I took them, figuring I might as well get something for all that effort. I'd been planning to sneak out to pawn them the next day, but Sophie caught me with them in the dormitory before I could manage it. I'd been sure she was going to rat me out, but instead she burst into tears. It turned out the books were hers. The only thing she had left from her father, who had been a poet and philosopher. Desperate to stop her crying, I'd shoved the books into her hands, telling her to keep them.

The books weren't worth much to anyone else, and if I couldn't have my locket back, at least someone might as well be happy. It wasn't like it was a big deal.

But ever since then, Sophie had insisted on acting like my friend. And, fool that I was, I hadn't been able to convince her otherwise. Now look at the mess she was in, all because of me! I wrapped my arms tight around my own midsection to keep myself from doing something ridiculous like hugging her.

"You didn't need to do that!" I hissed. "I could have handled it!"

"How?" she replied, crossing her arms. "By taking a job in an aether factory and turning yourself into a haunt?"

I waved my hands as if I could claw the answer out of thin air. "I would have figured something out."

"Factory whistle blows at eight o'clock. Even *you* can't steal that much silver in seven hours. Besides, you practically look like a haunt already. You need to sleep. Where have you been?"

There she went again, trying to take care of me. Thinking she knew better than me. Which she probably did.

For a moment I wavered. The entire night had been so strange, so unsettling. And Sophie was the smartest person I knew. Maybe she could explain why that blasted sword wouldn't leave me alone. She probably knew a million stories about the Nightingale. But if I told her about the sword, I'd have to tell her about breaking into the museum.

I cringed, already imagining her expression. It would be the same one she'd worn yesterday when she was telling me how the Council of Regents had refused to even meet with the representatives from the Aether Workers' Union. Lips pursed, brows drawn together. A look of pure disappointment.

"It's a long story. Doesn't really matter now." My fingers snarled in the tangles of my windblown hair as I tried to brush back the shaggy mess. "I'm going to pay you back, Sophie. I swear it."

"If it makes you feel better, I can charge interest," she said.

It took me a moment to remember what that was. Sophie had explained it once when she was off on one of her speeches about the banks taking advantage of poor folks. "That's when you pay a part of the money someone lends you back again, extra, on top of the original loan, right? How much do you want?" I asked, eager to settle the details.

Sophie rolled her eyes. "I'm joking, Lark! I'm not the Royal Bank, I'm your friend. I know you'll pay me back. I just want you to be safe."

Just be safe. Just pay her back. No big deal. Except that it *was*. That was why I hated when people did things like this. There was always a price for kindness. Sophie thought she was helping me, but it was only making things worse. Because now I didn't just have to worry about myself. A sickening suspicion began to twist in my belly.

"What about you?" I asked. "That was your emergency stash, wasn't it?"

Sophie was the cleverest of us girls with numbers and money. But even she had to keep up with her weekly boarding fees or she'd be kicked out.

Sophie turned away, heading toward the door to the dormitory. The sick feeling grew stronger. "Sophie? Will you be okay next week?"

"I'll be fine," she said. "You just worry about yourself."

But I couldn't do that. Sophie had given up her savings to keep me out of the factories for another week, and that meant I owed her. I had to find a way to pay her back. If I could find enough coin to pay off my own debts, too, even better. Ugh. If only that blasted Prince Jasper hadn't stuck his enchanted sword in the middle of a perfectly good burglary!

I was about to follow Sophie into the dormitory when a rattle sounded from down the hall. I scowled back in the direction of the umbrella stand. "Stay put! I'll find you in the morning," I hissed to the sword.

The rattling subsided. I continued into the dormitory, shutting the door behind me. The low, narrow room was crammed full with three bunk beds and the single vanity all six of us shared. A slight hush of sleep hummed in the air, punctuated by the deeper drone of our housemate Blythe's snoring.

The window was shuttered, but I didn't need streetlights or moonlight to find my way to the vanity. Not since Blythe and the twins had started working for Mr. Pinshaw. Cora and Nora were only thirteen, so they worked as dusters, collecting the loose aether powder that escaped the worktables. But Blythe was almost fifteen—old enough to be trusted as a grinder, crushing the raw aether rock into powder so it could be mixed with purified water and boiled into its liquid form: the syrupy, glimmering stuff I'd watched the prince pour over the sword earlier.

Back in the days of the Architect, there had been barrels of the stuff, enough to turn Lamlyle into a sparkling masterwork of aethercraft. It wasn't just the aether lamps and ephemera-boards. Artifice had been *everywhere*.

You could still see the signs, if you knew where to look: long-abandoned runemarks etched into the sides of buildings. Copper contraptions hidden away in closets, dull and dusty. There was even an enormous hulk of centuries-old brass moldering away in the middle of Prospect Park, now that the wars and the Dark Days had so reduced the supply of aether.

Of course you could still find plenty of aethercraft in the Cutlet. There was the normal stuff, like aethercraft chandeliers and doors that sprang open at a touch. Fountains that sprayed intricate streams of water lit in all the colors of the rainbow. Aetheric teapots that heated water and brewed your tea perfectly. But there were trickier, wilder contraptions as well. One of my best memories was of a grand exhibition Mum had taken me to in Prospect Park. We'd drunk lemonade and eaten spun sugar, and, best of all, we'd ridden an artificed horse. Mum's arms had held me safe atop its copper back as the creature trotted around the lake, metal flanks shimmering with runes, crystal eyes gleaming blue.

But all of it required aether. And that meant someone had

to mine it, scraping and scrabbling the dregs from the few pits that still had viable veins. Raw aether was noxious, sickening stuff. The entire Scrag stank of it, a sour stench like rotten cabbage that even Miss Starvenger's potpourri—sprinkled liberally around the house—couldn't completely drive away.

It clung to the folk who worked with it too. The luminous dust sifted onto their skin and hair, even with the special smocks and caps they wore to cover their clothing.

In the dim dormitory, the blue glow was hard to miss. The four sleeping figures gleamed with it. Cora and Nora were especially bright. Cora's hand, trailing out from under her blanket, shimmered like a ghost, her light olive skin frosted over with traces of aether dust from her work.

Sophie lingered by the vanity as I washed up. Her dark brows drew together as she watched me, making me feel like I was one of her columns of figures to be summed up. And that, somehow, the numbers weren't tallying.

"How did things go at the *Gazette*?" I whispered. It was always a good question to get Sophie going.

"I caught a mistake in the headline of tomorrow's ephemera-boards," she whispered back, grinning at me in the cracked mirror as I tried to tame my curls for the night. "'Prince Gideon Calls for New Mime Openings.' Can you imagine the letters they'd get if that had gone up?"

I stifled a giggle. "Not to mention all the disappointed mimes showing up at the palace looking for work."

Sophie snorted loud enough that Cora, in the nearest bunk, mumbled and tugged the blanket up over her gleaming head.

"At this rate I won't be surprised if you're running the entire rig a year from now," I added, lowering my voice.

Sophie tapped her chin. "Hmm. No, more likely five. But I mean to be managing editor in three years, by the time I'm fifteen."

As long as I'd known Sophie, she'd been on this path. She knew *exactly* what she wanted, and how to get it. Her first words were probably an essay on the right of toddlers to sufficient chocolate. Not that it was easy—especially not when some folk were foolish enough to look at her twisted foot and her limp and think it meant she was weak. But she knew what she wanted, and I envied her that certainty.

Me, I wanted something that might not even exist. I wanted to feel . . . *free.* To have enough coin that I never needed to worry about the roof over my head or the food on my plate. To escape the constant, gnawing fear that I was always going to be scraping and begging and stealing just to survive. And if I was rich enough, powerful enough, maybe *then* it would be safe for me to be responsible for something other than myself.

I padded over to the empty bunk bed, where I changed quickly into my nightgown. The tattered remains of my right coat pocket taunted me, but the heavier weight on the other side reminded me that I'd snagged something else from the market during the day.

I tugged the packet of waxy paper free, releasing a smoky, fishy scent that made Sophie wrinkle her nose as she crawled into the bottom bunk. "What's that?"

"Nothing," I said, tiptoeing lightly over to the bed beneath Blythe's bunk to slip the packet onto the pillow beside Willow's dark, curly head. She stirred, her breath quickening. One of her hands shifted, clutching the rough wool blanket.

Willow was Blythe's little sister, but her glow was different. Deeper. It lit her from within, so that I could almost make out the outlines of her finger bones, slender and gleaming beneath her light brown skin. She was the youngest of us—only ten. As far as I knew, she'd never worked a day in the aether factories. Blythe had made sure of that, working extra hours to cover board for her little sister. But their mother had been a factory worker too. The dust had touched Willow even before she was born.

It had changed her. She wasn't exactly a haunt. She'd been flickering in and out ever since she was born. Sometimes she'd go for an entire day, unable to eat, unable to speak, half-faded out of the world. So far, she'd always come back. I couldn't imagine what it must be like. For her. For Blythe.

I held my breath until her breathing slowed again, then crept back to my bed. Sophie watched as I climbed up to the upper bunk, slipping into it like a letter into an envelope. Lying flat on my back, I could press my palm to the patchy plaster ceiling above, feeling the spidery cracks in the one spot I always hit when I woke too fast and too suddenly from one of my nightmares.

"Why are you allowed to help Willow but I can't help you?"

Sophie's question floated up from below. I dropped my hand, turning over to curl under my blanket. "Ever since she started feeding those stray cats, they howl like banshees if she forgets them. Makes it hard to sleep."

A shifting creak. Then Sophie's voice again. "Oh. Right. That makes perfect sense."

I couldn't tell if she was being serious or having a go at me. It didn't matter. It made sense to me. People did things for you, and you did things for them. It was fair that way. No one did anything for free. I'd learned that lesson once, and I wasn't fool enough to need it twice.

CHAPTER FOUR

*I*t was three o'clock in the afternoon, and I was feeling desperate. I'd been working the crowds at the market in the Shank since before noon, and I'd still scraped up only a few pennies and a cheese hand pie, which I'd already eaten. The hand pie, not the pennies. At this rate I'd be paying off my debt until I was sixty.

"This is your fault," I hissed over my shoulder.

The sword twitched against my spine. So much for the aether wearing off. The blade was as magical and irritating as ever. Even worse, it had refused to stay hidden back at Miss Starvenger's. The blasted thing was lucky I hadn't shoved it down the incinerator. I didn't need any more trouble, and that was all the sword was right now.

Prince Jasper would surely be searching for it. For me. I shivered, remembering the fierce look in his eyes, just before I'd run off last night. He didn't strike me as the sort of person who gave up easily. But I couldn't pawn the sword while it was still all . . . *alive*-ish and bobbing after me like an eager puppy. And it wasn't like I knew a lot of expert artificers who could tell me how to turn it off.

In the end I'd had no choice but to take the sword with me, slipped down the back of my coat, with my cascade of red curls covering the hilt where it pressed against the nape of my neck, as if my coat were its sheath. So far it had been careful not to slice me, but just having it there was throwing me off.

Picking pockets was an art, one I'd learned from my first placement outside the orphanage. I still had hope back then. I still thought maybe someone would love me, that there were people out there willing to take me in and not ask anything in return.

At first I thought it was just a game—how Mr. Gadding had me try to slip the wallet right from his waistcoat without him noticing. How Mrs. Gadding gave me penny candies if I could sneak up on her and unclasp the bracelet from her wrist. Every purse I lifted, every ribbon I tugged from some rich girl's braid, earned me a smile. I wanted so desperately to be loved again that it didn't matter.

Until the day I made a mistake. I had the perfect mark. A woman, too worn and frazzled from tending her fussy baby to mind me sidling up beside her to slice her pouch. I had it heavy in my hand, was twenty steps from her when she noticed it was gone and started wailing about her lost coin, how she couldn't buy medicine for her sick baby now. And then it was no longer a game. I ran after her, holding out the purse, telling her it must have fallen. She tried to thank me, but I ran away, back to Mr. Gadding. Who had seen everything.

That was when I learned that the Gaddings' smiles had nothing to do with me. All they cared about was gilding their own pockets. I was a tool, nothing more. If I didn't do my job—if I gave in to any scrap of kindness or mercy—well then, I could skip my lunch. And dinner. And spend the night in the dank, windowless basement as punishment.

The Gaddings were loathsome, but I had to give them credit for teaching me how the world really worked. And for giving me the skills I needed to survive in it. That was what I had to focus on now. Surviving.

"Remember what I said," I whispered to the sword, ducking between a tanner's booth and a flower stall, keeping my eyes on my target. His violently green coat made him easy to follow through the crowd. I'd picked him out back at the alehouse, where I'd seen him cuff a delivery boy who was too slow to get out of his way.

Not that I was some sort of noble hero who only stole from nasty folk who deserved it. I'd stolen from folk as miserable as myself. Folk who hadn't done anything except been born poor, unlucky or ill-suited to what society expected of them. The memory of the things I'd done for the Gaddings still festered in my chest, like a bit of rotting cabbage I carried around with me and could never throw away. But these days I preferred to steal from folk who'd shown me they were maggots. Especially rich maggots, like this fellow.

I slowed, idling at the corner of a watchmaker's booth while the man in the green coat peered at the wares. The sword gave a wiggle that might have been warning or excitement.

"You just stay out of it," I told the sword. "Don't try to help. Got it?"

The sword gave a twitch I hoped was agreement. Meanwhile the man in the green coat had moved on to the hatmaker's stall next door, though he seemed more interested in admiring his ruddy reflection in the large mirror than observing the wares. He eventually plucked an emerald top hat from one of the displays and propped it atop his sculpted blond hair.

The hatmaker hastened over. "An excellent choice, sir," she effused. "And a perfect match for that stunning coat."

The man pulled a long face. "I don't know about that. The brim looks a bit uneven. And the ribbon is just a shade too dark." He sighed, adjusting the hat, then turning his head back and forth as he frowned at his reflection. "I suppose it might do for a less distinguished customer, but I'm afraid I expect a bit more."

Pink tinged the hatmaker's light brown cheeks, and by the way her jaw tightened, I could tell she was biting down on her response.

I sidled a step closer. Both of them were distracted now. This was my chance. Fortunately, Mr. Expect-a-Bit-More was wearing his pocket watch in the most ostentatious manner possible, the long chain swinging loose in a sweep of silver.

As the man turned slightly, pointing out another supposed imperfection in the top hat, I made my move. Keeping just out of his line of sight, I caught hold of the chain, giving it the tug that Gadding had taught me. The watch slipped into my palm. One quick twist and I had the clasp loose. My heart tripped over itself, frantic to escape. Slowly, slowly I started to back away, moving so that he wouldn't notice. I was a worm, a bug, something you didn't want to see.

Until the sword quivered, starting to inch up my spine, and I yelped.

The man startled, turning away from the mirror. Before I could lunge away, a hand caught my shoulder, spinning me around. The man loomed over me, yellow mustache quivering.

"What do you think you're doing?" he demanded.

I started to tuck the watch behind me, but his other hand shot out, wrenching my wrist forward. I gasped as pain ripped up my arm.

"N-nothing. You dropped your watch. I was trying to give it back." It had worked with the lady and her sick baby, but the man was clearly not buying it.

"More like trying to make off with it," he sneered. "I should have expected as much. These markets are filthy with rats like you. Won't do a day's honest work and think you can just snatch up someone else's fair earnings. Well, we'll see how you like working in the aether mines. I hear that's where they're sending criminaaahhhh—"

His voice quavered up into a startled shriek as the sword abruptly slid up past my coat's collar and brandished its glittering blade under his florid nose.

He released me at once, pressing himself back against the stall. One of the hat stands toppled with an enormous crash. Both the man and the hatmaker watched me—or rather, the sword—with a mix of amazement and horror.

Other startled exclamations told me they weren't the only ones who noticed the sword. I had to get away! But already the crowds were pressing closer, oglers and gossips starting to call out questions. In the distance, I even heard something that sounded fearfully like the whistle of a royal constable.

I could think of only one way out of this mess. I grabbed for the hilt of the sword. "Get us out of here! Quick!"

Instantly we were sailing upward, above the colorful awnings, above the tops of the lamps, then the buildings themselves. Finally we slowed to a halt and hung there, floating, the brisk breeze whipping my curls, and all Lamlyle laid out below.

My heart pounded, my fingers latched onto the hilt with a grip of iron. It was even more terrifying and exhilarating to do this by day. To be so high, so perilously free and floating. I wasn't hanging from the sword by my own strength, though. Something about its aetheric power must have made me lighter than air. I felt like a cloud.

Except that, once again, my perfectly good crime had been foiled by the sword!

"What was all that?" I demanded.

The sword flashed a bit of sunlight into my face, like a wink.

"Yes, right, you were very helpful getting me out of that mess, but you also got me into it in the first place," I said. "I need gold! Silver! Something to pay Sophie back."

The sword bobbed.

"You understand?" I said warily.

The sword gave no answer. Instead it suddenly swooped us away, toward the marble manors and elegant edifices of the Cutlet.

"Where are we going?" I tried to call out, but the wind stole the words away. It became clear soon enough. The shining tip of the sword veered slightly west, aiming for a building along the riverside that was capped by an enormous gleaming dome.

"The courthouse?" I demanded, my pulse ratcheting up another notch. "Are you going to turn me in?"

What should I do? I couldn't let go of the sword—I was still a hundred feet high, and smashing myself to a pulp was no better than getting arrested. I tried to tug at it, to turn the blade in a different direction, but it held resolute.

I braced myself to let go as soon as it was remotely possible that I could survive the fall without any broken limbs. But instead of taking me to the stern front gates, the sword only flew higher.

It was heading for the dome itself, I realized. More specifically, it was taking me to the very top, where a bright golden figure stood triumphantly, arms outstretched. The statue of Justice held a set of scales in one hand and a sword in the other. She lifted her chin bravely, staring out across the city with empty eyes that nevertheless seemed to watch me as the sword finally let me down onto the small pedestal.

As soon as my feet touched the stone, I let go of the sword. For a moment, I simply breathed. In. Out. In. Out. My insides felt as twisted as an old snarled bit of yarn, and I wasn't sure I could ever untangle them. At least I wasn't going to be arrested. I was high above, looking out over a secret world of rooftops and gargoyles.

The sword, meanwhile, was flitting around like an excited sparrow, pointing its tip at the statue of Justice.

The *golden* statue of Justice.

"You brought me here because I said I needed gold?"

The sword bobbed happily.

"I—well, thanks, I guess. But . . . it's not exactly easy to just carry off a three-ton statue."

The sword angled toward the figure of Justice, then back to me. Then back to the statue. In a single flash of steel, it slashed the hand holding the scales. Something plunked down onto the pedestal.

I picked it up. It was a single golden thumb. I grinned up at the sword. "That's more like it! Well done!"

The sword gave a happy wiggle in response, as I admired

the gleam of the gold in the sunlight. It would surely be enough to pay Sophie back. But that wasn't my only debt.

I glanced around. The dome was high enough that it was doubtful anyone could see us. Even so, I tugged the mask from my pocket—I'd mended the torn one earlier that morning—and tied it over my face. Then I gave the statue a considering look. "Can you take off just a bit more? Then I can pay off everything."

I'd be free. Finally! Free to go where I wanted. To do what I wished. Warm promise filled my chest like sunlight. Maybe having a magic sword following me around wasn't so bad after all.

That was when I noticed the sword arcing back, as if preparing for a mighty blow.

"Not too much!" I cried. "We can always come back if I need—"

Too late! The sword slashed again at Lady Justice. Only this time it wasn't just a thumb that fell away.

The sword cleaved the statue at the ankles. She toppled toward the roof with an enormous crash and started to slide away down the dome. Toward the edge of the roof.

I scrambled after her, dropping the thumb and making a wild grab for one golden foot. It was solid gold, but maybe if I could brace myself, I could slow it down. There were almost certainly people down below. I doubted anyone had noticed me yet, but that would change if a great hulking statue fell over the edge of the building. Or, worse, what if it fell on someone?

But it was sliding too fast. And now, so was I!

Down we both went, faster and faster toward the edge. I screamed, flinging up my hands, scrabbling at the slick marble of the dome. I couldn't stop myself.

Then a smooth hilt slid into my flailing hand. I stopped falling, as the familiar lightness of the sword's touch filled me. I floated up from the dome, spinning around just in time to see the statue of Justice crash into a cornice along the edge of the roof.

And there it hung, poised to topple at any moment. I barely dared to breathe. "We need to get it away from the edge," I hissed. "Before anyone notices us!"

The sword swooped me down toward the edge of the dome. Below, I could hear the hum of activity from the street. The jingle of horses, the rattle of carriage wheels, the jabber of voices. No screams, no alarm. Peering down over the edge, I could see clusters of figures in front of the courthouse. Several young men in stylish coats were standing on the steps, and an older woman rested on the bench directly below me. I let out a small sigh. I could fix this.

"All right, I'm going to grab the statue," I told the sword. "Then you lift us both away. We'll find somewhere safe to leave it." I just hoped the magic of the sword applied to whatever I was touching, or we wouldn't go very far. That statue was *very* heavy.

But before I could reach for the golden Justice, an ominous cracking sound echoed. The cornice, the only thing holding the statue in place, was crumbling away. In a blink, the statue was gone, toppling over the edge.

"Go!" I screamed, squeezing the hilt of the sword. "Down! There's a woman right underneath!"

My body spun; air, color, and sound all rippled over me in a rush. I might have been screaming. Then the old woman was there. I was flying toward her, with something massive and deadly hurtling down at us both. Would I make it?

I had to. I reached out, one arm scooping the woman up, tugging her with me as a terrible crash sounded just behind us.

My feet bumped down against solid stone. I staggered. Blinked. Felt my arms, my legs, all whole and uncrushed. The old woman moaned, stumbling as I helped her sit down on one of the wide marble steps of the courthouse. It was the least I could do, given I'd just nearly smashed her to paste. My stomach spun at the thought.

Dimly I became aware of other voices. Other bodies, pressing close. A clamor of confusion and fear and awe.

Did you see that? She almost got hit by the falling statue!

That masked girl saved her!

That sword!

She flew!

Just like the Nightingale!

Nightingale. My senses crashed back over me. I ducked my head, turning away from the crowd of curious faces. The old woman blinked up at me, her brown eyes sharp and thoughtful.

"Dear me. That could have been very uncomfortable. Thank you, dear. You saved my life."

But I hadn't. I was the one who'd nearly gotten her killed. And myself, too.

I stumbled back, letting go of the sword. It bobbed up, doing a sort of pirouette over my head, then dipping as if bowing to the crowd. They began to cheer.

They shouldn't be cheering me. They thought I was something I wasn't. Something I'd sworn never, ever to be. This was all wrong. I had to get away.

I bolted, diving for a gap in the crowds, pushing past the finely dressed folk and pelting away. I didn't even heed what way I went. All I cared about was escaping.

CHAPTER FIVE

S
o I ended up in the Heap. Fitting, I guess, considering it was a giant junk pile on the outskirts of Lamlyle, filled with useless, abandoned trash. Narrow alleys wove through crumbling brick and metal, past cracked glass baubles and fountains of copper springs, beneath fringes of wire and the arching ribs of fallen airships. I halted under the ruin of a metal sail. The only sound was the clatter of the metal tatters above, shifting in the breeze. These rusting hulks had been picked over by six generations of scavengers. There was nothing left.

This had been one of the brightest and most brilliant districts of Lamlyle, originally. I'd even heard rumors that the Architect himself had built his workshop here. But that had all changed two centuries ago, when the Crimson Knight turned against his creator and began a terrible rampage through the city. It had only been the might of the Nightingale that had stopped him, but their battle had utterly destroyed this entire district. And with the first Saventine war and the Dark Days that followed, there had been no resources to rebuild, so the Heap had ended up as a dumping ground for all sorts of broken or malfunctioning artifice.

Which meant there was no one around to see me scowling at the sword as it bobbed in front of me. If the thing were a dog, it would have been wagging its tail, clearly pleased with itself over the whole affair.

"What was *that*?" I demanded. "We nearly got that woman mashed to bits! 'A little more' doesn't mean slice down *the entire statue*!"

The sword twitched, then nodded its tip at me.

"Yes, we saved her!" I said. "Because we got her in danger in the first place. So you needn't look so pleased with yourself."

The sword dipped, disconsolate. I sighed. "Fine, yes, you did fly very fast. If you hadn't, I'd be in bits too."

I didn't know why I was bothering to make a magic sword feel better. It was just a bit of aethercraft, after all. But seeing the blade bob up happily at my words lifted something in my chest. Everything else had gone wrong, but at least I could still cheer somebody up.

I was about to order the weapon back into hiding when I caught a glimmer up on the trash pile beside us. Strange. Everything here was rusted. Even the copper had mostly turned green with age. There shouldn't be anything *shiny*.

Except there was: a small, round copper trinket, perched up at the prow of an old airship. It winked at me, setting a creeping tingle along my skin, as if I was being watched.

And maybe I was. I'd heard the Bright Brigade had spy-eyes all over the city. Just my luck if I'd stumbled into one. I shivered, backing up into a nearby alley.

"Keep an eye out," I told the sword as it retreated beside me. "Someone might have—ahhh!"

Something sharp stabbed into my spine, making me shriek. I whirled round, expecting to find a row of soldiers in blue uniforms, all of them jabbing aetheric swords at me.

But there was no Bright Brigade. Only the hulking remains of something that might have been either a war machine or a street sweeper, judging by the enormous rollers on the front, bristling with sharp spikes. I'd nearly skewered myself backing into one of them.

I sagged against a nearby bathtub fitted with a spidery attachment of mechanical arms, one still holding a tattered sponge. The sword jiggled worriedly. "It's all right," I said. "I'm panicking over nothing."

But the sword was still jiggling. No. *Pointing.* At something behind me!

I spun to find Prince Jasper standing at the mouth of the alley. Chin lifted, blue eyes blazing, he held something bright and glittering in his hands. Before I could move, before I could even speak, he hurled it at me.

The glimmering wires of whatever he had thrown enveloped me, sending me staggering back. I tried to bat the stuff away, but my arms wouldn't move, and my feet dangled above the ground. The copper web had plastered me up against the street cleaner, trapping me between two of its vicious-looking rollers.

"Let me go, you rusting rotter!" I twisted and tugged against the web, but it held me tight as a miser's purse strings.

"Oh, I will," said Jasper, sounding annoyingly smug. "Once I have my sword back."

He stalked closer, his gaze shifting between me and the sword, which was now quivering in the air beside me. It jabbed toward one of the wires binding my arms.

"No! Don't try to cut—" began Jasper, but the sword had already slashed at the web.

A loud crackle snapped through the air. The blade jolted back as if injured.

"Sword? Are you all right?" I glared at Jasper. "What did you do?"

"Nothing!" he protested, though his cheeks had flushed. Thankfully, the weapon shook itself off after a moment, like a cat that had just been doused with a bucket of cold water. Unhappy, but unharmed. "It's just a confinement matrix," said Jasper. "But the web conducts aether. It might have, er, unexpected effects for anything aetheric." He gave a frustrated shake of his head, addressing the sword. "Just leave her be. You're working for me now."

"No!" I blurted.

"It's not yours, thief," Jasper said. "Just be grateful I didn't bring the Bright Brigade to take you in."

He was right. Why was I so upset?

I'd been trying every trick I knew to slither free of my bindings, but it was as if they could tell what I was doing, tightening and loosening to match my movements. I should just shut up and let him have the sword. It wasn't as if I could stop him.

Jasper took a deep breath, staring intently at the weapon. "Sword, I command you to come to me. I am Prince Jasper, your new Nightingale."

I held my breath, the copper bindings still clamping me tight against the street cleaner. The hollow pinging was back in my chest, which was ridiculous. Of course the sword belonged with Jasper. He was a prince. I was a nobody, and the last thing in the world I wanted was to be any kind of hero.

But nothing happened. The sword simply floated there.

"Are you sure there's not some secret code word you need to use?" I said, after a moment. "I don't think it can hear you."

"Sword," Jasper repeated, more forcefully, "I command you to come to me."

This time the sword jerked from side to side. It could hear the prince. It just wasn't obeying him.

"Maybe you bodged up the ritual," I suggested. "It could just be a normal magic sword now. Maybe it's got nothing to do with the Nightingale." Maybe it might even be willing to stay with me, a nobody thief. But I knew better than to wish for that.

Jasper gave a gargle of frustration. "Or maybe *you* bodged

it up! You weren't supposed to be there. You weren't supposed to touch it!"

"I wouldn't have touched it if you hadn't been shouting at me about the Bright Brigade, you rusting bully," I snapped back.

Jasper tightened his fists, then slowly unclenched them. "It's fine. We can fix this. The sword listens to you. So you command it to come to me. Tell it I'm the one it's supposed to follow now."

I stared at him. Was it that easy? The sword flew closer. So close the blade showed me a slice of my own reflection: freckled pale skin, a gray eye wide with worry. The blue gems in the sword hilt glittered hopefully. Doggedly.

"What are you going to do with it?" I had to at least make sure the weapon was going to be all right. It had saved me, after all.

"Well, I'm not going to use it to chop the courthouse statue in half, for one thing," Jasper said dryly. "Do you have any idea how bad that could have been?"

The sword gave a guilty shiver.

"That's not fair," I said. "It was only trying to help me! And if you're only going to insult it, then you don't deserve to have it back."

Jasper ran a hand back through his hair. "That's not what I—look, that sword is one of the most powerful aetheric artifacts in the world. I'm not going to insult it. I'm going to do everything in my power to ensure it serves its true purpose."

I shot a quick look at the sword where it floated between us. The sensible part of me knew I should stop asking questions. I should just order the sword to serve Jasper and be done with it. But turning away now felt like when Mum was reading me bedtime stories from the *Tales of Violet the Valiant* and stopped just at the most exciting bit.

"What 'true' purpose?" I asked, unable to help myself. "You said it was the Nightingale's weapon. But the Nightingale is dead."

I half expected him to tell me it was none of my business, that I was only a thief from the Scrag. Instead he stared at me with his bright blue eyes for a long moment.

"The Nightingale isn't a single person. There have been at least five, according to the histories I've read. A new Nightingale is chosen by the sword in times of mortal peril to be the champion of Gallant and set to right whatever ills have befallen the land."

I stared at him, my brows lifting. "And you think that should be *you*?"

He shifted his stance defiantly. "Why not? My brother isn't the only one who can defend Gallant. This is my home. And I'm the one who figured out how to wake the sword up. It belongs to me." Jasper crossed his arms. "So go on. Command the sword to come to me and I'll free you. No charges. You can go back to doing . . . well, whatever it is you do."

I swallowed. Maybe he was right. But Jasper's opinion

wasn't the one that mattered to me. "Sword?" I asked haltingly. "What do you want? You know I'm really not cut out for this, right?"

The blade quivered for a moment, then swiveled, jabbing at something on the far side of the junk pile. I had to crane my neck, straining against the copper bindings, but I managed to glimpse a crumbling wall, the remnants of an old structure that had once stood here. Fractured bits of glass hung from the brick, jittery with shifting images and letters in stark black and white. An old ephemera-board! More than half of it was gone, cracked and fallen, but it must still be hooked into the network, judging by the bold headline:

THE NIGHTINGALE RETURNS! RESCUES WOMAN FROM MORTAL PERIL!

I gasped. Prince Jasper sputtered. It was only a short, flickering loop. Someone at the courthouse must have had a facsimilator. They'd caught only a few seconds of the scene, but it was enough.

There I was, swooping down out of the sky, the sword in my hand, to scoop up that old woman just as the falling statue was about to smash her. Over and over the stuttering image played out silently above us as Jasper and I stared wordlessly up at it.

If there was one thing in the whole world that I could

never, ever be, it was a *hero*. I wasn't some sort of starry-eyed do-gooder who was going to change the world. More likely I'd just get myself killed, like Mum. Only fools thought it made any sense to go around helping people for no reason. And I was no fool.

"I'm not," I managed to spit out, finally. "I'm not a hero."

The sword jabbed at the ephemera-board, unmoved by my protests.

"Try harder!" Jasper said urgently. "Command it!"

"I am trying!" I snapped, struggling against my bonds again. "Maybe if you let me go, I can try to talk some sense into—eek!"

A spark had just raced over my skin, following the lines of the copper wires still smooshing me up against the bulk of the cleaner. A moment later something rumbled, deep in the bowels of the ancient device.

"What's going on?" I shouted as a horrible grinding of ancient metal filled the air.

But Jasper was only staring at me in horror. Or rather, at the two enormous, spiky brushes on either side of me as they slowly began to turn. The spikes began to whir faster.

"Is this one of your 'unexpected effects'?" I shouted from my prison between the two churning rollers.

Jasper was backing away, his expression intent. "It's all right. It's a piece of junk. It probably can't even—"

He broke off as the ancient machine started trundling forward, slashing and flashing with deadly promise.

Jasper turned and pelted out of the alley. The coward!

The machine whirred after him, sweeping those fierce rollers from side to side, chopping up bricks, bits of rusted metal, broken glass, anything and everything that littered the ground. Craning my neck, I glimpsed a fine, glimmering powder being sucked up into the cleaner's body. Anything that got caught by those rollers would be ground like a handful of peppercorns.

I was safe, for now, tucked between the rollers, but I had no idea how long that safety would last. The sword zoomed above me, glinting watchfully, but so long as I was trapped in the net, it couldn't reach me. "Let me out of this thing, Jasper!" I shouted. "I can help you!"

"I'm a little busy!" The prince darted and dodged, racing along the twisting alleys of the Heap.

With every twist and turn, the cleaner followed right behind him. "Why won't the fool thing leave me alone?" Jasper shouted. "We're in the middle of a trash pile! Why is it after me?"

"Maybe it's smarter than you think."

The prince flung a poisonous look at me over my shoulder, then dove to the left, scrambling over a mountain of abandoned nose-hair trimmers. "You're not helping!"

"Right. Because *someone* decided it would be a bright idea to strangle me in a magic net."

The cleaner crashed into the trimmers, pulverizing them beneath the jagged spin of the rollers, sweeping away the dust as it chased after Jasper. I ducked my head as bits of detritus spattered over me, slashing tiny cuts along my cheek.

Jasper glanced back again. He had to be getting tired. His cheeks burned red and every breath was a gasp. He was still faster than the cleaner, but only barely. The slightest stumble, a single misstep, and he was going to be ground to bits.

And then he turned the next corner, and I saw what lay ahead. A dead end, choked with the gruesomely disembodied arms and legs of hundreds of metal automatons. He was trapped! There was no more time to waste hoping he'd release me. I had to try to help him.

"Sword," I said. "Go help him!"

The weapon made an anxious loop over my head.

"Please!"

The sword quivered, then arced away toward the prince. A painful hope woke in his face as he reached to seize the weapon's hilt. I tensed, expecting him to fly up, away, out of danger.

But nothing happened.

The sword tugged, but the prince barely moved. The flying magic wasn't working for him! His hopeful look splintered into despair, or maybe something harder and colder, as the cleaner rolled furiously toward him.

Then he reached for something in his pocket. He held the object up, twisting it.

And suddenly I was free. The wires holding me against the cleaner fell limp. I clung to the front of the wild machine to keep myself from tumbling down into the path of the rollers.

The cleaner was barely a dozen feet from Jasper now. The sword glinted at me, circling over the prince's head. There was no time to call it back. If I was going to do something, I had to do it now. Jasper had let me go because I was his last hope to get out of this.

He was counting on me.

Rot and rust, I had to try. Gathering every bit of grit I could, I leaped forward, down from the front of the cleaner and into its path. The moment my feet struck the ground I was running forward, legs pumping, driving, straining to reach Jasper before the cleaner.

"Sword!" I cried, lifting my hand, trusting the weapon to find me as I flung myself at Jasper.

The smooth, cool hilt slapped into my palm. A heartbeat later I seized Jasper, looping my other arm around his. Lightness bubbled through me, turning us both weightless, and then we were soaring up, away, safe, just as the cleaner churned into the bits of copper.

Jasper gripped my arm, clinging to me as he peered down at the terrible sight. He let out a long, ragged moan. Then a breath. Then, "Thank you."

I gritted my teeth. I didn't need thanks. It was Jasper's fault I was even in this mess. And yet the words lodged inside me, somewhere in my chest. They felt warm and bright, like I'd swallowed a star.

But that was just foolishness. It was over and done.

We swooped above the cleaner in a slow arc. The machine seemed confused now, churning into one pile of trash, then another. It might have made me laugh, if the device hadn't just nearly killed us both. "Is it still trying to find us? Is that why it's bumbling around like that?"

Jasper frowned. "I don't know. It should have been programmed to *avoid* people, not go after them. Maybe the runes have been damaged. Or someone tampered with it."

"Is it ever going to stop?"

"It'll run out of power. Eventually."

"Eventually as in a few minutes, or eventually as in a few hours?"

"I'm not sure." He paused. Swallowed. "So you need to stop it."

"Me? Why me? You're the one who set it off with your magic web and 'unexpected effects.'"

"You need to stop it," Jasper said, his voice bittersweet with resolution, "because you're the Nightingale."

CHAPTER SIX

No," I said, my heart galloping, trying to carry me away from the ridiculous notion. "I'm not. You are. You did the ritual."

"But the sword *chose* you. I don't know why. Maybe because you picked it up first. Maybe—" Jasper broke off, shaking his head. "Never mind. The important thing is it listens to you. So you need to use it to stop that cleaner before it gets out into the city proper."

"But I—"

"Look, it's almost at the edge of the Heap. Can you imagine what it'll do in a street full of innocent people?"

I could. And it was a horrible image. I shook my head. "That doesn't mean I'm the one who has to stop it. Call for the Bright Brigade!"

"They won't get here in time. You're the only one who can stop it."

"You don't know that. It might just squish me too! Why

should I risk my neck for Lamlyle? It's not like this city's done anything much for me."

"So that's it, you're just going to let it smash people?" Jasper scoffed. "When you have the power to stop it?"

A burning frustration filled my chest. He was making it sound like I was the villain here. But none of this was my fault! I was just trying to survive. It wasn't like I wanted people to get hurt, but I wasn't going to make the same mistake Mum had. I wasn't going to risk my neck for nothing.

For nothing. Wait. Maybe that was it.

Jasper was a prince. He must have plenty of money. Maybe I could solve both our problems in one go.

"Fine," I said. "I'll stop the cleaner. If you make it worth my time."

Jasper sputtered. "You want me to *pay* you? For being the Nightingale?"

"Not all of us are royalty," I snapped back. "Some of us need to earn our keep."

He made a dubious noise. "Is that what you were doing last night? Because it looked more like stealing to me."

"All the more reason to pay me an honest wage," I said. "You pay the Bright Brigade, don't you?"

"Well, yes, but . . ."

"So you can pay me. What's the problem?"

In the distance, the cleaner had just reached a row of abandoned carriages, the last barrier between it and the gate that led back into the city proper. In minutes it would be out on the streets.

"Fine," Jasper muttered. "I'll pay you. Now will you go stop that thing before it hurts someone?"

I grinned at him. "Of course. One Nightingale-for-hire, at your service. What do you think, should I slash it up?"

The sword quivered eagerly, flying us faster toward the machine as it continued its rampage at the edge of the Heap.

"Only if you want to turn all those knives and spikes into a giant cloud of death," said Jasper. "If you hit the motivating rune, the whole thing will probably explode. It's possible your third power might be invulnerability, like the first Nightingale, but I don't think we should test that hypothesis right now."

"Third power?"

"All the Nightingales have three powers. Obviously you can fly, and—*Oh!* That's it!" He brightened. "You summoned a freezing bolt last night! Try that again. If you can ice up the rollers long enough, I can reach the motivator and shut it off."

I gave the prince a sidelong glance. "You know how to do that?"

"I know a lot of things," he said, with a trace of wounded pride. "Even if I'm not the Nightingale."

I shrugged. I didn't see why he cared so much about being the Nightingale. He was already a prince, after all. But, so long as he paid me, I didn't need to understand him. I just needed to do this job. This very scary, potentially deadly job. What if the freezing bolt didn't work? How painful would it be to get caught in those slicers?

I swallowed, shoving down the useless thought. "Sword, get us closer."

The weapon swooped, setting us down onto the top of one of the carriages directly in the path of the cleaner. I let go of Jasper and took hold of the sword with both hands, aiming the tip at the cleaner.

Nothing happened.

"Any time now," said Jasper.

"Go on, Sword!" I said, wiggling it. "Ice it!"

Still nothing. Only the ravenous rollers, churning closer and closer.

"You did it last night," Jasper said. "You must have done something. Said something to trigger it?"

I shook my head. A fog of panic rolled over me, stealing my breath, making my chest tight. All I could see was the wall of spinning knives, coming closer and closer. And the glint of the blue gems, winking at me from the hilt of the sword. *Think*, Lark. What had I done last night? The prince had been coming at me, and I grabbed the sword and held it up and cried:

"Freeze!"

A stream of silvery light burst from the tip of the sword, slamming into the cleaner, shimmering over the rollers in a flurry of sparkling, glimmering ice. With a shuddering protest, the cleaner halted. But an ominous grinding from inside told me it was only a matter of time before it broke free.

Jasper wasted no time, darting forward to begin prying at something directly above one of the frozen rollers. "I've got to get inside!"

But the panel wasn't budging. And the ice was already beginning to melt, dripping from the hedge of deadly blades.

I ran to Jasper's side. "Stand back!" I hefted the sword, then slashed down at the bolts. Metal flew. The panel dropped away. Chunks of ice had begun to break free from the rollers. "Hurry!" I cried, as the blades shivered, starting to slowly, slowly creak into motion.

Jasper flung himself at the opening, reaching into the bowels of the machine, lips pressed tight, brows furrowed. "If I can just rework the main motivating rune and turn off the—aha!"

The horrible grinding drone stopped. The rollers gave one last faint hum, their spikes shivering to a stop an inch from Jasper's head.

Then the great metal hulk fell silent. Sleeping again.

"We did it!" I cried, stabbing the sword into the air in triumph, then gasping as the blade carried me up into a stomach-churning celebratory loop-the-loop. Even once it set me back down, I felt light. As if there were clouds under my feet. We'd done it. We'd stopped the cleaner!

I turned to Jasper and found him grinning back at me, though there was a wistful look in his blue eyes. "Good job, Nightingale."

Common sense caught up with me, dragging me back into the world where I had debts and couldn't, wouldn't trust anyone.

I stuck my hand out, palm up. "We'll see how good." I nodded at him. "Pay up."

His expression hardened. He patted his velvet coat, feeling in his pockets, then drew something out. He pressed it into my hand. "There," he said stiffly.

I stared at the two silver coins resting on my palm. "Two silvers? For nearly getting smashed to a pulp? That's it?"

"It's all I have right now," said Jasper, his voice chilly.

I shoved the coins into my pocket. It was better than nothing. I could pay Sophie back now. And a few more jobs would set things to rights with Miss Starvenger. Maybe I could even get Mum's locket back. That was the important part. Not whether some prince smiled at me. Let Jasper judge me. I didn't care. He couldn't possibly understand what my life was like.

"Oh, and you'd better take this." Jasper dug something out of the pocket of his coat and began fiddling with it. It looked like the magical snuffbox he'd brandished at me last night, except that now he'd opened it to reveal a mess of wires and gleaming crystal beads inside.

"That's what you were going to use to call the Bright Brigade," I said. "You called it an . . . aethercom?"

"Right. This one will let me send you messages, once I—" He grimaced, giving one of the wires a firm twist. "There! Now, when I have more work for you, this gem on the front will light up. I'm working on a way to have it transmit voices, but that's, er, not quite functional yet. But I did manage to rig it so the color will change. Green for normal missions, red for deadly emergencies. Either way, when you see it light up, come meet me on the roof of the Royal Museum. You can do that, right?" He held it out to me, clearly proud of his work.

I stared at the thing. It was like the bells the folk in the Cutlet used to summon their servants. Was that how he saw me now?

Jasper's enthusiasm faltered. "I know the crafting's a bit clunky—I should have done a better job welding the seam— but it'll work. I swear."

A twinge caught my chest. He had no idea why the aether-com irked me. He just wanted my approval. But he was a prince. He probably had a whole troop of retainers to tell him how wonderful he was. It wasn't *my* job to puff him up.

I took it. "What sort of missions? You said the Nightingale sets things to rights and defends the land. Who am I defending it from? Saventry?"

They were our greatest enemy, if you believed the ephemera-boards. A land ruled by mage-lords born with mysterious magical powers, who believed aethercraft was an unnatural abomination and had already made war on Gallant three times because of it. Jasper's mum, Queen Jessamine, had managed to negotiate a peace settlement to end the last war two years ago, but a lot of folks thought it was only a matter of time before another conflict broke out now that she was dead.

"I'm not sure," said Jasper. "Gideon's going to be crowned king at the end of the week, when he turns eighteen. He's convinced the Saventines are going to make a move against us.

And there have been strange things happening at some of the aether mines. Shipments going missing. Accidents."

"So you think the Savs are trying to bodge up our aethercraft."

"That's what you're going to find out. We need those mines. We need those factories. Our aethercraft is the only thing we have that gives us any hope of standing against Saventry if they decide to attack."

"What about the workers?" I asked. "Has anyone been hurt?"

"Minor injuries only. So far."

And I could keep it from getting worse. But this was exactly the sort of thing I'd sworn never to get involved with after Mum died.

It was also exactly the sort of thing *she* would have signed up for, no question. I couldn't help but feel like I'd be disappointing her if I turned away. And then there was the money. It was hard to say no to the prospect of a steady source of coin. Besides, I could always quit once I'd earned what I needed. It wasn't like I was promising to be the Nightingale forever.

Fine. I forced a reckless smile onto my lips. "I'll be there. So long as you've got coin, I'm your Nightingale."

First, though, I had a debt to pay.

By the time I got back to Miss Starvenger's, it was nearly

dinnertime. Which meant Sophie should have been in the dormitory, scrubbing the ephemera ink from her fingers so that Miss Starvenger wouldn't dock her supper for uncleanliness. But when I poked my head into the room, the only one there was Blythe, standing at the vanity and fussing with her long black hair. She'd recently taken to wearing it up, even though she was only fourteen. I stifled a groan as she caught sight of me, a frown creasing her forehead. As long as I'd known Blythe, she'd yearned to join the Bright Brigade. She was still too young to enlist as a cadet, but I knew she was saving every scrap of coin she could to pay the substantial fees for the entrance exam and uniform. And she loved to practice "military discipline."

Unfortunately, a lot of the time that just meant bossing the rest of us around.

"You're not planning to go to dinner like *that*, are you, Lark?"

For a moment I was afraid I'd forgotten to take off my mask. I ran a hand over my face but felt only bare skin. "Like what?"

Blythe sighed. "Like you got dressed in a rag bin." She pointed to my coat pocket, the one I'd mended that morning. "Take that off. Let me fix it."

I jerked back. The sword was still hiding along my spine. If I took off my coat, she'd see it. It was one thing to play the Nightingale for Jasper—that was just a job, and it needed to stay as far away from my real life as possible. Heroes were targets. Heroes got hurt. And so did the people around them. It was better for everyone if I stayed just plain Lark.

"I already fixed it," I told Blythe.

"Those stitches are lumpier than our morning porridge. Come on, Lark. Don't be pigheaded. It'll take me three winks."

"I need to go," I said, taking another step back, trying to close the door. "I have to find Sophie."

Blythe sighed expressively. "Why can't you just follow Miss Starvenger's rules, Lark? The rest of us do."

"You said it yourself," I snapped back. "I'm a pig, not a niminy-piminy sheep."

She flinched. So did I, as the sword, hidden along my spine, rapped its pommel lightly against the back of my skull.

But any twinge of guilt melted away as Blythe crossed her arms, scowling at me. "She's going to be cross with all of us if you make her mad."

"That's not my problem." I shut the door between us before she could say anything else.

I tried to set off down the hall but found that I couldn't move. The sword refused to budge, pinning me in place by the door.

"What?" I whispered furiously. "I can't take off my coat! She would have seen you."

The ridiculous blade only nudged me back toward the door.

"I am *not* apologizing," I told it. "Blythe only worries about not getting in trouble with Miss Starvenger. She doesn't actually care what I think of her." I shoved back just as the sword relented, and nearly spilled myself onto the carpet.

The door opened. Blythe poked her head out. "Sophie's in the basement. You're welcome." Then she snapped it closed again.

"See," I said. "She's fine. Now, are you going to let me go find Sophie, or do you want to wait in the umbrella stand?"

The sword subsided sulkily, but made no move to stop me as I headed back along the hall toward the stairs.

The basement was one of the few places in the boarding-house that Miss Starvenger didn't go, which meant the other girls used it as a sort of escape during the hours between work and chores and sleep. Sophie told me once that she thought Miss Starvenger was afraid of small, dark spaces, and it was true the basement was both those things. The low ceiling was cluttered with old copper pipes that had once flowed with aetheric power, back in the Golden Age when there was no Scrag, no slums, when all Gallant was filled with glory and magic.

I padded past the small nook decorated with Nora's sketches and the couch where Cora liked to sit and dream up new pranks to spite Starvenger, then through the laundry room, where Blythe had hung up a pair of trousers and a threadbare shirt stuffed with rags to serve as a makeshift fighting dummy. None of the artificed lamps were lit, since of course Miss Starvenger would never spare any aether for them. But the flicker of candlelight told me someone was here, back in the farthest chamber.

Sophie had made a den there, filled with musty old proofs

of the *Gallant Gazette* that she'd adopted from the office before they could be burned as trash. Normally, the space was dominated by a desk jury-rigged out of two cracked urns and an old wooden door. But now that had been pushed to one side, leaving the center of the room for . . .

"What's *that*?" I squinted at the collection of tubes and metal plates. It looked a bit like one of the waffle irons I'd seen in a fancy tea shop once, except about five times bigger.

Sophie yelped, jerking up from her hunched position. A handful of small bits went tumbling to the ground.

"Sorry," I said. "I didn't mean to startle you."

She groaned. "No, it's fine. It's not like I was getting anywhere."

I crouched down to help her collect the bits. They were all different sizes, some as tiny as the tip of my pinkie, others the size of my thumb. Each was inscribed with what looked like a letter or a number, except they were reversed, like looking in a mirror.

"It's an old ephemera press," said Sophie. "Can you believe it was only *three coppers* at the pawnshop?"

Honestly, I was surprised the shopkeeper hadn't paid her to take it away. The thing looked like it belonged in the Heap. But Sophie was beaming over it, the happiest I'd seen her in months.

I tried to smile, for her sake. "It, er, sure has a lot of pieces."

There was an entire box full of tiny backward letters. I ran my fingers through them, and they tinkled with a faint music.

"But why do you need an ephemera press?" I asked. "Don't they have one at the *Gazette*?"

Sophie scrunched her lips. "Yes. But Miss Parsival absolutely refuses to run any of my articles about the aether industry."

"Why not?"

"She says it's stirring the pot, and she doesn't want to get burned." Sophie scooped the fallen bits of type back into the box with vigorous energy. "But someone *needs* to stir the pot! The pot's poisoned! We can't just keep letting people eat out of it!"

"So what are you going to do?"

"Publish my own circular. I just need to work out how to link it into the ephemera network. The connection rune is all worn away."

"Without permission? Won't you get in trouble?"

"At least I'll be publishing something useful. Something factual! Did you see that nonsense all over the boards this afternoon?"

"Er, what nonsense?"

"Some foolishness about the Nightingale returning. But you could barely see the person. A blur in a mask isn't a legitimate news story!" She sniffed. "More likely it was freshers from the university pulling a prank."

I bristled. Sure, I might only be a Nightingale-for-hire, not a real hero, but that didn't mean I had no pride. "I thought the Nightingale was very dashing, saving that woman." The sword rapped the back of my head. "And that sword was brilliant. The way it flew so fast!" I added hastily.

Sophie waved a dismissive hand. "It's all just a distraction. That's why I need to get the truth out there, Lark. It's getting worse and worse. More people have ghosted in the last three months than in all of last year combined! And even more folk are flickering. We don't need the Nightingale. We need unions. And laws to protect our workers!"

She looked so fierce, so brave. So like Mum. It set a guilty twist in my belly. That was what the Nightingale *should* look like. Yet at the same time, a part of me was proud, just to see her like this. It made no sense. Why would I feel proud because of something Sophie was doing? I hadn't done anything. In fact, I'd made it worse. But it was time to make up for that.

I dug the two silver coins from my pocket and held them out to Sophie. "Here," I said. "I know it should be more, because of that interest thing, but I'll get you the rest soon."

She didn't take them. Her brows pulled together, and she bit her lip. "You should save it. You need it for next week."

"I'll get more for next week."

"How?" she asked. "How will you get more silver without a job?"

A lump formed in my throat. "You think I stole it."

She said nothing, her dark eyes pinning me.

"I didn't steal it," I said. "Not that it matters. Money is money. It's not like the constables are going to come after you."

"No, but they might come after *you*," she said. "Lark, it's bad enough here at the boardinghouse. You don't want to get sent to the mines. They're even more dangerous than the factories, especially lately! Did you know just last week the mine up in Fitchton lost five people because of a cave-in? They said the tunnel was perfectly safe, and then *pff*, it went just like that!"

"I'm not getting caught, because I'm not stealing," I insisted. "I—I have a job."

She still looked dubious. "Doing what? Lark, please tell me you didn't go to Mr. Pinshaw. It's bad enough Starvenger has Blythe and the twins trotting to his whistle."

"I'm not working at a haunt-shop," I said. "I swear."

"Then what?"

"I'm"—I scrambled for something believable—"running errands. For this nob in the Cutlet."

"Who? What's his name?"

"He doesn't want me to say. He's got . . . enemies."

Sophie narrowed her eyes. "You really think I'm just going to believe you stumbled into a job working for some mysterious noble?"

Of course she didn't believe me. Sophie was too clever for my lies. "Fine," I said, giving a helpless gesture. "You want the truth? I'm the new Nightingale. Prince Jasper gave me that money to convince me to help him keep Gallant safe."

Sophie rolled her eyes. "Your first story was better," she

said. She reached out, plucking one of the coins from my palm. "There."

"But I owe you two."

"Yes," she said. "But I was saving a silver to buy Blythe a birthday present. Now you can do that, and I'll have more time to work on this." She gestured to the printing press. "Just don't buy some gaudy trinket. Make sure it's something she'll really love."

I grimaced.

"What?" Sophie teased. "You're a professional errand runner now, aren't you? I'm sure you can fit it in tomorrow, between your other jobs. Just be sure you're back here by five."

"What's at five?"

"We're going to have a party while Miss Starvenger's at her ladies' tea. Nora's baking a cake, and Cora got lemons for lemonade. I promise you'll have fun. What, why are you looking like that?"

"I don't know if Blythe would want me there."

"Why not? You're one of us."

I winced. "Well, I might have just insulted her."

"How?"

"Er. I called her a niminy-piminy sheep."

Sophie sniffed. "Well then, I guess you'd better make it a really *excellent* present."

CHAPTER SEVEN

You wouldn't think it'd be hard to spend a silver. I'd whiled away plenty of dull and hungry hours imagining what I'd buy if I had coin to spare. A coat of fine velvet, soft as a kitten and blue as the twilight sky. A crystal hallowglass, artificed to show you glimpses of your own future.

But coats could be stolen. Crystals broken. That was just the way the world was.

All in all, sweets were the only safe bet.

Which was how I ended up in front of Madame Choux's Delights, trying not to drool as I stared at the confections displayed in the window. "What do you think?" I whispered to the sword, hiding in its usual place along my spine.

The sword twisted, nudging me away from the bakery and toward the dry-goods shop next door. "What's wrong with sweets?" I muttered. "Everyone likes sweets!"

A flutter of voices and laughter swept past just then. A gaggle of girls a few years older than me were on their way into the dry-goods shop.

They were all dressed alike: pale gray breeches, tall black boots, and blue coats. Each of them wore a smart blue cap decorated with a single silver star, except for one brown-skinned girl with her hair twisted into dozens of black braids, who was bareheaded.

They must be cadets from the Bright Academy. And as they strode past me, laughing and smiling and carefree, I understood exactly why Blythe was so eager to be one of them. They looked powerful, happy, confident. Free.

And if they were going into Pennywhistle's Dry Goods, then so was I.

I slid inside just as the door was closing, trying to stick close enough to the girls that I could tell which wares they fancied. A hum of excitement rippled through me.

"I'll get Blythe something a cadet needs," I whispered to the sword. "I should have thought of it sooner! It's brilliant!"

The sword bumped my shoulders.

"Oh fine, yes, it was *your* brilliant idea. But we're a team now, right?"

I lurked behind a display of woolen socks, watching as the cadets lined up along the counter, where a pale-skinned shop-keeper with a neat gray mustache had come forward to greet them.

"Ah, Miss Stella, you need another cap already?" He tutted at her.

The girl with the braids made a helpless gesture. "Sacrificed to the greater glory of my graduation trials, Mr. Pennywhistle.

But it perished valiantly in battle with a particularly vicious rumbleback that wanted my head very badly."

The cadets continued to chatter among themselves. I wasn't paying close attention, too busy trying to squint at the price tag on the blue cap Mr. Pennywhistle was fetching down from a shelf.

But a single word jerked me back.

"—the Nightingale, can you imagine?" said a blond cadet.

"Really Pris," said another, "you can't believe every bit of nonsense you read on the ephemera-boards. You know they say all sorts of ridiculous things just to get people to pay attention to the advertisements."

"No, it's true!" protested Pris. "They interviewed the woman the Nightingale saved! She *flew*. Actually flew down and scooped her out of the way!"

The chime of the register broke off their conversation. Stella had finished her purchase and now set the new blue cap atop her braids, tilting it to a jaunty angle. "All right, girls. Let's go celebrate and revivify!"

"Should we go to Madame Choux's?" suggested someone.

"No, this is a special occasion! We need somewhere that's really marvelrageous to celebrate our last week as cadets!"

"Oh, I know!" gushed Pris. "That new soda fountain, Dashlilly's, over on Quixby Street. They've got a hundred different soda flavors, only a copper each."

There was a general round of cheers and whoops as the entire pack set off into the streets, leaving me alone in the shop.

I'd tried to make myself presentable, braiding down my red curls, scrubbing my face. It didn't matter. Mr. Pennywhistle was still watching me as if I were going to snatch a bundle of handkerchiefs and run. I strode to the counter. I had silver in my pocket. That made me a customer. I had every right to be here.

"I'll take one of those caps," I said.

His brows arched. Turning, he started to fetch down a plain brown hat.

"No, one of the blue ones."

He hesitated, looking back at me. "The blue, miss? They're for cadets, you know."

"I know," I said, rubbing the silver coin between my fingers as he set the blue cap on the counter. My heart gave an eager bob. It was perfect. It even had the star pin winking above the brim. Blythe would love it.

"That'll be two silvers," said Mr. Pennywhistle, his voice utterly bland, even as his brows arched again.

The light feeling plummeted. My fingers tightened on my single silver coin. Of course. It was too much. Everything was always just out of my reach.

"Oh," I managed. "I—let me think about it."

The doorbell jingled, and Mr. Pennywhistle stepped away to check on the new customer. The sword nudged me toward the counter.

"What?" I whispered. "You want me to *steal* it?" To be sure, Mr. Pennywhistle was distracted by the new patron, a large man with deep brown skin who appeared to be after a particular shade of mauve handkerchief. "Sophie would never forgive me," I said urgently. "And besides, I'm supposed to be the Nightingale now, aren't I?"

The sword, however, clearly had a plan. The weapon zipped out of my coat to float above the counter.

"Stop that!" I whispered. "What if he sees you?"

The weapon slashed at the crown of the cadet hat. I gasped, clapping a hand to my mouth, horrified. The sword, apparently satisfied, slid back along my spine.

I let out a long breath of relief. The cap wasn't damaged. The sword hadn't cut the wool, it had only pried off the star pin.

Mr. Pennywhistle returned a moment later, cocking his head at the sight.

"How much for just the cap?" I asked. "Without the pin?"

He rubbed at his mustache, blinking. "Er, well that's highly irregular, but . . . I suppose I could let the hat alone go for one silver."

I slapped the coin onto the counter. "Done."

A minute later I was walking back out of the shop carrying a lovely pale green hatbox containing the blue cap, minus its star. The bells had just begun to ring the half hour. Perfect. Just enough time to get back to the boardinghouse by five.

"Good work, partner," I whispered over my shoulder.

The sword thumped my back, almost like a pat. I swung the hatbox by its ribbon, feeling the heft of it. I could already imagine the look in Blythe's brown eyes when she opened it. The thought made me feel like I'd drunk fizzy soda water. Sweet and bubbly. Maybe a party with the other girls wouldn't be too uncomfor—

Something in my pocket hummed.

I ducked around the corner, into the smaller alley alongside the dry-goods shop, and dug out Jasper's aethercom. It buzzed again, warm in my palm. The gem set into the bronze surface gleamed at me with a crimson light.

What had the prince said when he gave it to me?

Normal missions will be green.

If there's a deadly emergency, it turns red.

A feeling rippled through my chest. I wasn't sure if it was a chill or a thrill.

The sword, on the other hand, made its feelings perfectly clear, hovering excitedly before me and glinting rakishly.

Maybe it was a thrill. I'd never admit it to Jasper, but I actually sort of enjoyed stopping that street cleaner. After years of feeling helpless, like I had to wring every tiny bit of good fortune out of the wet rag of my life, it was nice to have the power to *do* something.

The hatbox hung from my arm, reminding me of my promise to Sophie. But surely this was more important? Maybe I could sort whatever the trouble was in time to make it back for Blythe's party. There was no time to drop off the gift. I felt an uncomfortable twist in my stomach thinking of Sophie waiting for me. Wondering where I was.

I'd bring the gift, one way or another. It wouldn't matter if Blythe got it a little late. Not when Saventine spies might be trying to blow something up. And of course it didn't matter to *me* if I missed the party. Sure, lemonade and cake would be swell. But what did you *do* at a party? I'd never been to one. What if I said the wrong thing? Or didn't know how to play the games?

I opened my eyes and slung the hatbox over my shoulder. Fortunately, I'd taken along my mask. No sense wasting a chance to earn more coin if it came up. I tied it over my face, then braced myself and grabbed the sword's hilt.

"Right. Let's go do our job."

I thumped down onto the roof of the Royal Museum a few very windy and wild minutes later, my heart still racing from the flight and the promise of my first official mission as the Nightingale.

Jasper came forward to meet me, a small notebook tucked under one arm and a fierce glower on his narrow face. "There you are. We need to get to the Wynchcomb Mine right away."

"Is it under attack?"

"No. But the miners are refusing to enter the mine because they say there's a monster in it."

"So, nothing's on fire? No one's about to die?"

"Well, no," Jasper admitted.

"Then how is this a deadly emergency?" I brandished the hatbox. "I do have a life, you know. I can't just drop everything and come running every time you want to go chase after some harebrained notion."

"It's not harebrained," Jasper protested, standing straighter. "What if there really is something in that mine?"

The bells were ringing again. Five o'clock. Sophie would be wondering where I was. But it was better this way, better not to get all caught up in the festivities. And I'd already made my decision. Even if Jasper and I had different definitions of "deadly emergency."

"All right," I said. "I guess we'd better check it out."

I landed us where Jasper directed, behind a scruffy stand of brush not far from a cluster of long, low buildings with flimsy walls and tar-paper roofs. We were on the very outskirts of Lamlyle, up on the southern heights. Looking back, I could see the golden wink of the clock tower reflecting the lowering sun. It was a quarter past five now. I wondered if the other girls had already started the party. Was Sophie upset? Probably.

Never mind. I'd made my choice, so I might as well stop mooning and get to work. There were more important things than cake and lemonade and party games. I'd made it this far in life without them, after all.

But as I started to move out from the bushes, Jasper caught my elbow. "Wait!"

"I thought we were in a hurry," I said. "Now what?"

"You can't just walk around like that. What if someone sees you?"

"They'll see the Nightingale," I said. "A girl in a mask with a sword." And a hatbox, but he hadn't given me much choice about that.

Jasper looked me up and down. He cleared his throat. "Don't you have anything a little more . . . heroic?"

"Oh, sorry," I said acidly. "My armor's at the shop getting polished."

For a moment he looked hopeful. "You have armor?"

"No! I'm a twelve-year-old orphan from the Scrag. Why would I have armor?"

He pinched his brows together, considering me. "All right. I'll see what I can come up with. But for now, you really need something more than that old thing." He gestured to my patched and faded but perfectly wearable coat.

"Ah!" he said, after a moment in which I debated using the sword to freeze his tongue before he could say anything more insulting. He untied a bit of ruffled silky cloth from around his collar, then held it out.

"You really think *that's* going to make a difference?"

"Well, not like this, but look. It's my prototype convertible ascot rain cloak. All you have to do is . . ." He flicked the cloth, and suddenly the handful had doubled, tripled, quadrupled in size, spilling out into a long, dark pool of fabric that shimmered faintly in the deepening dusk. I stared, confounded by wonder.

"Is it some sort of artifice?" I asked, after I finally found my tongue.

"Yes. The runes along the neckline control the density. You just give it a little twist to shrink it back down when you need to." He flicked it again, and the cloth abruptly fluttered back to neckerchief size. "Go on, try."

I took the ascot uncertainly. Even though I'd flown using a magic sword, I didn't quite believe what I'd just seen. But when I flicked the cloth, it swept down into a glorious black cloak, just as it had for Jasper. I secured it around my neck. The fabric swirled around me, almost completely covering my own worn trousers and coat. There was even a hood, coming down over my forehead in a faint point to shadow my face.

"Perfect! You look much more heroic now," said Jasper. "Er, though you might want to lose the hatbox."

"Fine," I said, thrusting it at him. "You carry it, then. Just make sure it doesn't get smashed."

He took it, slinging it over one shoulder with an air of distraction. "That reminds me. Make sure you don't get the cloak wet."

"I thought you said it was a rain cloak."

"I said it was a *prototype*. The density runes don't, er, work entirely well if they get wet. Might act a bit . . . odd. So best avoid liquids."

Before I could ask Jasper to explain what exactly he meant by "odd," he was striding off, heading for the cluster of buildings. I jogged after him, sword in hand.

We found a crowd of people gathered along a narrow rail track that ran through the compound. Nearly all of them must be miners, judging by their sturdy coveralls and the dinner pails slung over their arms. And the faint glow that clung to them, making them look almost like figures from an ephemera-board.

One of the brightest was a tall, spindly man who stood apart from the rest over by the entrance to the mine itself, which was a dark tunnel cut into the end of a long trench. He had his hands in the air, gesturing as he shouted. "We won't do it, Skinders. You can't force us to work under these conditions. It's bad enough when all we have to worry about is ghosting. I'll not have a single one of my people step inside that mine until you can promise us there's no pyrosaur down there."

"Come on, we need to get closer," whispered Jasper.

I followed the prince around the edge of the crowd. All the attention was on the shouting man and the unsmiling woman who must be Skinders. She was wearing a severe dark suit with a pearl-tipped pin stabbed through the lapel. Her expression offered little sympathy as she gave her pocket watch a close inspection.

"Mr. Caruthers, you know as well as I do that the last

pyrosaurs died out over five centuries ago. And you and your crew are now five minutes late for your shift. If you do not enter the mine at once—"

"You saw Tom's burns yourself, ma'am. You can't send us in there until whatever did that's gone. We risk enough already!"

Some of the other miners called out in agreement, but Skinders only folded her arms across her chest. "I assure you, last year's safety inspection revealed everything to be in perfect order. Perhaps if Mr. Foxwell had been more careful with his tea flask, he wouldn't have injured himself."

The gathered crowd gave an ominous rumble.

"Tea flask?" spat Caruthers. "You think hot water did that?" He shook his head. "Either you're a fool or a liar, and I'm not sure which is worse. But you'll need a better answer than that or you're going to be hearing from the Aether Workers' Union."

He tapped his chest as he spoke, gesturing to something I hadn't noticed before: a large blue-and-white pin. I was still too far away to make out the design, but I didn't need to.

I knew it. I knew it because I'd stayed up with Mum every night for a month, helping her paint it onto hundreds of metal disks just like the one on Caruthers's chest. A crossed chisel and flask, white on a blue background. The symbol of the Aether Workers' Union. I'd helped her hand them out, too, at one of the organizational meetings. I'd been so excited to be a part of it all. To be a hero, just like Mum, standing up for people who needed help, dreaming of changing the future.

My insides seemed to drop out of me, leaving a hollow ache. I couldn't stop staring at the pin. I know it sounds ridiculous, but somehow, it was like Mum was there. Like if I could just squint hard enough, I could see her there beside the man, her hand on his shoulder. If only she were here. Everything would be so different.

"You're the ones in violation of your contracts," Skinders was saying. "And I have the authority to inform you on behalf of the company that if you don't return to work at once, you will all be fired immediately."

"Oh?" Caruthers said. "And who's going to work the shafts then?"

"There's plenty of convict labor available," said Skinders.

Protests burst from the crowd. Shouts and exclamations. Some of the miners started moving forward, as if they meant to enter the mine. Others leaped to block the way. Two burly women ran to one of the nearby rail carts and began shoving it, clearly meaning to tip it over.

An ember deep in my chest flared to sudden heat. A whisper of memory tickled my mind, something Mum used to say. *If you have power, and you don't use it to do good, you're as much the enemy as the folks who use their power to do ill.* I had the power to do something. I just needed to be brave enough to use it.

"That's it, then!" Skinders shouted. "You're all—"

"No!"

My shout barely rose above the din, but I hadn't only called out. I'd plunged the sword upward, flying into a high arc, then swooping down to land right in the center of the scene, my cloak furling majestically. I brandished the sword of the Nightingale, so that all of them could see the brave sweep of the wings at the cross guard, the bright blue eyes of the hilt.

"No!" I repeated, in the sudden silence. "No one's getting fired!"

My voice sounded thin. I took another deep breath, trying to imagine what a real hero would say. Mum always told me that you needed to believe in yourself, if you wanted other people to believe in you.

"I am the Nightingale, champion of Gallant!" I announced. "And I am here to aid you! I will enter the mine and face whatever foul monster lies—" I stumbled. Was it "lies," or "lays"? Ugh. Well, hopefully they got the point. "Lies within! Fear not!"

A stir of murmurs wove around me. I could hear some of it.

"She flew!"

"That sword!"

"Saw her rescue a lady on the ephemera-boards!"

Jasper sidled up behind me, clearly trying his best to keep a low profile. "You don't need to talk like you're starring in a cinema drama, you know," he whispered.

"Hey, it's working," I whispered back, before giving Skinders and Caruthers my best heroic smile. "So, do you accept my assistance?"

Skinders blinked. "Er. Well. I suppose we can hardly refuse."

Caruthers frowned. "The Nightingale? Aren't you a bit young for that?"

I planted the sword in front of me. "So you don't want my help?"

"No, we do, we do," he said hastily. "But do you really mean to go in there all alone?"

Jasper gave a meaningful cough and stepped forward. Caruthers's brows furrowed as he looked the prince up and down. Then he slapped a hand to his forehead, as if remembering something. "Right. Of course. I should've recognized him at once."

"That's perfectly fine," Jasper began. "Really, there's no need to—"

"It's the Flea!" proclaimed Caruthers. "The Nightingale's trusty sidekick!"

I leaned closer to Jasper. "Why didn't you tell me about the Flea?" I asked. "I didn't know I got a sidekick!"

"Because the Flea is completely made up! He's from a serialized adventure of the Nightingale's life that was published in the ephemeras fifty years ago. They added him for comic relief!"

Jasper was obviously not finding this as amusing as I was. I choked my giggle into a cough. "That's right," I announced. "Of course I need my trusty Flea to, er, carry our supplies."

Jasper gave me a sour look as he hefted the hatbox. I relented, turning back to the business at hand. "Right, then, where is this pyrosaur, exactly?"

"Tom said it came out of the south shaft," said Caruthers.

"Those tunnels were closed down since we mined it all out two years back. Should just be empty caves now."

"I guess we'll find out," I said. I turned to Skinders, giving her my sternest hero-of-the-realm look. "No one else goes in until we make sure it's safe."

She pursed her lips, but nodded.

I turned to Jasper. "Ready, Flea?"

He looked at me archly. "As ready as you are, Nightingale."

CHAPTER EIGHT

I wasn't ready. Not really. Not for an enormous dark tunnel that held some sort of terrifying, flame-breathing monster that I'd just promised to defeat. Sure, folks in the fancy colleges and libraries *said* pyrosaurs were extinct, but I'd heard Cora telling Willow about one that had burned down her grandfather's farm. And everyone knew about Toozie, the pyrosaur who lurked in Lake Toozwell up in the far north.

I wished now that I hadn't been quite so heroic. Maybe I should have just offered to go in and take a look. But I'd gotten carried away with it all, seeing that pin. Remembering Mum.

Now I was probably going to get burnt to a crisp in a pitch-black pit.

Though it wasn't truly pitch black. Thin lines of gleaming blue light traced the walls like spiderwebs, casting an eerie glow to light our way. We kept close to the metal rails and wooden ties of the tracks that ran along the tunnel. The deeper we went, the brighter the aether in the walls seemed to glow. The veins grew larger. Here and there cracks and crevices opened, looking like luminous mouths breathing blue light into the tunnel.

"Do you think it might really be a pyrosaur?" I asked, as we crept forward.

Jasper snorted. "Pyrosaurs are extinct."

"Are you *sure*? What about—"

"All the supposed sightings of Toozie have been thoroughly debunked," said Jasper. "So yes, I'm sure. If there's a monster down here, it's a human monster. The same fiend who's been causing all the other mining accidents. And we need to find him, before he causes any further harm."

I let out a breath. I suppose Jasper was probably right about pyrosaurs. Still. A villain who might be trying to blow up the mine was almost as bad.

A flicker of movement caught the corner of my eye. I gripped the sword tightly, but there was only another wall threaded with aether. And aether didn't move. Except that some of these gleaming blue lights *were* moving. Scuttling along the wall, from vein to vein.

I yelped, jerking back. "It's moving! What is it?"

"Ooh!" Jasper bounded forward. "Dazzlebugs!"

"Dazzlebugs?" I still had the sword lifted between me and what I realized were luminous beetles. I could see them now: each was about the size of my thumb, with a shining shell and six quick legs. The sight of them swarming along the wall made my stomach flip, but Jasper didn't seem to care. He was peering so closely at one large beetle that its long, thready antennae nearly brushed his nose.

"Well, technically *Blattella aetherus*, but the miners call them dazzlebugs because—cover your eyes!"

He flung himself away from the wall as a great burst of light filled the tunnel. I squeezed my eyes shut, but the brilliance stabbed through my eyelids. The next moment it was gone, leaving me, well, dazzled.

"Because they do that," Jasper finished. "It's a self-defense mechanism."

"To keep away nosy princes?" I blinked rapidly, trying to clear the spangles of leftover light floating in my vision.

"I prefer the word 'curious.'" Jasper brushed a protective hand over his nose, which was, in fact, rather large, though it suited his face. "And no, *Blattella aetherus* have several other natural predators, including—"

"I didn't come here for a biology lesson," I said, cutting him off. "I came to find out if someone's going to blow up the mine. And we're not going to figure that out just standing here. Come on, let's go to that south shaft."

I set off again, striding more quickly along the tunnel. This was just like any other job, I told myself. The nerves might be fluttering and flapping in my belly right now, but once I knew what I was dealing with, they would settle. Jasper followed, though his silence held a certain air of injury.

"You can tell me about the dazzlebugs while we walk," I

said, relenting. It might be useful information, after all. And maybe it would help distract me from worrying about what exactly we might find down here.

"They're such extraordinary creatures," he said, his voice cheerful again. "They don't have lungs like us. They breathe through holes called spiracles that connect to tubes that bring air into their organs. So, technically speaking, they can live without their heads!"

"How?" I asked, curious in spite of myself. "Are they magic?"

Jasper rolled his eyes. "Magic doesn't exist."

"Oh, really? Would you like to tell that to my flying sword?" I let go of the hilt so that the sword could do a small spin around Jasper before giving him a sort of tut-tutting gesture.

"That's aethercraft. It only seems like magic because we don't understand exactly how runes work. The dazzlebugs, that sword, even the mage-lords in Saventry, all of them get their power from aether. All of them follow rules. Call it magic if you want, but it's really just science with rules we don't completely understand."

"Oh."

"It's nothing to be sad about," Jasper said after a moment. "It's a good thing. Isn't it more exciting to know that there *is* an explanation, even if we don't know what it is yet? It means you can always find an answer, so long as you don't give up."

"I guess." It irked me to admit it, but maybe there was more to Jasper than a fancy coat and delusions of heroism. He was probably the sort of person who stopped reading a book every time he hit a word he didn't know to look it up in the dictionary. Hungry for answers, hungry to understand everything. It made something in me sit up, wake up, wish for more. It would be nice to feel like everything in this rusting world made some sort of sense. That there was no puzzle we couldn't solve, no problem we couldn't fix.

"There's so much about aethercraft we can learn," Jasper burbled on. "Not just the things we lost from the Golden Age, but new inventions too. Devices to cure diseases. Or to do dangerous jobs for us. Or—listen to this, it's *amazing*—I found one old treatise talking about how we might even be able to make artificed flying machines that could take us up into the stars. Can you imagine?"

Maybe it was the passion in his voice. Maybe it was the shimmer of the aether spattering the ceiling and walls, making me feel as if I was walking through the night sky. But for a moment I could believe it. Could feel an echo of Jasper's bright-burning enthusiasm.

"Like the Moon Maid?" I asked.

"The what?" asked Jasper.

"The Moon Maid. She lives on the moon and has a great golden boat with silver sails that she can fly across the sky. I know they're just stories," I added, flushing. "But my mum used to tell them to me when I was a little kid."

I hadn't thought about those stories in years. Not much time to look up at the sky these days. And anyways, I probably shouldn't have said anything. Jasper wouldn't care about fairy tales. I looked down, tracing my foot along one of the gleaming blue seams that ran along the tunnel floor.

"Stories are important too," said Jasper. "And it's curious that her boat has silver sails. One of the treatises I found proposes the construction of something rather like that. Giant wings made of a thin metal film powered by sunlight and aether." He grinned at me. "So maybe there's some truth to the Moon Maid."

I found myself grinning back. Then I remembered what was hidden under all that glittering innovation.

"Yes," I said softly. "But is it worth people ghosting away in the factories to get us there?"

"Pff. The factories are perfectly safe, so long as you follow proper safety protocols. And my brother says ghosting is actually extremely rare."

"How many factories have you visited?"

"Well . . . none. But—"

"You're the one going on about understanding things. Maybe you ought to actually see for yourself and then decide how safe they really are. Come have dinner with my housemate Willow on a bad day, and watch her try five times just to swallow a spoonful of soup because she's flickering. Or go down to the cemetery and see the shrines to all the workers who've ghosted off for good."

Silence.

"Or maybe you don't believe me, because I'm just a kid

from the Scrag who never had any fancy tutors and doesn't know the right word for dazzlebugs."

"I believe you," he said, after a long moment. "It's just . . . aethercraft is *so* amazing. I mean, look at you. Look at that sword, and what you and it can do together! There must be a way we can have both. Make the factories better. Change things."

I wanted to believe him. Jasper was actually a decent fellow. But his dreams were like dazzlebugs: so bright and flashy that they kept him from seeing the rest of the world like it really was.

"That's a nice idea. Too bad the folks with all the power like things the way they are and smack down anybody who interferes." Sophie. Mum.

"That's not—"

"Let's just focus on the job." I walked faster, tired of being underground, tired of the walls pressing around me like a fist. Jasper's steps scuffed behind me, following, but thankfully, he didn't continue the conversation.

"That must be the southern shaft," he said as we came to a junction. A wooden blockade had been put up across the left-hand tunnel. Large letters in an alarming shade of yellow warned us KEEP OUT.

We halted, listening. Even the sword tilted its blade as if cocking an ear to detect any hint of danger. There was nothing but the faint scuttling of dazzlebugs. So why did I feel like I was being watched?

"Do you want to go first?" I asked Jasper hopefully.

He quirked a brow. "I'm the sidekick. Remember?"

Fine. I could do this. I'd once stolen a gold ring off the finger of Agatha the Axe, one of the most brutal prizefighters in the Scrag boxing rings. I knew how to move quietly, to keep my head and stuff fear down deep when there was a job to do.

And I wasn't alone. I had the sword. "Ready?" I asked.

An eager spark ran up the length of the blade.

I slipped past the barrier, moving slower now, alert for any danger. The tunnel widened before opening into a vast natural cavern. Jasper followed after me, his breath rasping almost as loudly as mine in the silence.

"Look over there!" Jasper pointed to the far side of the cave.

There was a giant ragged hole in the ceiling, opening onto the distant twilight sky. Giant boulders and rough rock littered the sandy floor beneath. Among the rubble lay twisted bits of metal and broken glass. We crossed to examine the mess more closely.

"Is it mining gear? Something they left behind when they closed up this cave?"

"I don't think so. Not unless miners have a use for a grade-five torque wrench with a quixology reduction rune. And this!" He bent to collect one of the bits of metal. It didn't look much different from the rest as far as I could tell, but Jasper was marveling at it as if it were a piece of the moon.

"Look at this! Red steel! If I had to guess, I'd say it's part of a Golden Age relic! Maybe even the work of the Architect himself! I've never seen this sort of embedded wiring before. . . ."

I couldn't make out the rest of his mumbling, but that was fine, because something else had just caught my attention: a wide depression in the sand, about the size of a large dinner platter. Maybe someone had set down a heavy bucket? And yet . . . there was something strange about the shape. It wasn't round, or even oval. It was *foot*-shaped. But no human would have a foot that size—not unless they were ten feet tall.

"Jasper," I said, "come look at this. What do you think made it?"

I heard a gasp, then a gargled exclamation. I turned, expecting to find the prince lost in reverie over some new bit of broken metal he'd discovered.

Instead I found him struggling in the clutches of a tall stranger. The man had one arm locked around the prince's neck from behind, turning Jasper's cries into muffled gasps. With the other he tugged at the metal, trying to tear it from Jasper's grasp. Rust it! The villain must have been hiding behind one of the boulders!

I couldn't tell how old the man was. Or really much of anything, except that he was tall and thin. He wore a dark bowler hat pulled low over his forehead. Round, tinted spectacles covered his eyes, setting off his pale skin. The collar of his black overcoat was turned up, concealing the lower part of his face.

He looked like a hundred men I'd seen on the streets in the Shank; I'd have called him decent and respectable if he weren't trying to strangle Jasper.

"Hey!" I shouted at the stranger. "Let him go!"

Jasper continued to wriggle and writhe, but the man had an iron grip.

"What do we do?" I asked the sword. "I can't freeze him—I'll get Jasper, too!"

Just then something scuttled across the sand in front of me, gleaming and chittering. Aha!

I snatched up the beetle. "Jasper, *Blattella* coming your way!"

The prince caught my eye, gave a quick nod. He scrabbled at the villain's face, knocking the dark spectacles askew. "Do it!"

I threw the beetle straight at them, then flung my arm across my face as a bright light burst out around us. The man growled. Jasper shouted. By the time my vision cleared, everything had changed. Jasper had broken free, still clutching the red steel. The villain crouched a few paces away, rubbing his eyes.

"What are you doing here?" I called out to the man. "Who are you?"

He straightened, slowly, as he carefully readjusted his dark spectacles. Then he gave me a vicious smile and plucked something from the inner pocket of his coat. He held it up like a prize.

"Is that supposed to be an answer?" I asked.

"No," said the man, in clipped tones that matched his suit. "It's supposed to be a vortex generator."

He tossed the object toward Jasper and me, then turned and raced away down the tunnel, leaving the round, silvery device ticking ominously in the sand. I stared after the man. Who was he? And what was he doing here?

"We've got to get out of here!" Jasper croaked. "Quick! Before—"

The vortex generator gave a loud pop and opened, revealing a whirling twist of darkness. Instantly the air began to rush inward, sucking me toward the gadget. I tightened my grip on the sword as it fought to fly us free.

"Hold on!" Jasper yelled over the sudden roar. He'd grabbed onto one of the giant boulders, clinging to it to avoid certain annihilation.

I tried to fly to him, but the pull of the vortex was too powerful. I couldn't move, could only hang there in midair, the sword humming in frustration.

"We need to get out before the vortex maximum density is reached!" Jasper shouted.

"Before what?"

"Before it sucks in enough stuff to fill it up. It's powered by a gravity rune, so it compacts all the mass it absorbs and squishes it to the size of a pin." Jasper huffed, swinging himself to the side as a large rock flew past. "Once it's full, it'll explode."

He tried to regain his grip, but more and more stones pelted him. I could hear him yelping. Sand, loose rock, the tools and bits of metal, the entire contents of the cavern whooshed away, vanishing into that spinning dark.

I had to do something! But what?

"Will it explode right away?" I called. "Or will we have time to run?"

"Maybe five seconds. Plus or minus three seconds."

Better than nothing. I had to try, or both of us were going to get squished, or exploded, or both. I craned my neck. A large stone outcropping rose below us, not too far from the vortex. Perfect.

"Sword," I said, "we need to fly back toward the vortex and chop that stone free."

"What?" Jasper cried. "You're flying *toward* it?"

I had no time to respond. The sword had already answered, swooping us around to face the vortex. Faster and faster, no longer fighting the pull, we zoomed straight at the stone. I gripped the sword as tight as I could, gritting my teeth.

The blade slashed through the rock as if it were jelly. With a great *crack!* the stone broke free, enormous chunks flying straight into the spinning void. As each piece vanished, the vortex seemed to swell like a throat, swallowing down a great gulp. The pitch of its drone climbed higher and higher.

Please let it be enough! Sword and I were caught now, rushing closer and closer to pin-size doom. Then, suddenly, everything stilled.

The silver orb closed. The vortex vanished.

"Five seconds!" Jasper shouted hoarsely.

I grabbed the orb. It was heavy and warm and humming like an angry bee. "Go!" I screamed to Sword. "Up! Fast as you can fly!"

We flew. High. Swift. Sure. Up through the ragged hole in the ceiling, into the deep blue twilight, stars just beginning to wink out. *Four. Three.* "Stop," I called to Sword as I flung the vortex generator upward, arcing it into the heavens.

Two.

We dove back toward the cave, my stomach lost, my heart racing. *One.*

CHAPTER NINE

Brightness blazed above us, followed by a clap like thunder. I braced myself, clutching Sword's hilt to my chest as we flew back into the cave. But there was no burning lick of flame on my back, no sharp cut of shrapnel. Only a patter of fine grit and pea-size stone.

I let out my breath in a long gasp of relief. Before I knew it, my feet were touching down onto stone, and Jasper was there, his eyes crinkling with concern. "Are you all right?"

"I think so." I leaned against one of the remaining boulders, letting the solid stone prove that I was still alive, that the world had stopped spinning.

There wasn't much left in the cavern. The vortex had sucked away and exploded every possible clue. I sighed. "So much for the Nightingale's first mission. We nearly died *and* we let the bad guy escape *and* we lost all the clues that might've told us what he was up to."

"Not all the clues." Jasper held up the bit of metal the man had tried to steal. The sword hovered nearby, tilting its blade curiously at the thing.

I cocked my head. "What does *that* tell us?"

"Well, he clearly knows something about artifice. Maybe he was working on some sort of project down here. Something dangerous—that must be what burned that miner. The question is: Why?"

"Not *who*?" I asked. "Shouldn't we be trying to track him down? He did just try to murder us." Sword bobbed in agreement, then made a stabbing motion.

"*Why* will lead us to *who*," said Jasper. "I'm going to run some tests on this red steel. Maybe I can figure out what he was using it for."

"If he knows about artifice, he probably wasn't a Sav, right? They hate aethercraft."

Jasper nodded. "And he sounded like a Gallantine. Someone who has it in for the mines and factories."

I bit my lip. Did the prince think the union was behind this? That was ridiculous. The union didn't want the mines or the factories shut down. That would put everyone out of work. They just wanted to be safe, to be treated fairly. At least, that was what Sophie and Mum wanted.

Ugh. If only I'd managed to capture the villain, then we would know for sure! A proper Nightingale probably would've spotted him the moment she stepped into that cave. I should have done more. I flushed, feeling Jasper watching me. We had to find that man.

"You did good work, Nightingale. If that explosion had happened down here, it wouldn't have been just us in trouble— it could've set off a chain reaction in the aether. The entire mine might've been destroyed. But you stopped it."

It was too much. The way he was looking at me. Like he really thought I was some sort of hero. But foolishness like that was just going to get us both hurt, one way or another. It was one thing to do a few missions, but I couldn't afford to have him start expecting me to save the world.

"I'm not here to be the champion of Gallant," I said, biting out the words. I held out my hand, palm up. "I'm here because you're paying me. Remember?"

Jasper stiffened. For a moment he looked hurt, before a chilly remoteness froze his narrow face. "Right." He patted his pockets, then ran his hands up the lapels of his dark blue coat. "This will have to do." He unpinned a silver brooch from his collar and held it out. "I don't have an allowance for paying off mercenaries."

"*Mercenaries?* You think it's mercenary to expect to be paid a fair wage for your work?"

The sword hovered between us, blade tipping anxiously from me to the prince and then back again. But what did it expect me to do? I wasn't just going to let Jasper say something like that. He had no idea what my life was like. This was exactly why it was a bad idea to start palling around with a prince.

"This isn't normal work," said Jasper. "It's righting wrongs and doing good deeds. There's a difference."

"I've still got to fill my belly," I scoffed. "I've still got to pay my debts. Not all of us live in palaces."

I bit down on my tongue before I could say more. Jasper didn't need to know all the sordid details of my life. He didn't even know my real name. I was just the Nightingale. That was what mattered to him.

"Listen—" he started to say, but I cut him off.

"Never mind. You don't understand." I snatched the brooch from him, then shoved it into my pocket. "I've got to go, I have a party to—wait. Where's my hatbox?"

I scanned the cavern, then fixed my gaze back on Jasper. "You said you'd keep it safe."

He flushed. "I did. That is, I meant to. But I must have lost it when that man attacked me, and then the vortex started sucking everything up, and . . ."

He trailed off, pacing a few steps to the right, then bent down to pick up something from the ground. It was a tiny scrap of once-proud blue felt.

Fantastic. On top of everything else, Blythe's birthday gift had been destroyed.

I didn't know which made me feel worse: the fact that the gift Sophie had trusted me to buy had been reduced to scraps, or the fact that I had completely missed the party. I'd left Jasper behind to straighten things out with the miners and flown straight home, but we were still a good two hours late. Even if the girls had delayed supper, they'd surely be done with the cake by now.

I raced downstairs from the roof just as the clock downstairs began to chime seven o'clock, sprinted through the main hall, and turned the corner. I burst into the kitchen, breathless. "I'm here! Sorry I was late!"

Four faces turned toward me. Sophie and Willow, over at the kitchen table, looked up from Willow's arithmetic lessons. Blythe glanced over from the sink, where she was elbow deep in the washbasin, rinsing dishes. Cora spun around from the silverware drawer, where she'd apparently been juggling three of Miss Starvenger's spoons. All but one clattered loudly to the floor in the sudden silence. Only Nora continued working, setting clean glasses back in the cupboard. Cora tugged her arm a moment later, signing to her sister. Then Nora, too, was staring at me.

Blythe rolled her eyes. "Apologies won't change anything, Lark. You know the rules. If you miss dinner, you get Beastly Porridge. So you needn't try to wheedle anything better out of me."

I hesitated. Had I gotten the day wrong? But no: aside from Blythe, the other girls were all giving me very odd looks. Especially Sophie.

"Er, Beastly Porridge is fine," I said.

It wasn't, actually. It was beastly, like its name, a horrid stew of undercooked split peas and overcooked carrots that Miss Starvenger's cook made every day. Normally dinner was a cup of pease porridge—as it was properly called—and a sausage roll, or sometimes even a slice of cheese pie or egg custard. But if you weren't clean, if you weren't on time, if you looked at Miss Starvenger with too much cheek, well then, all you got was Beastly Porridge.

I headed for the table, where a covered bowl waited for me. Sophie slid closer along the bench, whispering furiously. "What happened? Are you all right?"

"I'm fine," I said. "I had a last-minute job. That's why I'm late. But . . ." I took another look around the kitchen. "What happened to the party?"

Blythe had returned to work, humming one of the Bright Brigade training songs, but Cora and Nora were huddled conspiratorially near the cupboard. Nora signed something at Sophie. I'd picked up only some of the language Nora used to communicate, having been deaf since she was a baby, but I recognized the sign for "now" and her questioning expression.

Sophie shook her head, mouthing the word "wait." Then she turned to face me again. "We were waiting for you, of course," she said. "We couldn't start without you."

A warm feeling puffed me up, just long enough that I could come crashing down the next moment when she added, "I hope you found a good gift."

Rust it. Sophie had been counting on me to get Blythe's gift, and I had failed utterly. Not only was I late, but I had nothing. Nothing except . . .

I pulled Jasper's brooch from my pocket, holding it out under cover of the table. "Here," I said. "I got her this." I stuffed down any prickles of concern over giving the thing away. I'd just have to do some more hero-ing and earn another. Jasper probably had plenty of trinkets in that fancy palace.

Willow, who had inched over to join us, gave an approving "Ooh," her dark eyes widening with delight. But Sophie did not look pleased. In fact, she looked downright angry.

"I told you Blythe doesn't care for jewelry," she whispered furiously. "And she especially won't care for jewelry whose real owner might come calling for it!"

"He won't! This was a . . . gift from my boss. To make up for me being late. I didn't steal it!"

Sophie stared at me.

"I swear, Sophie. On my mum's memory. I did get a gift, it was brilliant, but there was an accident, and it got destroyed by . . . my boss's dog. So he gave me this instead."

"The dog ate the gift? *That's* your excuse?" She was frowning, but there was hurt in her eyes.

And I couldn't do anything to fix it. Not with the magic sword quivering against my back, not with the silver trinket in my hand. Somehow, I'd managed to mess everything up. This was why I didn't get chummy with people. "Sophie," I started to say, but she'd already turned away.

"Never mind. We'd better get going. Wouldn't want Miss Starvenger walking in on an unauthorized party." She signed to Cora and Nora, and the two girls scampered off toward the pantry. Willow, meanwhile, bounced up and headed toward the lights.

A moment passed in which I sat cringing on the bench beside Sophie. Then Cora and Nora returned to the kitchen. Nora carried a large cake with pale blue frosting and fifteen gleaming candles, while Cora balanced a pitcher of lemonade and a handful of glasses. Willow dimmed the lights. Blythe turned to look at us in confusion.

"Surprise!" the twins and Willow and Sophie called out. "Happy birthday, Blythe!"

Sophie nudged me with her elbow. "Surprise!" I added my echo, as Willow flung up her arms and did a little jig of excitement. Blythe's stern expression melted into surprise, then delight.

Then alarm, as she looked past us toward the door to the front stairwell.

"A surprise, indeed," said Miss Starvenger, standing on the threshold, still wearing her fine purple evening coat with the ruffled collar. She scanned the scene, taking everything in as her lips pressed tighter and tighter. "A surprise to find my young ladies demonstrating such appalling disdain for house-hold rules."

She turned to Willow. "Miss Willow, turn up those lights." Then to Cora and Nora, "Misses Razakan, bring those here.

And Miss Treadwell, do stop dripping dirty water all over my kitchen floor."

Blythe snatched up a dish towel. Cora and Nora exchanged a dire look, then moved reluctantly to the table, where they set down the cake and lemonade. All of us watched with a sense of deep foreboding as Miss Starvenger leaned down, swiping a finger along the rim of the cake. She licked the frosting off her finger thoughtfully.

"Very rich," she said. "Too rich for children. I'm afraid I'll have to confiscate this."

"But we baked it ourselves!" Cora blurted. "We bought the eggs and the flour and the sugar and the butter! We didn't use any of your things, Miss Starvenger."

"Did you use my oven?" Starvenger asked mildly. "And I believe this is my pitcher," she added, tapping one long fingernail against the frosted glass.

Cora looked mutinous, balling up her hands into fists. Nora caught her sister's elbow, shaking her head.

"Did you ask my permission?" asked Starvenger. "For any of this?"

"No," said Sophie. "But that doesn't give you the right to—"

"*I* am the only one who has rights here," said Miss Starvenger. "You girls are my responsibility. I would be a poor guardian if I didn't teach you the value of rules. Or if I let you indulge in such unhealthy, frivolous behavior."

Willow's lips were wobbling. Blythe had a protective arm around her sister's shoulders and looked utterly mortified.

"Very well. I'll see that this doesn't go to waste," said Starvenger, nodding at the cake and lemonade. "And you girls have evening chores to do. So off with you now. You need your sleep if you're going to be good workers tomorrow," she finished with a bright, cheerful smile that showed far too many teeth.

Blythe instantly began herding Willow toward the door. Nora and Cora followed. I waited for Sophie to slide out from the bench before I started to follow, but as I stood, Miss Starvenger caught my wrist. "What's this?"

It was the brooch, still in my hand. Starvenger plucked it abruptly from my grasp.

"It's—it's a birthday gift. For Blythe," I said.

Starvenger's eyes narrowed, as she turned the bauble in her hands. "Hmm. It almost looks real. Well, it will do to cover the costs, I suppose."

"What costs?" demanded Sophie.

"Did I not make it clear you girls had broken my rules?" She gave a long-suffering sigh. "The world is not a kind place. Especially not for young ladies from disadvantaged backgrounds. I know you think it's cruel, but I assure you that all of this is for your betterment. Rules exist for a reason. You will need to learn to follow them if you want to make something of yourselves. Just consider yourselves fortunate that this is your only punishment. The world out there will be far crueler to you than I could ever be."

She closed her fingers over the brooch and tucked it into

her pocket. Then she made a shooing motion toward the door. "Go on. The laundry won't wash itself, now will it?"

Frustration burned through me. My fingers trembled, itching to grab for Sword's hilt. To turn Starvenger into an ice cube.

But that wouldn't solve anything. I trudged to the door, walked out into the hall, and started to follow Sophie down into the basement.

Sophie thrust an arm across the way, blocking me. "Where do you think you're going?"

"To help with the laundry," I said.

"I think I've had enough of your help for one night," she said. And with that, she shut the basement door in my face.

When Mum died, I had to stitch my heart back together, all by myself. And I've never been a very good seamstress. Now it felt as if someone had snipped at those ungainly, lumpy stitches with a pair of very sharp scissors.

I should never have agreed to buy Blythe's present. If Sophie hadn't been counting on me, waiting for me, they'd have had the party on time and Miss Starvenger never would have caught them. I wouldn't have ruined everything.

I swiped my hand across my eyes, then plucked a pair of damp stockings from the laundry basket. The others had washed everything last night, leaving it to me to hang the garments up on the roof the next morning, on the line strung between two chimneys. It meant lugging the heavy basket up four flights of steps from the basement, but ever since the aetheric dryer broke down five months ago, it was the only option.

Besides, up on the roof there was no danger of anyone seeing Sword as it zipped around, trying to help me. Shoving its hilt into the basket, it rose with one of Willow's pinafores draped over its cross guard. "Thanks," I said, taking it, then starting to clip it to the line. "Not very heroic, is it?"

Sword said nothing.

I wasn't expecting it to, not exactly. I mean, it was a piece of metal. Artificed and magicked up with a dose of aether, yes, but still only a thing, surely. And yet in the past few days I'd started to feel like it was speaking to me again, like it had when I'd first picked it up. Like if I could just turn my head to the right angle, I could hear its voice.

"I suppose the other Nightingales were fancier than me. I mean, they were from the Cutlet or the Shank, I bet. They went to schools, knew how to do things like fight and make speeches and be all impressive and brave and that sort of thing. Right?"

The sword gave a noncommittal wiggle.

"I wish I could talk to one of them," I admitted. "This would all be a lot easier if I knew what I was doing. If there were some set of instructions."

This time Sword bobbed excitedly.

"There are?" I stepped away from the clothesline. "Where?"

The weapon flipped itself sideways, angling its blade so that it ran parallel to the ground in front of me. Squinting, I could just barely make out the symbols etched into the blade itself. The same ones that had glowed when the prince first woke it up with his aetheric woo-woo back in the museum. Unfortunately, I had no idea what the etchings said. But Sword was obviously very proud of itself, judging by the way it kept twitching its hilt at me.

I sighed. "Thanks. That's . . . useful information."

Useful to someone who understood whatever ancient and obscure language—if it even *was* a language—the Architect had used to craft his masterworks. And I just happened to know someone who was utterly obsessed with that sort of thing.

"Maybe Jasper knows what it says. He's got a lot of artifice stuffed into his brain. Even if he can't do a simple job like keep a hat safe." I paused my work, tugging the aethercom from my pocket to check that it wasn't lit.

"Still nothing," I told Sword. "I guess he hasn't figured out what Dark Spectacles was up to. Too bad. I could use a good fight right now. Maybe do something right for a change. Getting paid again wouldn't be bad either."

I hung the last bit of laundry on the line, then slumped against the ledge bounding the roof. The rusting factories belched out so much smoke these days, my eyes were constantly stinging. I rubbed at them.

A moment later Sword was hovering beside me worriedly,

with a handkerchief caught over one wing of the cross guard. I took it, dabbed my eyes, and gave a soggy sigh. "I know, it shouldn't really matter what they think of me. It's not like I need friends. I just wish . . . I wish I could *fix* it. But it's not like I've got spare cash lying around to throw a party and buy a new cap. Ugh." I pressed my hands to my face, trying to cool the flare of heat on my cheeks.

Something fell into my lap. A small but heavy weight. I lowered my hands and looked down to see a bright blue gem sitting against the dark gray of my trousers. Where had it come from? I started to reach for it, then stopped, looking up at Sword in dismay as I realized the answer.

The weapon hovered in front of me, hilt up, showing the spread wings and bird's head of the hilt clearly. Where two sapphire eyes had once winked at me, now there was only one.

"Did you do that *on purpose*?" I demanded.

The sword gave a sort of bow.

"No." I seized the gem, thrusting it back at Sword. "I can't take it."

But the weapon floated out of my reach. Then it pointed its tip at my head.

"Yes, it's more than enough to get another hat. But it's your *eye*," I protested.

The sword spun, as if turning its back on me. I breathed in. Out.

I suppose I should have expected this sort of wild, extravagant gesture from a magic sword meant for a self-sacrificing hero. And it wasn't that I didn't appreciate it. I did. It made me feel like . . . like I *mattered*. But it was just like Sophie giving me her coins the other day. If I accepted this, it meant something. Something that squeezed my belly with nerves and at the same time bubbled up in my chest like fizzy lemonade, sunny and sweet.

I closed my fingers over the sapphire. "Fine. I'll take it to the pawnshop, and we'll get it back again as soon as I get my next payment from Jasper. Agreed?"

The sword spun around again, bobbing in agreement.

Something tugged in my heart. I was the one who'd gotten the gift, yet it was Sword who seemed the happiest about it. "Hey," I said. "Thanks. I . . . I appreciate this."

Sword flew closer then, its one remaining blue eye seeming to stare into me, before it gave a little twitch, as if to say *Pshaw, it was nothing*.

"All right," I said. "Let's go fix this."

CHAPTER TEN

My pockets were full of coins and my chest was fluttering with a jittery uncertainty. Mrs. Wixwell had taken the sapphire for six silvers. I could've gotten more from Eddie Crimp, but I trusted Mrs. Wixwell to keep her word and hold the gem for the two weeks she promised. Six silvers was plenty. I'd save two for my next payment to Miss Starvenger and one for emergencies. The rest would help me set things right with Sophie, Blythe, and the others. I'd already spent one coin on a new blue cadet cap, tucked securely under my arm in its hatbox.

Now I just needed to convince the other girls to go along with the rest of my plan. I'd found the perfect spot to wait for them, at the corner of Appleby and Comstock. Sophie would be coming down Appleby from the *Gazette* office, and the other girls from the factory down Comstock. We could pick up Willow at the boardinghouse after.

I paced back and forth, waiting for the factory whistle,

running over what I was going to say. The sword lay hidden against my back as usual.

Then it twitched, the hilt edging up slightly, rapping against the side of my skull to make me turn. "What?" I expected to find someone in need of saving, or perhaps another runaway street cleaner, but all I saw was the large ephemera-board that covered the top half of the warehouse across the street. An image flickered there: Prince Gideon, flashing his bright smile for the facsimilators, blocky black text scrolling below.

> Speaking from the palace's grand balcony, Crown Prince Gideon called on the people of Gallant to unite against the efforts by as-yet-unknown persons to sabotage the Wynchcomb aether mine—efforts that are rumored to have been thwarted by the Nightingale herself. "We must all practice vigilance in the face of these attempts to undermine our industry!" said the crown prince. "Aether is the lifeblood of Gallant, and any person or organization that seeks to sow dissent or interfere with our mines and factories is a traitor to all that our nation stands for!"

Wait, what did he mean by "organization"? It almost sounded like he was blaming the explosion at the mine on the union! That made no sense. If Jasper and I hadn't foiled Dark Spectacles's plan, he might've blown up that cavern while the miners were already at work. Besides, the union wasn't like that. They advocated for safer conditions, better pay, and fair treatment. At least, that was the purpose of the union Mum had helped form. Could it have changed?

A familiar voice tugged me from my thoughts. I searched the street and found four figures walking toward me along Comstock Street.

"So it's always like that?" Sophie was asking. "They lock the doors to the workshop and only the foreperson has the key? But what if there's an emergency? What if you need to use the lavatory?"

"That's why they do it," said Cora. "So you have to ask permission. You can't just nip out and take a break without them docking your time."

My mind tried to make sense of the words. And the fact that Sophie was coming from the direction of Pinshaw's.

"Sophie?" I blurted out. "Why do you care about the rules at the factory?"

She looked up at me, a trace of guilt in her dark eyes. Then she squared her shoulders. "Because I work there now, as a duster."

"But . . . what about your job at the Gazette?"

"I don't work at the Gazette anymore."

"What? Did they sack you?"

"No. I quit."

"But—"

"Why are you here, Lark?" she cut in, turning the questions against me.

"I—oh, um . . ." I stumbled over my words, forgetting everything I had planned out. A part of me wanted to just stop there, turn and run. But I owed it to Sophie, to Blythe, to set things right. Besides, it would be . . . nice. Wouldn't it? At least it would help take my mind off Dark Spectacles while I waited for Jasper to do his experiments on that metal bit.

"I came to make up for last night," I said more firmly. "I'm going to take you all somewhere really *marvelrageous* to celebrate Blythe's birthday."

"*Marvelrageous* isn't even a real word," said Sophie. Her voice was cold. So were her eyes, watching me. My insides shivered, but I pressed on. She was logical. She was fair. She'd see the truth if I could just convince her to give me a chance.

"Wait until you see this place, and then decide that," I told her, hoping very hard that those cadets knew what they were talking about. "I know things went to rust last night. But I swear, I'm going to make up for it. Really, Blythe."

Blythe pursed her lips in consideration as Sophie continued to watch me with an intent, slightly suspicious expression. But Cora and Nora broke into identical expressions of delight. Nora clapped her hands together, then made one of the signs I'd picked up. *Where?*

"Come on," I said. "I'll show you."

❧

"That's it, Quixby Street," I said twenty minutes later, after we'd stopped by the boardinghouse to collect Willow and made our way into the Shank. Thankfully, Miss Starvenger had been distracted by a new edition of her favorite ephemera tabloid, the *Gallant Gusher*, and was too deeply invested in the Earl of Prim's secret love affairs to notice us leaving. The evening skies were a high, clear blue that called people out into the streets for a ramble. "We're nearly there."

Or so I hoped. Quixby wasn't a very long street. It had to be here somewhere.

"But where's *there*?" asked Blythe. "Where are you taking us, Lark?"

Nora began signing excitedly, pointing to something ahead.

"Here!" I said triumphantly, as we all goggled up at the enormous sign shaped like a soda glass full of pale green froth, topped by a bright red cherry, with the word DASHLILLY'S inscribed along the length in ornate letters that gleamed with a shimmer of aether, slowly changing colors from bright pink to green and back again.

Cora read the smaller golden text beneath: "One hundred flavors! Penny sodas, ices, and creams! Come in and enjoy a fizz!" Then she squealed. "Ooh, do you think they have mango? I've always wanted to try mango!"

"I want to try them *all*," proclaimed Willow. "Oh, I hope I don't start flickering before I get to chocolate!"

Even Blythe wore a tentative smile. She touched her dark

coiled hair, watching a trio of smartly dressed older girls walk into the shop.

Sophie still looked serious, searching the wide glass windows painted with an enormous list of flavors. "I don't think you'll be able to try them all today, Will," she said. "Maybe start with one."

"She can have more than that," I said, and thrust out my hand, showing them the two silver coins. "Twenty to share between us, that's—"

"Three each," answered Sophie, staring at them as if she expected they might suddenly vanish like an image on the ephemeras. "Plus two extra. But Lark, where did you—"

"For Blythe," I said, cutting off her questions. "It's her birthday. I mean, it was. So let's enjoy it, right? You do like fizzes, don't you, Blythe?"

Blythe grinned. "I'm starting with coconut."

Sophie still looked suspicious, but the other girls seemed to . . . be excited? Happy? Maybe this was actually going to work.

A few minutes later, we were crowded around a table, seated in one of the curving booths that rippled along the walls of the shop. The interior was enormous compared to any other shop I'd been inside, and felt even larger because of the mirrors covering every wall.

The soda fountain stood at the center, a mountain of glittering copper and crystal that must have been a good three stories tall, rising up beneath the even higher vault of the glass-domed ceiling. Clear tubes spiraled in the air and looped out along the walls, weaving in complex patterns as they carried the bubbling torrent of soda here and there. A dozen dispensers encircled the fountain, each bearing several different levers that the attendants manipulated to pour streams of colorful liquid over goblets filled with cream or shaved ice. Servers in pink-and-green-striped uniforms darted about the tables, some whisking away empty glasses while others arrived balancing great gilded trays of fresh sodas.

"That must be Miss Dashlilly!" said Blythe, pointing to a woman gliding among the servers, giving orders. "Isn't she glamorous? She used to be a famous actress, traveling all over the world to perform, even Saventry."

I could believe it. She moved like someone used to having every eye on her. Her smallest gestures seeming to be magnified, infused with mortal drama and high emotion. And she was so elegant, her curly black bob decorated with a band holding several pink-and-green ostrich feathers, to match her fuchsia-and-emerald gown. The black mole on her brown cheek gave her just the faintest aura of mischief.

Blythe lowered her voice. "Some people say she was secretly a spy during the war, you know. I can't believe I get to see her in person!"

"Too right," said Cora, ogling the aetherlights that sparkled in clouds of blown-glass bubbles along the ceiling. "This place is amazing!"

Nora, reading her sister's lips, nodded eagerly, then signed something that Cora translated: "It's like being inside a glass of fizz!"

It was. Maybe that was why my chest felt so light and buzzy, even though our first round of sodas hadn't even arrived. Blythe was giggling with Willow over the ridiculous hat a woman at a nearby table was wearing. Nora had taken out her notebook and pencil and started sketching the fountain. Cora was swaying to the lilting music that seemed to come from nowhere and everywhere at the same time.

I had done this. I'd brought them here, and made them happy. I knew it wasn't the same thing as saving a woman from being smashed by a falling statue, but it felt like just as much of a victory, somehow.

Sophie frowned up at the ceiling, her head cocked. "They must have a telharmonium," she said, then sighed. "All that aether, all that work, just so we can listen to music and put bubbles in drinks."

The lightness in my chest winked out. Sophie caught my expression. "No, don't look like that, Lark. I didn't mean that coming here was a bad idea. It's just that after today, after I saw how bad it is, I can't stop thinking about it."

"Sophie," I said softly, "did you really quit your job at the *Gazette*?"

"Lark," she said, with a touch of mischief, "did you really think that ascot was a reasonable fashion decision?"

I tugged at my collar, where I was, indeed, still wearing

Jasper's ascot rain cloak. I flushed but didn't let her distract me. "Sophie."

She rolled her eyes. "Fine. Yes. I did."

"But why? You said anything was better than working at the factory. You made me promise—"

"I'm not working at the factory for money," she said. "I'm doing research for a new article. The *Gazette* won't tell the truth. All they put on the boards are that rusting Prince Gideon's lies about how safe it is. Maybe if folks understand how much all this really costs, they'll make real changes."

And here was Sophie, bravely thrusting herself right into the heart of it. Not because someone gave her a magic sword, but because she saw something wrong and wanted to fix it.

"Especially," Sophie went on, lowering her voice, "once they find out Pinshaw is building a new aether factory."

If the sword against my spine hadn't already been making me sit bolt upright, that would have done it. "What? What new aether factory? Are you sure about that?"

"That's the only thing I can think of to explain the evidence," she said. "Something big is going on. Increases in the manufacturing of copper tubing and crystal pipes. A whole crew of workers from Pinshaw's were supposedly sent to go help at one of the workshops up north, but according to public record, that workshop was shut down two years ago. It doesn't add up."

I bit the inside of my cheek. Should I tell her what I knew?

Maybe this was connected to Dark Spectacles. That would take the heat off the union. "Er, so, what else have you learned?"

Sophie sighed. "Not much yet. The conditions at Pinshaw's are disgraceful, of course, but I need more than that to make folks actually pay attention. That's why I need to find out about this new factory. Where are they building it? What are they going to do with all the aether dust? Is this why more people have been ghosting lately?" Her glower was powerful enough that even Sword, hidden behind my back, gave a quiver.

Her words also set a tiny warning bell tinging in my chest. "Sophie, you need to be careful. If it's a secret, they probably won't want you poking at it. It's dangerous."

"Not as dangerous as ignoring it all. Besides, I needed this," said Sophie, pulling something from the pocket of her pinafore, showing it to me under the cover of the table. It was a small glass jar holding a few drops of gleaming blue liquid aether! Not as much as Jasper had used on Sword, but still enough to be worth several gold.

"Sophie!" I hissed. "Did you *steal* that?"

"I need it to run my ephemera press," she said unrepentantly.

"I can't believe this! After all the times you've twitted at me for thieving to survive, you go and do this? Do you know what would happen if they caught you?"

She sat up straight against the booth. "Sometimes you need to do things because they're the right thing to do. No matter the risks."

I set my fists on the table, scowling at her. But for all my irritation, I was also suddenly, desperately afraid. Sophie was clever, but she wasn't sly. Her gift was telling the truth. Sooner or later, someone was going to find out what she was up to.

"Promise you'll be careful," I said, my voice tight. "Please. You need to stay safe, Sophie."

Her deep brown eyes held mine. "Lark, you don't need to worry—"

"I'm not worried," I said quickly. "It's just that Willow would hate it if you got sent away. And the other girls too."

"The other girls." Sophie looked amused. "But not you."

"I suppose I'd miss you too. You're my housemate. And who knows who Starvenger would bring in to take your bunk?" Why did she keep looking at me like that? As if I were an old dress she'd just decided to make over fresh?

Thankfully, our drinks arrived just then, and I filled my mouth with a great gulp of cherry-flavored fizz. Around the table the other girls did the same, and for several minutes we were united in the silence of deep satisfaction.

Cora finished first, leaning back against the booth with a sigh. "That was amazing. I don't even know what a mango is, but it's my favorite thing in the world now."

"It's a fruit from Anzel-Hara," said Sophie, around her own last slurps of vanilla cream soda. "My father said his grandfather grew whole orchards of them. Papa always said fresh, ripe mangoes were the one thing he missed most when he immigrated to Gallant." She looked away for a moment. "I'll have one of those next."

"I almost wish they didn't have so many flavors," said Blythe, tapping her metal straw against the base of her empty glass. "It's too hard to choose. I was sure I was going to get mint next, but now I don't know if I should get that or mango." She looked across the table to me. "This was a brilliant idea, Lark. Thank you."

I flushed. Everyone was looking at me. Sophie nudged my shoulder with hers. It felt strange. Not bad. Maybe even nice. But it wasn't what I was used to. Fortunately, I had a reason to change the subject.

"Now you have to open your gift. It's from Sophie and the other girls, and I was supposed to pick it up, but I got delayed last night."

I placed the hatbox on the table, then slid it across to Blythe. Willow was practically bouncing on the booth beside her. Blythe set her hands along the lid of the hatbox, her fingers tugging it free, then peeling back the layers of pale blue tissue paper inside. Her hands abruptly froze. She seemed to stop breathing for a moment, her mouth open in an O of surprise or alarm.

Oh, rust me. Had I picked the wrong thing?

Blythe lifted the blue cap out from the nest of tissue with trembling fingers, turning it this way and that. And she was smiling now, a wide, reckless, delighted grin. "It's a cadet cap!"

"We know you can't use it right away," I said, glancing toward Sophie. She gave me an encouraging nod, almost like she was proud of me. Warmth flooded my chest, and I continued, "But we figured you'd need it soon."

Blythe's light brown eyes glittered. "I—I don't know. I need to study for the entrance exams, and I'm so tired at night, and I know the book I have is ten years out of date, and . . ."

Nora made a sharp gesture that needed no interpretation.

Blythe swallowed a soggy sigh. "I can't try it on. I'm not a cadet yet."

"Of course you can," said Willow. "I want to see what you look like."

Cora had already started chanting, "Cadet Treadwell!" under her breath, with Nora giving a salute.

"It doesn't have the star, so it's not technically part of the uniform. You wouldn't be violating any regulations," said Sophie, who had apparently swallowed a Bright cadet manual. She gave me a knowing wink. I grinned back, relieved she understood.

Blythe set the cap atop her coiled dark braids. She turned left, then right, hands still raised as if to snatch it off at the slightest hint of danger.

"You look perfect!" crowed Willow.

She did. It was almost like artifice, how the sharp blue lines and jaunty angle made Blythe look older, braver, more capable.

I reached up to my own collar, fiddling with the ruffle of Jasper's ascot rain cloak. Maybe that was why the Nightingale wore a uniform. Was it easier to believe in a hero who wore a mask and armor? Surely no one would look at me now and believe I could save the realm from anything more terrifying than an angry cat or an especially large spider.

"Come on, then," said Cora, edging out from the booth, pushing Blythe and Willow ahead of her as Nora did the same to Sophie and me. "Let's show you off to the attendants. Nora likes that girl over on the left, the one with the dimples. What, no, I didn't say that!"

Nora was signing furiously. Cora rolled her eyes. "She says she just wants to see her close up, so she can sketch her properly." Nora slapped her lightly with the sketchbook as we all jostled up to the counter.

It was . . . nice, all of us together like this. It wasn't the same as being with Mum, being a family. But it was the closest I'd felt to that in a long time.

"What flavor will you get, Lark?" asked Willow.

"I'm still deciding," I said, peering up at the list. "Maybe— oh!"

My answer turned into a gasp of alarm as I caught sight of a familiar figure on the far side of the fountain. A man in a long overcoat and dark spectacles. The villain from the mine! Had he followed me? His round, tinted lenses swept across the crowd. I ducked back behind Sophie, just to be safe.

"Lark?"

"You order first," I said, letting her walk ahead of me to the dimpled girl at the counter. "I need to . . . think more."

Right. *Think, Lark.* Was he just craving a cherry bubbler, or was he here for some sort of criminal mischief?

I slid a hand into my pocket and gripped the aethercom. But it only worked in the other direction—I had no way to let Jasper know about the danger. Which meant that whatever this was, I had to handle it myself.

I started edging my way around the counter, trying to look as if I were just reading my way through the voluminous menu. Meanwhile, Dark Spectacles skulked closer to the fountain, his attention fixed on the aetheric device itself. A large crowd of young men bustled up between us, blocking my view of him. Rust it!

I ducked past a server balancing a tray of drinks that swirled bright yellow and vivid green. By the time I had a good view again, the man had slid past the counter, right up to the shimmering copper chassis of the soda fountain. Then he opened one of the panels.

Before I could move, before I could even shout out a warning, he tore something from the very heart of the device: an intricate contraption of tubes and crystals that pulsed with an aetheric glow. There was a sudden flare of bright blue light tracing agitated lines across the copper surface of the fountain, then an enormous *whomp*!

"What's happening?" someone shrieked.

All the taps on the soda fountain began to foam. Attendants shouted in alarm, rushing around the device, flipping levers and switches. But nothing happened, except that the bubbles began to rapidly grow larger. And larger. And larger.

Chapter Eleven

*W*ithin moments, hundreds of sticky bubbles had filled the air. I gritted my teeth, trying to spot Dark Spectacles, but I'd lost him in the bubble-filled chaos. All around the shop, patrons were screaming, trying to flee the frothy deluge.

One of the attendants batted at a particularly enormous bubble as it loomed over him. But it didn't pop. Even worse, he couldn't seem to pull free as it wrapped itself around his hand. He yelped, tugging at his arm. "I'm stuck!" Another bubble enveloped his head, turning his cries into faint, tinny echoes.

Miss Dashlilly climbed up onto the counter and was calling out, "Everyone stay calm. It looks like there's been a minor power fluctuation of the viscosity agent. I'm afraid that can have some unexpectedly potent effects on the bubbles, but it's easily undone. Someone needs to get to that conduit." She pointed to the web of wires and copper tubes coiling around the very top of the fountain. "Cut that, and it will—"

But whatever else she'd been going to say was lost as a tide of bubbles surrounded her. For one long moment I stared around the room, waiting for someone to step forward and take charge. To say that the Bright Brigade was on the way.

No one did. There was no one to save us.

Except me.

I squinted up in the direction Miss Dashlilly had been pointing. I was pretty sure I could see the conduit she meant. And it'd be simple enough for me to fly up and slash the tube as the Nightingale.

But I wasn't the Nightingale right now. I was Lark, and I was surrounded by people who knew me. I still had the artificed cloak and my mask, but I needed to find somewhere to put them on, before the rusting bubbles turned everyone into Dashlilly's hundred-and-first flavor.

Blythe had already walked Willow over to the door. I could see her craning her neck, probably looking for the rest of us. Cora and Nora reached her a moment later. But where was Sophie? I didn't see her trapped in any of the bubbles. Had she gotten out some other way? There was a crimson sign reading EMERGENCY EXIT that was pointing toward the rear of the shop.

I jogged toward it. "Lark!" came a cry behind me.

"Sophie!" I cried, relief lifting my chest. She was standing in the doorway of what looked like a supply closet. "We need to get out of here." I'd lead her outside, then go back in.

But she stood her ground. "No, we need to help! There's a

ladder in here. If you help me get it out, we might be able to reach that conduit."

"It's not your job to fix this, Sophie. You need to get out. I'm sure someone will be here soon to take care of it."

"That might be too late! Look at them." She gestured to Miss Dashlilly, who was now fully encased in one of the bubbles, beating her hands against the inner surface. "They don't have much air. We need to stop this and find a way to get everyone out!"

Another tide of enormous bubbles was heading our way. "Watch out!" I cried, pushing Sophie back into the closet.

"Lark! Don't—"

I slammed the door. "You'll be safe in there," I called. "Don't worry. I'm going to get help!"

Then I ducked into a niche beside the closet and pulled on my mask. The sword zoomed out from its hiding place and flew to my hand, just as the cloak unfurled around me, covering my normal clothes.

Meanwhile, I could still hear Sophie shouting from inside the closet—she sounded furious. But this was for her own good. I was the Nightingale, and this was my job. I had to keep her safe.

Confidence rippled through me. I knew what to do. I was ready for this.

"Let's go, Sword." I slashed at the bubbles surging toward me. The blade sliced through them, splitting the surface and making them each fall apart with a loud *pop!* We flew, broken bubbles disintegrating around us.

Now I just needed to cut the conduit. But which one was it? There were three different tubes coiling around the top of the fountain. I floated for a moment, staring at them. "It was the one on the left, wasn't it?"

The sword glinted encouragingly. Below, the bubbles had nearly filled the entire shop. I didn't have time to waste. "I really hope this works," I said, then swung Sword at the pipe.

Sploosh! A gushing tide of chocolate syrup spurted from the slashed pipe, dousing me. Wrong pipe! My flowing black cloak snapped, abruptly closing around me like a clamshell. I gasped, barely keeping hold of Sword.

Rust it! Jasper had warned me not to get the cloak wet! I'd assumed he meant it would get stained, or maybe the seams would start to go or something. Not that it would try to strangle me! Meanwhile, the bubbles continued to flow, and dozens of people were being suffocated inside their own sticky prisons.

I had to do something. But how? With my cloak twisted around my arms, I couldn't maneuver Sword to cut myself free. But if I let it go, I'd fall. I tried to glimpse the ground below. Even though it was covered in bubbles, I knew it was a long drop. At best, I'd break something. At worst . . .

I couldn't see any other way. There was no time to fly back down to untangle myself and get help.

"Sword," I said, "listen to me. I'm going to let go of you."

The blade wobbled in my hand.

"It'll be all right," I said. "You can do this. As soon as I let go, you fly over there and slice that other pipe. We need to stop the fountain."

Another more urgent wobble.

"I know, but you're fast. You can do it and get back in time to catch me. I know you can. Ready?" For a moment it lay still in my palm. Then it gave a sort of spark, a flicker of warmth that shivered up my arm. "Good," I said. Then I let go.

My own weight caught me, jerking me down toward the ground again. My stomach flipped. Everything was rushing past, color and syrup and bubbles. And only one thought filled my mind: it had to work.

But what if it didn't?

The slash of a blade sounded in the distance. *Good, Sword, that's it.*

I fell farther, faster, tangled in the cloak that was about to become my shroud. Then silver flashed. Fabric ripped. The cloak flapped loose again and I reached out to feel a solid heft smack into my palm. Lightness billowed me up again.

I couldn't feel my own heartbeat. It wasn't even a beat. Just a high, swift thrumming.

"You did it!" I told Sword as it bobbed us both in the air, only a few feet above the ground. My cloak hung in chocolate-stained, sword-slashed tatters, but I was *alive*. "I knew you could!"

A flash of pink-tinged light ran up the blade, almost like a blush. Then it spun me around until my breath caught again. "Yes, yes," I told it, grinning. "You're a very good sword. But we're not done. We've got to get everyone out of those bubbles now."

We flew around the shop, Sword slashing and piercing and poking, until every last bubble had burst, leaving a crowd of sticky folk wheezing but free. Last of all, we sliced open the bubble holding Miss Dashlilly.

She staggered, gasping. Her eyes widened as she looked me up and down. She straightened her feathery circlet, then gave a graceful curtsy.

"The Nightingale, I presume?"

"Er, yes, it's me. The Nightingale." I gave an awkward salute. What was I supposed to do? Strike a dramatic pose? I was still covered in sticky chocolate that probably made me look as if I'd been sweeping out chimneys, not saving citizens from certain death by soda fountain.

"Thank you," said Miss Dashlilly. "I don't know who that villain was, or why he wanted my effervescence modulator, but I do appreciate your swift and capable assistance!"

"That's the thingy he ripped out of the fountain?"

"Indeed," she said. "It was quite the antique. Repurposed from the workshop of the Architect himself!" She shook her head. "Well, I suppose I'll have to make do with one of the newer models, even if they never do get the balance right for the citrus drinks. And in the meantime . . ." She gave me a dazzling smile, snatched a fizzing green goblet that had been abandoned on the counter, and lifted it high. "Three cheers for the Nightingale!"

The rest of the crowd took it up, until everyone was cheering and hip-hip-hooraying and calling out, *"Nightingale! Nightingale!"*

The applause seemed to shimmer over me, filling my chest with—well, not bubbles, those no longer felt entirely celebratory to me—but whatever the feeling was, I liked it. It reminded me of putting on new clothes, ones without any stains or patches.

Then I saw Sophie. Someone must have let her out of the closet. Now she was standing a few steps beyond the rest of the cheering crowd, with her arms crossed and an intense look on her round brown face.

Did she recognize me? Or was she just upset with the Nightingale? Either way, the sooner I got out of there, the better. Dark Spectacles was probably long gone, but I had to tell Jasper about him stealing the modulator. It could be the key to figuring out what he'd been up to in the mine.

"You're very welcome," I called out. "But I have other evils to vanquish! Goodbye for now, people of Gallant!"

Fortunately, there were skylights in the high arched ceiling above the soda fountain. I jabbed Sword upward to carry me through one, up and away from Sophie's penetrating stare.

It took me three swoops around the palace, peering in windows, before I spotted Jasper. He was in a sort of study, decorated in dark wood and crimson velvet, standing at stiff attention in front of a desk. I couldn't see the person to whom he was speaking, but they must be important, judging by how rich the furnishings were. Then again, it was a palace. Maybe even the chimney sweep had fancy apartments. Though I doubted Jasper would have a look of utter awe and desperation on his face during an interview with the chimney sweep.

The sword landed me on a wide balcony outside the room, allowing me to creep up to the set of floor-length windows that had been left cracked open. If only breaking into the museum had been so easy! Then again, I did have a magic sword now.

"So you see why I had to investigate the incident," Jasper was saying. He stood like a soldier at attention, stiff-shouldered, hands behind his back. Nothing like the cheeky, geeky boy I'd come to know. "There's been a pattern of attacks. Someone needed to do something, Gideon!"

Gideon? As in Crown Prince Gideon, soon-to-be king of Gallant? I cringed, suddenly aware of how disreputable I looked, covered in chocolate sauce, my slashed cloak only barely covering my patched coat and trousers. Well, it seemed to be a private conversation anyway. I'd just wait here a bit and see if I could catch Jasper's attention.

"Jasper, Jasper, Jasper," said the elder prince. I could see the back of his blond head shaking as he spoke. "I do appreciate your enthusiasm"—Jasper perked up at this—"but you really must leave these matters to those who have the skills and experience to make sense of them. What were you *thinking*, running off like that?"

The trace of relief in Jasper's expression froze into brittle dismay. Then frustration. "I was thinking that I've got a duty to Gallant, just like you," he said, in a rush of words. "I want to help, Gideon! I *can* help! I'm not a little boy anymore. You don't have to keep me safe."

"Apparently, I do," said Gideon. "Given you nearly blew yourself to bits. You'd do far better putting your energy into your lessons. Armsmaster Hrothsina says you're weeks behind her other students."

"But I didn't get blown up. The Nightingale saved my life. And I found a clue, Gideon. Look, see this bit of metal the man was working on, it's—"

"The Nightingale? You mean that girl from the ephemeras? Come now, I hardly think *she* could be the hero of Gallant reborn." He chuckled. "She doesn't even have a proper uniform."

The sword nudged me meaningfully. "Shush, you," I whispered furiously.

I must have spoken louder than I meant, because Jasper's eyes suddenly darted to the window, then went wide as he spotted me. Oops.

"Is something wrong?" Gideon said, starting to turn.

I flung myself to the side, into the shadow of the balcony wall, just as Jasper spoke up quickly. "No. Just that I remembered I, er, have a history lesson to finish up. I'd better go over to the museum to finish my research."

"That's the spirit," said Gideon bracingly. "And maybe when you're finished, we can get in a round or two in the training hall. I can teach you a few things Hrothsina doesn't know. Help you get a leg up on the others. How does that sound?"

"Really? You're not too busy? I mean, yes, that'd be great, Gid. Really swell."

I peered back inside in time to see Jasper practically bouncing up into the air. It reminded me of the way I'd been with the Gaddings. So eager to please, so eager for their attention that I didn't care if all they gave me were scraps. I scowled at Gideon. He'd better keep that promise, or he might just get a visit from a very real and very angry Nightingale.

"Just remember," Gideon added. "No more gallivanting around trying to be a hero."

Jasper hunched. "Don't worry. No chance of that."

Gideon hesitated, then set a hand on his brother's shoulder. "You know it's for your own good, Jas. You're all I have left. Saventry took Mother, but they're not getting you. I'm going to keep Gallant safe. I'm going to make us so strong that no one will even think of attacking us, ever again. But I need you on my side if I'm going to do that. I need you to listen to me. Can you do that?"

"Yes," said Jasper, in a strange, strangled voice. "I can do that."

"I wasn't sure you'd be here," I said, when Jasper finally found me on the roof of the Royal Museum a few minutes later. "Didn't you just promise your brother to give up hero-ing?"

He gave a twisted smile. "Well, we've already established that I'm only the sidekick. So no worries."

"Jasper, just because—"

"Why did you come here?" he asked abruptly. "Or were you just spying on me for fun?"

"I wasn't spying," I said. "I have information. And you're the one who gave me a one-way aethercom. Why are you such a grouch tonight?"

Jasper sighed, running a hand through his hair. "Sorry. It's just . . . Gid never takes me seriously."

"Well, I do," I said. "And I seriously need an aethercraft genius right now, to explain what Dark Spectacles might want with an"—I hesitated, trying to remember what Miss Dashlilly had called it—"efflatulence modulator?"

Jasper gave a choked sputter.

"What?" I asked, alarmed by his expression. "Is it something horribly dangerous? Why would Miss Dashlilly have had it in her soda fountain, then?"

Jasper coughed. "Are you talking about an *effervescence* modulator?"

"Right, that's what I said. Well, close enough. Anyways, Dark Spectacles nabbed it, right out of the fountain at

Dashlilly's. Made the whole thing go haywire. Fortunately, the Nightingale was there to set things to rights," I added, grinning to Sword as it gave a triumphant little loop above me.

"So I see," said Jasper, eyeing my chocolate-stained clothing. "Hmm. An effervescence modulator."

"Right. An antique. Dashlilly said it was from the Architect's own workshop."

Jasper began to pace, his brow furrowed.

"What's wrong?" I asked. "Does that mean something to you? Is it going to help us find Dark Spectacles?"

Jasper frowned. "Come on, I need to show you something."

CHAPTER TWELVE

The grand gallery of the Royal Museum was an impressive room at any time of day, but it seemed even more overwhelming in the shadowed, early evening light. The vast open chamber was echoingly empty of any visitors except Jasper and me. It rose four stories tall, wrapped with ornately carved walkways that left the center open to display the museum's collection of pyrosaur fossils. The enormous petrified bones of the ancient reptiles were wired into place, caught in fierce poses. There were even several hung from the lofty roof, soaring or swimming through the air with a strange, alien grace.

Jasper led me past a giant three-horned beast whose mouth came straight out of my nightmares to a smaller display at the very center of the room. Two display plinths stood there, each spotlit by an aetherlight.

"So, what did you want to show me?" I asked.

Jasper gestured to the larger of the two plinths, which held a giant red-tinged cauldron. "That."

"You brought me here to show me a rusty old cook pot?"

"It's not a cook pot."

I frowned at the thing. It *was* roundish and made of metal. But if it was a cauldron, it was wrong side up, with the opening on the bottom. And there were two marks along the front that looked an awful lot like eye slits, above a mouthlike grate. I realized, finally, what it was.

"A helmet?"

"The Crimson Knight's helmet," said Jasper.

I let out a long breath. "It's big enough to boil a watermelon."

"You don't *boil* watermelons," answered Jasper.

"That's not the point. He must have been gigantic."

"Ten feet tall, according to the records that survived the Dark Days."

I shuddered. "I can't see how anyone ever stopped him."

The sword bobbed up at that, pointing at me, then wiggling its cross guard like a proud young soldier, throwing back its shoulders to stand at attention.

That was right. It was the Nightingale who stopped him two centuries ago, after the knight turned on the Architect who'd made him and began a terrifying rampage through Gallant. That was what had sparked the first war with Saventry, when their mage-lords decided that aethercraft was too unnatural and dangerous to be tolerated so close to their borders.

"All right. So what's it got to do with Dark Spectacles sabotaging the mines?" I asked.

Jasper's lips pressed into a grim line. He pulled something from one pocket. It was the piece of metal he'd found in the mine.

"Notice anything?" he prompted, setting it on the display beside the helm.

I squinted. Then stared. Then shook my head, not wanting to believe it. "Just because they're the same color doesn't mean anything. Maybe lots of things from the Golden Age were made out of red steel."

"No," said Jasper. "I've checked all the records I can find. Only the Architect himself knew how to create red steel. And he only ever crafted one thing out of it: the Crimson Knight."

"Right, and the Nightingale destroyed the knight, so that's the end of that story."

"It's not so easy to destroy the works of the Architect," said Jasper. "According to the legends, the Nightingale only managed to break the knight apart, not finish him completely. No one knows exactly what happened to all the pieces, but it's possible that Dark Spectacles found one or more of them. And that he's trying to reconstruct the knight."

"Then wouldn't he need more of that . . . red steel stuff?"

"Yes. But no one knows exactly how the Architect made red steel. You'd have to infuse molten metal with gaseous aether. The heat required is tremendous."

"You think that's what burned that miner?"

Jasper nodded. "It also explains why he was after the

effervescence modulator. He probably needs something like that for the infusion process."

My stomach felt like the insides of an aetheric dryer, tumbling and tumbling and tumbling. "Who would want to re-create a monster that nearly destroyed Gallant?"

He shook his head. "Someone desperate or foolish, or both. We have to find Dark Spectacles and stop him. Fast. If Saventry learns that the Crimson Knight is back, they won't care who's responsible. They'll just attack and say we broke the peace accords." He looked away across the hall. I followed his gaze.

A portrait of Queen Jessamine hung there, looking serene but capable, the barest hint of a smile at the corner of her mouth. She was dark-haired, like Jasper.

"Look, I know this is just about the coin for you," he said after a moment. "But it's more than that for me. My mother hated war and despised what it did to Gallant. After the Battle of the Rhee, she said there was no way anyone would ever really win. That was when she started the peace negotiations, even though she'd been wounded. She put off being treated properly because it was more important for her to finish the accords. And she did it. She convinced the mage-lords to agree to her terms . . . and then she died."

The words fell into utter silence. I stood there, not wanting to move or breathe or speak.

The prince finally met my eyes. "The peace accords with

Saventry were my mother's greatest legacy. I can't let them get broken."

The way Jasper was looking at me now, all burning, bright blue passion, was even worse than one of Sophie's stares. As much as I didn't want to care, a part of me did. For Jasper, the peace accords were like my mum's locket. The last piece of her he still had. Of course he wanted to fight for them.

"We won't let that happen," I said fervently. "I mean, you still have the helmet here. Dark Spectacles needs that to finish the job, right? So we still have time to find him."

A trace of relief crossed Jasper's face. "Yes. We do. And I've got something that might help." He reached into his pocket and tugged free a lump of wires and crystals. It looked as if he'd swiped a handful of trash out of the Heap, but he brandished it proudly.

"What is it?" I asked.

Jasper tapped one of the crystals. Immediately the device began to shriek. I hadn't heard anything that loud since Miss Starvenger discovered that someone—Cora, probably—had replaced her favorite shampoo with spoiled milk.

"Great," I shouted, covering my ears with my hands. "You invented a Very Loud Noise Generator."

"No. Listen." Jasper took a step backward, and the siren grew suddenly quieter. Another step and it had dimmed to a distant murmur.

Cautiously, I unplugged my ears. "I still don't—"

Jasper stepped forward again, moving past me toward the

helm of the Crimson Knight and the bit of red steel from the mine. The shrieking returned, louder than ever.

"It's a red steel detector! All you need to do is fly around the city until it starts making noise, and then go in the direction that makes it get louder! If Dark Spectacles is trying to remake the Crimson Knight, this should lead you straight to him. You can sneak up on him and—"

"Sneak?" I cocked my head as the tinny siren continued to shriek its warning.

"Ah." Jasper rubbed the side of his nose. "There may be a slight flaw in my plan." He waved his hands. "Well, the tracker can at least point you in the right direction. Just turn it off when you get close." He clicked the crystal again and the device fell silent.

"Better than nothing," I said, taking the device and stuffing it into my pocket. "One Dark Spectacles on ice, coming up." The sword swooped back and forth as I spoke, sparking with obvious excitement.

Jasper frowned. "Just be careful. We barely escaped that vortex generator last time. He might have more tricks than that."

"Well, so do I, right? Back when we were fighting the cleaner, you said the Nightingale has three powers. We know about the flying and the ice blast. So, what's my third power?" I looked at Jasper, then at Sword.

The weapon only shrugged its cross guard.

"It probably doesn't know," said Jasper. "Aside from flight,

the sword's powers have been different for every Nightingale."
He stepped over to the only other display. As I followed, I
noticed the plaque along the plinth: THE MASKS OF THE
NIGHTINGALES. Jasper pointed to the mask on the far left,
which was so battered it barely looked like a mask anymore.
Half had been torn away, the ragged edges blackened. But you
could still make out the impression of a beak, how the leather
had been carved with a design of feathers.

"The first Nightingale was the one who destroyed the
Crimson Knight," said Jasper, pointing to the tattered mask.
"She couldn't be physically harmed so long as she was holding
the hilt of the sword."

"Then why does her mask look like it's been chewed by—
oof!" Jasper had just elbowed me in the side, jerking his chin
at the sword. It had sunk low, drooping like a mourner at a
funeral. Oh. Was that how the first Nightingale died? Because
she wasn't holding Sword, and it couldn't protect her?

"Er, never mind. And what about that one?" I pointed to
the middle mask, which was much larger than the first.

"The second Nightingale saved Gallant during the great
floods last century. He could breathe underwater when
he was holding the sword," said Jasper. "The masks of the
third and fourth Nightingales were never recovered, but that
one on the right with the aetheric wiring belonged to the fifth.
That's the last one before you. They saved my great-grandfather
from a terror group of Saventine mages called the Order
of Silence. Supposedly they could summon an enchanted

song that caused anyone who heard it to fall into a trance."

"So the powers are completely random?"

"I don't think so," said Jasper, growing animated. "If you correlate the different powers to the environmental challenges each Nightingale faced, there's a distinct pattern. My hypothesis is that the powers manifest in direct response to the nature of the specific threat to Gallant."

I had no idea what the words "hypothesis" or "correlate" meant, but I could ask Sophie later. I still got the point.

"I can make Sword shoot out ice," I said. "Does that mean there's going to be a fire?"

"More likely it has to do with the Crimson Knight. According to the histories, he could conjure handfuls of flame."

I winced. "Invulnerability would be pretty handy, then."

Jasper bounced up on his toes, a slightly unsettling gleam in his eyes. "We need to conduct an experiment."

"What do you mean?"

He started pacing, shaping the air with his hands in his excitement. "It's a scientific principle. We perform a test in a controlled environment to demonstrate the validity of a hypothesis."

There was that word again. I shook my head. "I don't follow."

He made a gesture like he was stabbing something. "We try different things and see which of them you are immune to. Knives, drowning, flesh-melting acid, uncontrollable sneezing. Ooh! I have a new electric scrambler that we could test!"

"No!"

"But we could practice proper safety protocols. It would be perfectly—"

"I'm not letting you try to stab and drown and fry me just to see if I'm invulnerable. Sword and I will figure this one out."

Jasper seemed disappointed, but nodded. "Oh, and I suppose you'll be wanting payment for that business at the soda fountain." He fumbled in his pocket, then drew out a glimmering chess piece. A rook, I thought. They were the towers, right? At first I thought it was copper, but it was too bright, too sunshine-pale.

I stared at the chess piece. "Is that *gold*?" I asked, my voice faint.

He turned it over in his hand, frowning. "Is it not enough?"

I shook my head. "It's too much."

He groaned. "I don't understand you, Nightingale. I thought you *wanted* to be paid. I'm trying to give you want you wanted. So why do I still feel like I'm doing it all wrong?"

"Because it's ridiculous that you can just hand me a rook made of solid gold, la-di-da, as if it's nothing!"

"It *is* nothing. I mean, my dog Gadget steals them all the time, so we have an entire backup set."

But it wasn't nothing to *me*. It was enough to buy my future back. A part of me wanted to toss it back in his face, to make him understand how big a deal it really was.

Before I could come up with the right words to explain it

all, Jasper's attention shifted abruptly to Sword, who bobbed between us.

"What happened?" he blurted out. "One of the sword's eyes is missing!"

Rust it all. I forced a look of surprise onto my face. "What? It must've come loose during one of the battles. But look, it still works fine. Right, Sword?"

Sword angled at me for a moment, then executed a complex series of loop-the-loops.

None of it had driven the fierce frown from Jasper's face, though.

"It's all right," I told him. "I'll go look for it. And if I bring it back, you can fix it, right? I mean, you're some sort of artificing genius. Does it even need a second eye, really? Anyway, I'll go now."

I snatched the golden rook from his hand and fled before he could ask me any more questions I couldn't answer without lies.

The sword might've turned my whole life into a tangle, but all of that seemed to fall away when we were soaring above the city. It was as if the only thing in the world was me, and Sword, and the vast, empty span of blue. Somehow, up here, everything felt possible.

I hadn't had that feeling in a long time. Mum and I used

to have picnic dinners out on the fire escape, and she'd tell me about our future, how one day we'd have our very own apartment, where we could paint the walls whatever colors we liked and I'd have a whole room of my own. That one over there, she'd say, pointing across the forest of rooftops to one tall building of pale gray stone, near the edge of Prospect Park. *See that light, right at the top? That's where we'll live. Up in the sky, where we belong.* She poked me, making me giggle with the joke of it. I had my father's last name—Granby—to honor the memory of a kind man who had died of a fever before I ever knew him. But my first name, Lark, was my link to my mother, Louisa Larkin. *Birds of a feather,* she used to say.

Until she tried to fly too high, too close to the trees where the vultures lived, and they struck her down. And here I was, daring the same thing. Searching for a villain who might well be trying to re-create the most dangerous aethercraft in history.

I glanced at the wiry mess of Jasper's tracking device, tied to my wrist. I'd been flying back and forth above Lamlyle all morning, but it hadn't given a single peep. Well, except for the continuous squeal it made whenever I got near the Heap. I'd spent two hours trying and failing to narrow down the source before I remembered my history: the Heap was where the Nightingale had fought the Crimson Knight. The entire place was probably littered with bits of red steel, chipped away during that climactic battle.

We were over the Scrag now. I'd left it for last, partly because Dark Spectacles looked too posh to belong there, and partly because, well, it stank of aether fumes. Especially where I was, just south of Pinshaw's factory. And right above Wixwell's pawnshop. I could fly down right now, turn in Jasper's gold chess piece, and fill my pockets with enough silver to pay off every last bit of my debt. I could get Mum's locket back.

Three days ago, that was all I'd wanted. That was the only reason I'd even agreed to become the Nightingale. But everything was different now. I flew on, above the hulk of the huffing, chuffing aether factory. The truth was, I'd started to *enjoy* being the Nightingale. It felt good to help people, to be able to make a difference. I'd stopped that bomb in the mines. I'd saved my housemates and the other folks at Dashlilly's. Mum would be proud of me for that.

And then there was Jasper.

And Sword.

Sword, who had become something like a friend. Maybe more than that. A partner. It had chosen me, and it expected something from me. Sometimes I even thought that maybe it *cared* about me.

Maybe, in spite of everything, I was turning out to be a proper Nightingale after all.

"All right," I told Sword. "One more pass here, and if we don't find anything, we'll go back to—"

I broke off, as the device tied to my wrist gave a sudden shrill cry. We had found something.

CHAPTER THIRTEEN

There was no question about it. The closer I flew to Mr. Pinshaw's factory, the louder the tracker wailed. Unlike the Heap, this was clearly no wild-goose chase. I landed on the roof. As I swung the tracker in a slow arc toward the left, the wailing increased. The red steel was on the far side of the factory. My heart began to thunder in my ears. What if it was the Crimson Knight? For all Jasper had said about him not being complete without his helmet, he didn't really know for sure. And even if it was just Dark Spectacles, he might have another trick like the vortex generator up his sleeve.

But I couldn't afford to panic. Fear made your hands tremble during the take. Doubt made you miss the perfect pluck. This wasn't a bit of thieving, but I had to be strong all the same. I could do this. And I wasn't alone. I had Sword. I gripped the weapon's hilt tighter. "Come on," I said, clicking off the shrilling tracker. "Let's see what it is."

I marched to the edge of the roof, took a bracing breath,

then peered down. A tangle of pneumatic tubes erupted from the back wall of the factory below. I'd never been this close to them, but I knew what they were, thanks to Sophie: a system that carried the factory waste off to be dumped into the Rhee. The tubes were made of crystal, which meant I could see very clearly the swirl of glimmering dust inside.

And the girl trapped along with it: Sophie!

She was on her hands and knees, inching her way forward with grim determination. Rust it, how had she gotten stuck in there?

"Let's go!" I jabbed Sword in the direction of the tubes, sending us flying down. I landed atop the tube Sophie was in with a dramatic swirl of my only slightly chocolate-stained cloak. "Don't worry! I'll save you!"

I heard Sophie make a noise. Why did it sound more like a groan than a cry of relief? Rust it, the aether dust must be getting to her. I had to get her out, fast!

I swung Sword down at the crystal tube a few feet ahead of Sophie. The blade slashed through the crystal once, twice. A great chunk fell away, releasing a cloud of gleaming dust. Holding my breath, I flew closer to seize Sophie's arm.

Before she could even thank me, I was swooping us down to the ground at the back of the factory. "There," I said, as I set her down gently. "You're safe!"

Sophie winced as she put her weight on her right foot. I held out my hand, but she ignored it. Instead she was glaring. At *me*.

"You again," she said, as if I were a rat that had turned up in her larder too many times. "Just who do you think you are?"

Had she seen through my mask and cloak? Honestly, it might be for the best if she'd figured it out. We could work together to thwart Dark Spectacles. Jasper was clever, no doubt, but he wasn't Sophie. But before I could respond, Sophie answered her own question, her tone scornful. "The Nightingale," she said. "Champion of Gallant."

I blinked. That wasn't the reaction I'd been expecting.

"Er. Yes. So, um, will you be all right?" I looked her up and down. Normally it took a couple of months for someone to start ghosting, but I didn't know how much aether dust she'd been exposed to while trapped in that tube.

Sophie brushed off her smock, then set her fists on her hips. "No. I'm *not* all right." She jabbed a finger up at the tube. "Look at that! Look what you did!"

I gulped. A stream of glittering dust was wafting from the hole I'd cut while I was rescuing Sophie. Oops.

"Don't worry," I said, pointing Sword's tip at the breach. "I can fix it. Watch this. Freeze!" A jet of ice burst from the blade, covering the hole in seconds. "See?" I said proudly.

"And what happens when it melts?" Sophie scoffed. "What are you and your fancy sword going to do then?"

The sword twitched, trying to tuck itself back behind me like a puppy hiding behind its master. I let it go and crossed my arms instead. "Well, *excuse* me for trying to help."

"I didn't *need* help." She shook her head, the fire of

conviction glinting in her dark eyes. "I wasn't trapped! I was trying to figure out where all the extra dust is coming from! I just know Pinshaw is up to something. He doesn't think anyone'll notice that he's venting twice as much aetheric waste as usual, but he's wrong. People deserve to know the truth. He's poisoning the Scrag! So if you really want to be a hero, Nightingale, maybe you should worry about *that*. Not running around stabbing your sword into things you don't understand!"

I felt as if a vortex generator had just opened inside my chest, sucking all the words, all the air out of me. I gaped at Sophie. "I—I thought I was helping."

"Indeed," said a polished voice nearby. "You've been a great help, Nightingale. You've identified this radical unionist before she could do anything to further interfere with the proper functioning of my factory. Thank you."

I turned to see a man in a neat dark suit, flanked by several dangerous-looking factory guards. It took me a moment to recognize him. It had been four years since Mum's funeral. Mr. Pinshaw had lost most of his dark hair, and what he had left was dashed with gray. But I could never forget those watery blue eyes. Couldn't forget them staring at me with all the feeling of a dead fish, as he shook my hand and told me how sorry he was about Mum's "accident." How he'd be happy to offer me a job in his factory once I was a bit older. Anything to help.

I'd been so angry, so wretched, all I could do was snap that I was never, ever going to work for him. But my words hadn't mattered. I was just a fly. Not even worth swatting. He just blinked his dead-fish eyes, smiled, and walked away.

And now, here he was, *thanking* me! I started to shake my head, but Pinshaw went on, his clipped tone cool and controlled. "I'll have my people repair the tube. The girl's mischief won't cause any long-term damage to our production quotas."

"I—but—" My lips felt numb, as if I'd accidentally iced myself.

"And as for you, Miss Tam," Pinshaw continued, frowning at Sophie. "By rights I should summon a constable to arrest you for this destruction of property. But I can be a forgiving man. You are quite young, after all." He crossed his arms, dipping his head benevolently. "I'll say nothing of it, provided you leave these premises at once. You're fired."

"What?" I exploded. "No! Just because she figured out you—"

"Shut up!" Sophie snarled at me. "I told you to *stop helping*!" She stared Pinshaw straight in his dead-fish eyes, and said. "You're going to regret this," she said. "All of it. The truth will win out." Then she turned and began slowly pacing away, toward the street, head held high.

Rust it all! What a mess. I glared at Pinshaw. "She's better off without you and this haunt-shop."

Pinshaw considered me coolly. "Careful, Nightingale. You're supposed to be the champion of Gallant, aren't you? Crown Prince Gideon would hardly approve of you aligning yourself with such traitorous and disruptive elements."

The man clearly didn't realize how close he was to becoming

a human ice cube. But right then, I was more worried about Sophie. I gave him one last glare before dashing off after her. She'd already rounded the corner but had stopped to rest her foot and was leaning against a streetlamp. Her expression darkened when she saw me.

"Go away."

"I'm sorry," I began, "but I was only trying to—"

"I know exactly what you were trying to do, Nightingale. But we don't need you to protect us. We need laws. We need the rusting crown prince to admit that the factories are dangerous. You can fly around and do a few good deeds, but that's not going to change anything, not really. You can't fix everything. And today, you just made it worse."

The lump in my throat choked me. I'd disappointed Sophie before, but never like this. Never so much that those dark brown eyes stabbed into me like unforgiving knives. A part of me wanted to blurt out the truth, to tell her who I was, that I was her friend, to demand that she forgive me. But what if she didn't? What if she despised me just as much when I was Lark? I didn't know if I could bear that. So instead I turned, grabbed Sword, and flew away from her accusing eyes.

It took five loops above the city to drive the stinging from my eyes and to steady the crackling feeling in my chest, as if a single word might shatter me. But even Sword couldn't fly high enough to escape the memory of Sophie's accusation.

Or the queasy, uncomfortable suspicion that she was right. Sophie was clever and wise. I trusted her. I respected her. So. Maybe I couldn't fix everything. But there was one thing I *could* repair, so I might as well go do that.

"We're going to get your eye back," I told the blade as we made our way over to Mrs. Wixwell's shop. The weapon was back in hiding under my coat, the mask was in my pocket, and the cloak was wrapped around my neck as a frilly collar. I needed a break from being the Nightingale, at least until Sophie's angry words stopped echoing in my head. If I was just Lark, I could at least pretend they had nothing to do with me.

There was no door to the pawnshop, only a small barred opening above a narrow counter. Display windows flanked the entrance on either side, covered in a wire mesh, revealing an assortment of valuables whose owners had never returned to claim them. An ivory fan, spread to show a painted scene of some distant green land. A brass spyglass. Silk gowns, gemmed cuff links, and a set of tiny teacups crafted from some luminous, pale green stone.

I slid my receipt under the bars. "I'm here to collect. This should more than cover it." I set the gold rook down beside the receipt with a satisfying *clunk*. That was the nice thing about gold. It didn't have to give you an approving nod. You didn't have to worry about disappointing it. You always knew what it was worth, and what it cost.

Mrs. Wixwell adjusted her spectacles and touched a hand to her close-cropped gray hair. She did not look like a woman about to turn a tidy profit. She looked like someone about to deliver unpleasant news.

"Oh, Miss Granby. I'm afraid the item in question has already been resold."

"What? But you said I had two weeks!"

I seized the receipt, shaking it. I'd had enough trouble for one day.

"Well, yes, under normal circumstances, but you'll recall that there's a clause saying that if another buyer offers more than twice the item's worth, I am free to sell it at any time."

I had a vague recollection of her saying that. But who in the Scrag would buy a gem for so much more than it was worth?

"Who?" I demanded. "Who bought it?"

"I'm afraid I can't reveal that information."

I gave a groan of frustration, then pushed the gold rook closer to the metal grate. "How much will you give me for this, then?" I had to track down whoever had the sapphire and get it back. Coin was always good for loosening lips.

But before Mrs. Wixwell could respond, a hand darted between us, snatching up the rook. "Hey!" I spun toward the thief, ready for a fight or a chase. But there was no thief.

It was Miss Starvenger.

She was wearing one of her most devastating outfits, striped cream and navy, the skirts caught up with dark blue bows, and a matching hat that framed her freshly curled brown hair and keen blue eyes.

"My, such an industrious girl you are," she said, turning the chess piece in her hand, admiring it. "It seems you have a most generous employer. First that silver brooch, and now this?"

Uh-oh. I had a bad feeling about this.

"He is," I said, my eyes fixed on the rook, waiting for her to put it back down. "So I'll have more coming. I'm going to pay off every last penny I owe."

"Mmm." She sounded as if she were finishing off a particularly delicious tart. "Tell me, dear Lark, who is this generous man? He sounds like someone I would be most eager to meet. What's his name?"

Her hungry eyes searched my face. "Er, Mr. Jasper," I blurted out.

"It's fortunate he trusts you with such work, Lark. I hope you won't disappoint him." Her expression made it clear she had her own significant doubts on that count. "Remember that you have the reputation of my household to maintain. I won't have you tarnishing the Starvenger name."

"Of course not, Miss," I said. "I know how hard you've worked to make it mean something." Something rotten. But I smiled at her, knowing better than to say it. "May I have my rook back, please?"

Her lips pursed. "*Your* rook? I'm afraid you forget yourself, Lark. You own nothing. You are my ward. Whatever monies you acquire come to me directly. We'll call this your payment for this week's room and board." With that she turned and began pacing away from the pawnshop, the golden rook still in her hand.

"Wait!" I left Mrs. Wixwell gaping after us as I raced to block Starvenger's way along the street. "That's not fair! It's worth more than that!"

Starvenger paused, smiling the smile of someone who was quite sure she had the upper hand. "It's worth what I say it is, if you want to get your mother's locket back."

I quivered with the injustice of it. I wanted more than anything to snatch Sword from my back, to transform then and there into the Nightingale and freeze the selfish, lying woman. But I couldn't risk Mum's locket. I breathed in, trying to find something, anything, to convince Miss Starvenger to relent. But all I could manage was a croaking protest. "Why?" I asked. "Why do you have to be so cruel?"

Starvenger's jaw tightened. "Kindness doesn't get you anywhere in this world, Lark. Hard work. Tenacity. That's what you need, not foolish sentiment." For a brief moment she almost looked sad. "I was like you, once. Trust me, you'll be considerably better off the sooner you give up such fantasies. That's what I'm trying to teach you girls. These are the skills you need to survive."

"No! Please! Don't you have any idea what that locket means to me?" I swallowed, trying not to panic. Trying to figure out some way to reach her. Sophie said one of the best ways to win someone over in an argument was to make them feel what you were feeling, see themselves in your shoes. "Don't you have anyone *you* miss? Someone you lost? Your mother—"

"No," snapped Starvenger. "It's foolish to miss those who are gone. We can't change the past, and regret accomplishes nothing, save to tarnish the future." But even as she said it, one hand slid to her neck, touching the gold chain. Her eyes went distant. Was she remembering something? Had I actually reached her?

Then she gave a small shake of her head, shattering my hopes. "This is a good lesson for you, Lark, not to place such value on material things. You may have the locket back when your account is settled, and not one minute earlier. And this," she added, holding up the rook, "will cover five silvers of your debt. That's fair, isn't it?"

My eyes stung, and I had to blink quickly. Tears would only make this worse. She probably wanted me to cry, to see that she had that power over me, horrid woman.

Then someone else spoke. "No. That rook is worth considerably more."

Jasper stood a few paces away, leaning casually against a contraption that looked like one of the velocipedes you sometimes saw rich nobs riding in the Cutlet, except that it had two large bellows attached to the sides. Even without the strange device, he would have stood out against the grim gray of the Scrag, though, in his blue coat and trousers, the royal insignia glimmering on his velvet-trimmed lapel.

"Prince Jasper!" I said, as a mixture of relief and panic flooded me. What was he doing here?

Miss Starvenger's mouth opened. Nothing came out. She started to shake her head in disbelief. "P-prince Jasper?"

Jasper smiled, pointing above us to a nearby ephemera-board, which was currently displaying a story about Crown Prince Gideon's upcoming birthday. The image showed Gideon and Jasper standing together on the palace balcony.

"As you see," he said.

And there was no question about it. I'd gotten used to being around the boy who got excited about glowing bugs and desperately wanted someone to tell about his latest inventions. My partner. Yet all at once, Jasper was royal. Formidable. The sort of person who could cow even Starvenger.

She still looked disbelieving, giving a small shake of her head. "Here? In the Scrag?"

"Actually, I'm here to visit Lark. On royal business," he added sternly.

She turned on me, accusation in her eyes. "You're working for the prince?"

"No," Jasper said, before I could respond. "She's my friend. And that gold chess piece was a gift. So I suggest you return it."

CHAPTER FOURTEEN

Miss Starvenger sank into a deep curtsy. "My apologies, Highness. I'm afraid my ward did not inform me of her connection to your esteemed self. Please forgive my ignorance."

"Your ward?"

"Yes," said Miss Starvenger, fixing a weirdly bright smile on her lips. "I run a boardinghouse for girls like Lark here, who have nowhere else to go. Of course it's a challenge, keeping them all in line, making sure they're well fed and brought up smartly, but I feel it's my duty to Gallant, one I undertake most humbly."

Jasper's nostrils flared. He glanced at me, then back to Miss Starvenger. "Is that so? Then why were you confiscating that chess piece?"

"There are significant costs involved in clothing and feeding my charges. So it's only right that any income they earn should help support our household."

Jasper's black brows drew together. "She shouldn't be earning income. She should be in school."

"All my girls study their lessons at home," Miss Starvenger added quickly.

"In any case," said Jasper, "the rook was a gift, not a payment. So I trust you will return it before there's any further misunderstanding."

Miss Starvenger's fingers tightened on the piece. She glanced at me, then at the various curious passersby who had halted, watching the scene. Finally she gave a strangled smile. "Of course." She passed the chess piece back to me. "I'll see you back at the boardinghouse, Miss Granby," she said, with the barest trace of a threat. She dipped another curtsy to Jasper. "Good day, Your Highness." Then she whirled away and retreated down the sidewalk.

I stared at the gold figurine. It felt as if the last several minutes were some sort of strange dream. Jasper didn't belong here, in the Scrag. He didn't belong in this part of my life. He wasn't supposed to see any of this. A tightness caught in my throat. Before it could choke me, I set off toward a side street, ducking away from the commotion. I needed a place to breathe. To stop the whirl of my thoughts.

Jasper's quick steps followed as I sank onto the ledge of an old fountain, the pool dark and dank behind me. He sat beside me. "Lark."

"What?" I still didn't look at him.

"That's your real name."

"Yep."

"And you really live with that horrid woman?"

"I don't have much choice." The words came out sharper than I meant them to, but something inside me was still full of teeth, wanting to bite back at the world.

"Oh. Er. Sorry."

Silence yawned between us, like one of the gaps between ephemera broadcasts, when the screens all filled with a strange, buzzy static.

It wasn't that I didn't appreciate his help. I was glad to have the rook. It was only that . . . it was so easy for Jasper to come in and fix things. But just for today. What would it matter, tomorrow? Miss Starvenger was going to make me pay for that scene. And where would Jasper be then? Back in his gilded palace.

Rust it. Was this how Sophie had felt, earlier, when I'd tried to swoop in and fix things for her? Some things were too big, too complicated to fix so easily. Even for the Nightingale. Or for a prince.

But that didn't mean it was wrong to try.

I slid a sidelong look at Jasper. He was tinkering with the fountain, spinning one of the levers. "Thanks, Jasper," I said. "I don't know how you ended up right where I needed you, but I'm glad you were there."

"You're welcome." He tugged free a bit of metal tubing

from the fountain. "I'm glad I was here too. D'you know, this is the first time I've been in this part of town? And that's wrong. I need to do better. I *will* do better."

He fiddled with the tube, cleaning it out, then fitting it back into place. "There, that should do it." He wiggled the lever again. A half-dozen sprays of water suddenly burst from the dank pool, forming a sort of flower. The stagnant water began to clear.

I slumped against the side of the fountain pool. "Jasper," I said. "I didn't lose the sapphire. The sword gave it to me, to pawn, because I needed money. But I meant to get it back. That's why I was there at the shop, but some rich sot had already . . ."

I trailed off as Jasper pulled something from his pocket and held it out to me with a sheepish grin. "You were wondering why I ended up there at the pawnshop just at the right time? Well, when you told me the sapphire was lost, I figured someone might find it and try to sell it. I sent word to every pawnshop and jeweler in the city, offering a reward. Which led me to this."

It was Sword's sapphire eye. I sucked in a breath. "*You're* the rich sot!"

"Serves me right, I guess. If I'd waited another ten minutes, you'd have gotten it a lot cheaper. But I was angry. I thought . . . well . . . I didn't understand. But now I do. And I'm not angry. Not at you, anyway."

I let out a long, soft sigh. "Really?"

"Here," he said. "Tell your sword to come over and let me fix it."

"You can do that? Right here and now?"

"I always come prepared." He grinned, drawing a vial of liquid aether from his pocket, along with a tiny paintbrush.

The sword had already slid free from its hiding place. I gestured it toward the prince, who set the sapphire back into the hilt, then began carefully inscribing a rune onto the surface of the gem. A shimmer of light flickered over the blade. I held my breath.

The sword bobbed up, both eyes glinting blue, and flew a joyful circle above our heads, before floating down to nudge at my hand.

I sighed again. "This was easier when it was just a job."

"So it's not anymore?" asked Jasper. "Not just a job?"

"No," I said. "I mean, I still think I should get paid. I am risking my life, after all. But now I care."

He snorted. "Noted. But Lark, is it a *bad* thing to care? I mean, isn't it better that way?"

"No," I said, my voice small. "If it's just a job, then I can quit. It doesn't matter if I let people down. That I can't fix everything." I squeezed my eyes shut for a moment, thinking of Sophie.

"No one's asking you to fix *everything*," said Jasper.

"Then what's the point?" A burst of fury ripped through me. "What's the point if we can't actually make things better?

The first Nightingale died stopping the Crimson Knight, but there was still a war. And now this rusting Dark Spectacles wants to start it all over again. Heroes die all the time, and nothing really changes. Like your mum. And—and mine."

"Your mother?" Jasper prompted softly.

"She was trying to make things better in the factories. She helped organize the first Aether Workers' Union. But Mr. Pinshaw didn't like it. He threatened her. Sent a man to our apartment to tell her if she didn't stop, they'd make her. And then, one day, she—" My throat closed, unable to say the words. "She was going to a union meeting. She said she'd be back late. Not to worry. But she didn't come back. Some folks said she must've ghosted, but I don't believe it. They got rid of her. Just like they promised."

Jasper let out a long breath. "Oh."

"And afterward, all her friends kept telling me I should be *proud* of her. That she was an inspiration. That she'd made a real difference. But nothing really changed. The aether factories are hurting people. And anyways, I'd rather still have her with me. I don't need to be proud of her. I just want her to be *alive*—"

I broke off, my voice catching.

"I understand," said Jasper.

"I know. So you see why I have to figure out what's going on with Dark Spectacles. Your brother is already blaming it on the union. That's *my* mum's legacy. And I'm going to fight for it."

Jasper sighed. "I don't want the culprit to be the union,

Lark. Just like I don't want it to be Saventry. But until we find that man, people are going to be looking for someone to blame."

"Then we need to find him!" I said. "I've been flying all over the city with this thing, and the only time it ever made a peep was when I was above Pinshaw's aether factory. Wait." I sat straighter. "The pneumatic tubes!"

"You think he's hiding in the pneumatic tubes? That seems rather unconventional."

"No. But my friend Sophie says there's more waste in the tubes than there should be. She's investigating it. She thinks someone's building a secret aether factory somewhere."

Jasper's brows arched into the dark swoop of his bangs. "A *new* aether factory? Like the sort of place where you'd create red steel and repair an ancient murderous metal knight?"

I nodded. "Exactly like that. So if we follow the tubes, we could figure out where the waste is coming from. Right?"

"It's worth a shot," said Jasper.

I seized Sword's hilt. "Let's go find out."

"He's in the Heap? That makes no sense," I said, as we flew west from Pinshaw's aether factory. We'd traced every other set of pneumatic tubes. Most went from the factory to the river, while others curved north toward the railway, where the deliveries from the mines came in. If any of the tubes was going to lead us to a secret aether factory, it had to be this one, which ran above the streets of the Scrag, straight toward the ruin of the Heap.

"On the contrary, it makes a considerable amount of sense," called Jasper, zooming along in his velocipede beside me. It turned out that the two strange bellows attached to the sides allowed it to float, though he couldn't get much higher than the tops of the town houses. It also had an unfortunate tendency to start plunging back down toward the street any time he stopped pedaling. "Hardly anyone goes there anymore. And there's plenty of raw materials."

"No, I mean, I already looked here," I said. "It's all just rubble! Do you see anything that looks like an aether factory?"

"No," he puffed. "But maybe that's because it's not *in* the Heap. It's *underneath* it." He pointed to the pneumatic tube we'd been following. Just ahead of us, the crystal pipe plunged down abruptly, straight into the ground. "That might also explain the haywire cleaner," he added as we landed in the nearby clearing, under the shadow of a shattered dirigible. "Maybe it wasn't just a random accident that it was chasing after us and ignoring the rest of the trash. Dark Spectacles could have put it there to keep people from poking around."

"So how do we get in? Through the tube?" I hefted Sword, eyeing the crystal column.

"Maybe we don't have to," Jasper whispered, pointing. "Look!"

I caught a glimpse of someone in a dark coat, moving through a nearby alley. The piles of rubble and tattered metal screens shielded him from full view, but the glint of dark where his eyes should have been told me all I needed to know.

"Dark Spectacles!" I followed Jasper's lead, diving sideways behind the broken hull of the dirigible. We peered out through a crack in the thin metal as our enemy advanced into the clearing. He halted beside the tube and peered up and down the length of crystal. His back was to us.

I held my breath. Should I attack now, while I had the element of surprise? I glanced at Jasper and brandished Sword.

He shook his head sharply, then tapped his eye and pointed back at Dark Spectacles. I stifled a sigh. Fine, yes, I supposed it made sense to see what the man was up to. We did need to find out how he was getting into whatever was hidden below the Heap.

The man had taken something from his pocket and was holding it to his ear. "I've checked the pneumatics. There doesn't seem to be any permanent damage. We can proceed as planned."

He went silent, head tilted, as if listening to something.

"Aethercom," Jasper said quietly. "Sounds like he's talking to a partner."

"Yes," the man went on. "You have my word. Project Red will be fully functional on the day of the coronation. And I've kept the work completely secret—no one suspects anything."

Jasper turned toward me, his eyes wide. "They must be planning an attack on my brother," he whispered. "That's why they're trying to re-create the Crimson Knight!"

"Who do you suppose he's working for?" I asked, keeping my voice low. "I thought everyone loved your brother."

Well, everyone except Sophie. And others like her, folk who wanted a different sort of progress than what Gideon had promised. But it couldn't possibly be Sophie. She'd been just as keen as I was to find this hidden workshop.

"I suppose there's the Council of Regents," said Jasper, though he looked dubious. "They've been effectively ruling for the past two years, but once Gid turns eighteen, he'll take charge. If they bump him off, they stay in power, at least for another five years."

Rust it. If only we could hear the voice on the other end of that aethercom. But all I could make out was a distant hum. Dark Spectacles nodded. "Yes. I think that would be wise. The union will be the perfect scapegoat, and we might just kill two birds with one crimson stone." He chuckled.

A surge of fury rose up my chest. He was using the union as a scapegoat!

"Of course. Good day." The man tucked the aethercom into his pocket, then strode over to a crumbling section of brick wall. He pressed a hand to one of the bricks. With a hum and a faint crackle, the old wall vanished, melting away to reveal a much sturdier, much newer copper door.

"Some sort of ephemera technology," Jasper murmured. "Fascinating."

There was no handle, only a row of crystals along one side. Dark Spectacles tapped the topmost one, and the copper door slid sideways into the ruined wall.

"Right, then," I told Jasper. "Stay here."

"What are you going to do?" Jasper whispered.

"What do you think I'm going to do? I'm the Nightingale. I'm going to stop the bad guy before he gets away!"

Because of this man, the union was in danger. Because of him, I'd nearly been blown up. My friends had almost been bubbled to death. Now I'd tracked him down in his lair, and it was time to end his villainy before he did anything worse, like actually rebuilding the Crimson Knight.

I crept out from behind the dirigible. Dark Spectacles had his back to me. This was my chance to take him out, before he vanished into his hidden workshop. I pointed Sword's tip at him, aiming for his legs. I still wanted to be able to ask him some questions. *"Freeze!"*

The man must have heard something, because he started to turn, but he was too late. By the time he'd given a startled yelp, his entire torso and legs were sheathed in ice.

"Aha!" I cried out. "Now we've got you! And now you're going to tell us exactly what you're planning to do with the Crimson Knight! And why you want to blame it on the union!"

The man did not move for a long moment, as if I'd frozen

all of him, not just his legs. Slowly he cocked his head, looking over one shoulder at me.

"Ah. Nightingale. You just don't know when to leave something alone, do you?"

"I'm not letting you rebuild the Crimson Knight," I spat. "I'm not letting you murder Prince Gideon! And I'm *definitely* not letting you blame it on the union!"

One gray-flecked brow arched above his spectacles, as if I'd surprised him. Then his lips quirked. He gave a low laugh. "You have no idea the forces you're tampering with, girl. This is not a game. And it's no place for children who think they're heroes."

"I'm not playing games. The Crimson Knight could destroy all of Gallant! Not to mention break the peace treaty with Saventry!"

"As I said, a child's views," he scoffed. "You've let fears consume you. You refuse to accept that aethercraft is Gallant's greatest strength, one we must embrace fully if we're to restore the glory of the Golden Age. And that includes the Architect's greatest creation: the Crimson Knight."

I shook my head. "The Crimson Knight murdered the Architect! And nearly destroyed the city! I'm not letting you unleash him again."

Another laugh. "Oh, really? Well, then, there's someone you should meet."

His teeth glinted like a dagger over the upturned collar of his dark overcoat. Something about it snagged me, like a bit of spiderweb across a door, sticking in my thoughts, tugging uncomfortably. I'd seen that smile before.

I had to get a better look at him. Without the dark lenses. But even as I started marching forward, the villain jabbed a finger at the crystals along the copper door. Not the top gem, which had opened it. The one on the bottom, large and ominously crimson.

Thoom! The earth shivered, sending a thrum up through my heels, up my spine, rattling my teeth. The ground began to peel back, revealing an open shaft large enough to swallow a pyrosaur.

"The Nightingale is here to see you," called Dark Spectacles from the far side of the sudden chasm. "Why don't you come up and say hello?"

A strange grinding and whirring hummed from the depths. I gripped Sword tighter. It wasn't possible. The helm was in the museum!

But the enormous figure rising up from the shaft told me it was, in fact, more than possible. Two feet, large enough to crush me with one step. Two fists the size of boulders. A torso that rose up, up, up as the platform lifting him came to a stop.

The Crimson Knight was incomplete. But that didn't make him any less terrifying. Even headless, he was a good seven feet tall. A glimmering blue rune had been etched into his chest, while the rest of his monstrous body gleamed a dark bloodred.

"Ah, there you are, my beauty," said Dark Spectacles. "Look. Do you recognize this girl? Perhaps not, but surely you know the sword she carries. The sword that once destroyed you."

A rumbling growl came from somewhere deep in the metal monster's chest. It almost sounded like a word, but it was too garbled for my ears to make sense of. Tendrils of oily black smoke coiled from his neck, lashing the air hungrily, as if searching for what was lost.

Dimly, I was aware of Jasper joining me, both of us staring up at this terrible thing that should not be. That *could not* be.

"What was that about the Crimson Knight not working if he's not whole?" I managed to croak.

"Obviously my conjecture was wrong. But really, how much harm can he do without—"

The rest of Jasper's words were drowned out by a great hissing, as something exploded from the palm of one of the knight's hands. A crackling ball of crimson flames hurtled toward us.

CHAPTER FIFTEEN

I leaped, shoving Jasper to the side as a wave of heat rushed over my back, the air snapping and sizzling behind me. A cloud of dark smoke hazed the air. As it cleared, I could see that the knight's flaming blast had shattered what was left of the dirigible, opening a passage into the Heap beyond. If that blast had hit me—

I gulped. My legs felt like jelly.

"Just keep moving!" Jasper cried as he scrambled to his feet, tugging me after him. "He's bigger, but you're faster. I'm going to get some backup."

"Seriously?" I said. "You want me to fight that thing? He's huge! And in case you missed it, he just *shot fire out of his hand*!"

"And you have a magic sword," said Jasper. "So use it!" Then he turned and pelted away, out into the Heap. My breath came in gusty heaves. This was impossible. I didn't belong here. My fear rose up, no longer a manageable tangle I could shove deep. It was too big. It filled my chest, my mind, driving out everything else and leaving me frozen.

Something flashed in my vision. The sword. It had tilted, just a fraction, so that the blade glinted my own reflection back at me, a slash of wide, terrified eyes peering out of a black mask.

"I don't know if I can do this," I whispered to it. "I don't know if I'm really her."

The weapon shivered in my hand, and a ripple of blue aetherlight arced up the edge of the blade. Deep in my skull, voices murmured together. *Nightingale.*

I breathed in. The sword was as bad as Sophie. Both of them *expecting* things from me. Things I didn't think that I actually had.

We never know our own strength until the world tests us, Mum had told me once. I'd found her staring at the painted placards she was making for the union's first strike, hugging herself. I could tell she was scared. But she wouldn't let that stop her. *Being brave doesn't mean you're not afraid,* she had said, hugging me tight. *It means doing what you need to do, even if it's scary.*

I'm pretty sure she wasn't expecting the scary thing to be a giant murderous metal monster, though. And it was true, no coin was worth this. But maybe I wasn't doing it for the coin.

I swung the blade up, doing my best to direct the tip at the Crimson Knight as I shouted, "Freeze!" Silvery-pale ice exploded into the air. I stumbled back, the recoil thrumming through me even as the Crimson Knight bellowed.

It had worked! A column of ice encased the metal monster's leg, pinning him in place. But before I could make another attack, the knight pointed a hand toward his frozen leg. Flames burst from his palm, and a great cloud of steam rose up, sizzling and sputtering.

When the steam cleared, my ice was gone. He was free once more.

I had barely enough time to leap for cover as another bolt of flame smashed toward me. The blast hit a section of brick wall, shattering it and pelting me with sharp fragments of stone.

Pain sliced my temple. Something hard slammed into my chest, driving the air from my lungs. I fell, shoulders slamming into the earth.

A heavy slab of wood lay across my midsection, pinning me there.

"Sword! Get us out of here!"

That was when I realized my hands were empty.

I'd thought I'd been scared before. But it was nothing compared to the churning inside me now, as the Crimson Knight loomed over me, one giant foot lifted directly above my head. I had a single moment of clarity in which I recognized the shape of that foot. The same shape I'd seen in the sand of the mine.

What a rusting useless last thought. Mum. I should be thinking of Mum. I should be acting brave like her. Instead I was trapped, too dizzy to even struggle. Jasper had said he was getting backup. What sort of backup? It didn't matter now—he was too late. I was done for.

As the Crimson Knight began to lower his massive foot, I gathered all my strength, trying to roll to the side, but I moved barely an inch. I didn't even have the breath to scream.

And then I heard a familiar churning, whirring noise. I craned my neck to see a spinning wall of sharp spikes surging forth from the Heap.

It was the cleaner! And Jasper was perched in the driver's cockpit, cackling as he drove it straight at the knight. As the ravenous machine crunched into the knight's leg, the red menace toppled to the ground, off-balance.

Jasper leaped down and dashed to my side. He crouched over me, his eyes so blue and clear. But the rest of him was strange. "You're fuzzy," I said. Or tried to say. My tongue didn't want to cooperate.

"You're bleeding!"

"S'fine." I tried to smile. "Guess . . . my third power's . . . not invulnerability."

"Come on, we need to get you away. Where's the sword?"

"Lost it."

"Call it back. Come on, Lark, stay with me. The sword won't be able to help if you're unconscious. I need to get you out of here. You need to order it to fly us away! Quick!"

He looked past me. I wanted to try to see what was making him grimace, but it hurt too much to turn my head, which felt like it was full of sharp bits of glass and damp wool. Whatever had distracted him was making a tremendous racket. "Sword?" I managed to slur out. "C'mere. Take us . . . somewhere safe."

I heard a skittering of metal, then saw the glimmer of something floating over me anxiously. I lifted one hand, groaning in pain, but managed to wrap my fingers around the smooth hilt. Lightness filled me, turning the weight of the wooden beam to thistledown. I felt another hand close over mine, gripping tight, as if to keep me from letting go. Then a rush of air. Then nothing at all.

I woke in a strange, bright room that made it seem as if I were inside some enormous piece of artifice. My head still felt broken and cluttered, but the other pains were duller now, only distant throbs.

"Careful," said Jasper. "I put healing salve on your cuts, but that won't help with the bruises. I think you took a pretty big bump to the head. How do you feel?"

"Like a useless dazzlebug that got stomped by a giant metal monster."

"Don't be so hard on yourself," said Jasper. "You survived. That's something. Besides, that was only your first time facing the knight. I'm sure you'll do much better next time, once you're properly prepared."

Next time.

There was going to be a next time. Because I was the Nightingale, and the Crimson Knight was my nemesis. The thought opened up a vortex generator in my stomach, sucking in every bit of relief I'd been feeling.

"Sword?" I called, my voice jittery. Then the weapon was

there, slipping into my hand. I gripped it tightly, feeling instantly better. "You took us somewhere safe." I was talking to Sword, but really I was trying to convince the spinning void inside myself.

"Yes," said Jasper. "We're safe. No one knows this room even exists. And the only entrance is under the Royal Museum. The Crimson Knight can't find you here."

I groaned, pushing myself upright, releasing Sword to bob beside me. I'd been lying on a low couch. Now I sat, staring at my surroundings, the safe place Sword had taken us to. "What is this?"

"It used to be a control room for the cthonibus system," said Jasper. "But since the rails broke down in the Dark Days, no one bothers to come down here anymore. So I turned it into my workshop."

The walls were copper, fitted with shelves and cubbies and hooks, all of them chock-full of wires, bolts, springs, and countless other artifice supplies I couldn't name. Two long worktables occupied the center. One was filled with more metal bric-a-brac, while the other held several large sheets of paper covered in carefully drawn designs, a towering pile of old books, and something that looked like an enormous pair of spectacles set on a stand.

This was good—the room gave my scattered attention something to focus on. I tried to pretend I was just a thief again; there were so many fascinating treasures here to steal. Some of the tightness in my chest relaxed. I squinted at something that looked like an aetheric tea service, mentally calculating how much it would be worth for trade at Mrs. Wixwell's. Not that I was really going to steal from Jasper, but it made me feel better. To remember I was Lark. Not the Nightingale, not the hero who'd just nearly died. *Lark.*

A clattering and yipping came from one of the corners of the room. Jasper smiled, dropping to one knee as a medium-sized brown-and-white dog came bounding to meet him. Or rather, bounding and rolling, since the dog's hindquarters were fitted into a sling between two wheels.

It didn't stop him from slobbering all over the prince in greeting. "Hey, Gadget," Jasper said, his voice rising the way Willow's did when she was talking to her cats. "Did you keep watch over the workshop while I was gone? Good boy!"

Gadget barked again, his stubby tail wagging as he licked Jasper's face. "Enough, enough." The prince fumbled in his pocket for a bright copper wrench, which he dropped onto the floor. "Here, take this. You know what to do."

"You feed your dog tools?" I asked, peering dubiously at the creature. Aside from the wheels, he looked like any other dog, slobbery and furry and far too eager to love anyone he could.

"No, I'm training him to clean up the workshop. Watch."

The dog snapped up the wrench but didn't eat it. Instead he trotted away with it, over to the other end of the room. A device stood there, a ramshackle contraption of wires and hoses and springs. The dog dropped the wrench into a trough along the bottom of the machine, then backed up, head cocked, as if waiting for something to happen.

And it did. The wrench tipped the trough to one side, sending the tool onto a sort of conveyor belt that carried it up toward one of the nearby shelves. A spring released, followed by a series of clatters and clacks from inside. A moment later, a dog biscuit fell from a small chute onto the floor nearby.

Gadget trotted forward eagerly to collect his reward.

"Is he some sort of artifice?" I asked, as I watched him crunching and slobbering.

"No, just a normal dog. But his back legs don't work, so I built him that roller-sling. So long as he has that, he can do almost anything he'd be able to do otherwise. And he's a big help. Aren't you, boy?"

Having finished his treat, Gadget padded over to investigate me. I froze, uncertain how to respond. Most of the dogs I'd met before this were rough, hungry hounds running loose in the streets. The sort you kept your distance from.

"Don't worry," said Jasper. "He's very friendly."

I reached out a tentative hand to skritch the dog's head. He responded by thrusting himself closer, drooling happily onto my leg. It was amazing how such a disgustingly slobbery creature could make everything feel better. Gadget leaned even closer, hot breath wafting over my face. "You like that?" I said softly. My panic felt farther away now—still there, looming in the back of my brain, but muffled now by Jasper's chatter and Sword's steadfast presence and the warm press of a dog against my knee.

"Just be careful about—"

I yelped as a zap of energy suddenly raced up my arm.

"—the aetheric charge that builds up in his wheels."

I shook my stinging fingers. "Sorry." Jasper grimaced. "I haven't figured out a way to dampen it without interfering with the movement rune." He sighed. "There's still so much I don't know."

"Seems like you know more than a lot of folks," I said. "This place is *amazing*."

Jasper blinked, then rubbed a hand through his black hair. "Really? You think so?"

"Look at all this stuff," I said, sweeping a hand at the scattered devices, the heaps of copper bits and bobs, the shelves full of tantalizing artifacts. One of them looked like some sort of mechanical badminton racket. Another reminded me of a hallowglass, but much larger, with about a dozen extra lenses. "You could make anything down here. How did you find it?"

"My mother brought me here. She wanted to see if she could get the cthonibuses working again." He coughed. "But then the war broke out. And once I was on my own, I needed a place to work. Somewhere I could experiment without, er, setting fire to my bedroom drapes or accidentally trapping the war minister in a magnetic field that deconstructed his dress armor. In the middle of a council meeting."

"Whoa," I said. "Good thing you're a prince."

Jasper made a face. "Maybe if I was more like Gideon. All it means for me is that I'm constantly disappointing people. I'm a barely tolerable swordsman. I never know the right things to say at parties. And the one thing I'm actually good at, no one takes seriously."

I bit my lip. Part of me wanted to snap at him, say that a little disappointment didn't seem like a bad price to pay for golden buttons and a royal pantry and not having to constantly be afraid your life was going to fall apart. But I could hear the pain in his voice. The hurt.

And it made something in me ring back in sympathy. Even a prince's life wasn't perfect, apparently. "Maybe you just need to stop caring what they think."

He looked at me. "Is that what you do?"

It was what I *should* be doing. What I'd meant to do ever since I'd arrived at Miss Starvenger's. And yet . . .

I thought of how happy Blythe had been when she opened up her hatbox. How Cora and Nora had squealed and sighed together over the list of soda flavors. How the crowd had cheered for me after I'd stopped the haywire fountain. Or how it felt knowing I'd saved those miners.

It had felt *good*.

Dangerously good. Because Jasper was right. Disappointing people you cared about was horrible. The only problem was, I wasn't sure I could go back to not caring, now that I'd started. I thought after Mum died, after the Gaddings turned out to be such miserable disappointments, that the part of me that cared had died. I'd hollowed it out, so the sharp broken bits could rattle inside me without piercing anything else soft and tender.

But somehow Sophie had crept in there. And Willow, and her rusting cats, and the other girls. Even Jasper.

Which made the fact that the Crimson Knight was back from the dead ten times worse.

If I didn't care, I could just run away. There wouldn't have to be a next time. I could learn my lesson from nearly getting squished once. The lesson I thought I'd learned when Mum died. Being a hero meant sacrifice. It meant dying alone, defeating evil. It meant your reward was saving everyone else. But there was no one to save *you*.

Jasper's question still hung there, like a crooked picture on the wall.

"I wish I could," I said finally. "But I don't think the Nightingale can afford to stop caring. Jasper," I added, my voice small. "I don't know if I can do this."

I glanced to Sword, worried the weapon might get upset like it had the last time I said something about not being the Nightingale. But it only hung there, waiting.

Jasper cleared his throat. "You don't need to do it alone, Lark. You've got me, and Gadget, and Sword. And once I tell my brother what's going on, you'll have the entire Bright Brigade too."

"You think he'll believe you?"

"He'll believe *you*," said Jasper. "The Nightingale. The hero of Gallant. I know he wasn't your biggest fan before, but this is a threat to his life. He'll see that you're both working on the same side once you tell him everything."

I huffed, looking down at myself. "D'you think he'll even let me speak? I don't look like much of a hero right now." I wasn't covered in chocolate, at least, but I was smeared with grease and blood. My poor cloak was in tatters, half of it burned away. Even my trousers and jacket looked as if they'd lost a battle with a giant metal knight.

"Ah!" Jasper bounced up, crossing the room to a cabinet. "I've got something for you that will take care of that. A new costume. A real one, this time."

He returned with a bundle of shimmery blue cloth, boots, and a mask.

I stared at it. A mask. A *real* mask. For a real Nightingale. The sort of Nightingale who meant to do battle with the Crimson Knight. Not just a girl who'd accidentally grabbed a sword.

Jasper didn't seem to notice my hesitation. Instead he pointed to a door along one wall. "You can wash up and change in there."

He looked so expectant that I forced myself to reach out. To take the bundle and step into the privacy of the washroom. With the door closed, I took a long breath. It felt strange, as if I were standing at the end of a long bridge that was about to carry me to some new and distant land. Silly, I told myself. It was just a costume. It wasn't going to change who I was inside.

The washroom was small but fitted with artificed piping

and a nozzle that squirted out cinnamon-scented soap from the wall. I stripped off my burnt and bloodied clothes and gingerly scrubbed the blood from my face and arms. The healing salve had already worked wonders, though I had a couple of spectacular bruises.

I tugged on the pair of close-fitting dark blue trousers and matching jacket. Everything fit perfectly, smooth and silky, but stretching with my movements. I wiggled, twisted, lifted my arms, and kicked my legs. It was as if I was wearing a second skin of beautiful dark blue. Even the midnight-colored boots seemed as if they'd been molded exactly to my feet. They had a pattern of feathers carved into the surface, the outlines gleaming faintly with aether. Last of all was the mask, fine enough to match the ones up in the museum display case. Like the boots, the leathery substance had been worked with gleaming feathers, which swept back from a birdlike mask.

They were the most comfortable, most lovely clothes I'd ever worn. And they *did* make me feel different. Powerful. Graceful. Strong.

Like I really was the Nightingale.

I stood for a long moment, eyes closed. A part of me didn't want to leave the room. Maybe I didn't really look as good as I felt. Maybe I just looked like a kid playing dress-up. Or like a thief who'd stolen a magic sword and ended up in over her head.

Right, enough dawdling. I opened my eyes, then marched to the door and flung it open, stepping out into the workshop in my new costume. Jasper, Gadget, and Sword were all waiting for me. And all of them, somehow, wore the same expression. Even Sword, who didn't have a face, managed to look astonished. The weapon began to quiver, then zoomed around in the air several times over my head.

"Does it look all right?" I asked, then immediately regretted the question. The answer was clear enough on their faces. They obviously couldn't believe it was me. I started to take a step backward, into the washroom.

"You look *amazing*!" Jasper burst out.

"Really?" I searched his narrow face for any sign of laughter, for any hint that he was teasing. But I found only a sort of puffed-up delight. Like he was proud of me.

"Really," he said, grinning. Then he seemed to catch himself, his excitement turning into something more serious. He bowed, pressing one hand to his heart. "Welcome back to Gallant, Nightingale."

I shivered, remembering the voices that had whispered in my head when I first held Sword. Maybe the weapon remembered too, because it flew to my hand, and as I took the hilt, a ripple of energy went up my arm, into my heart.

Like nothing was ever going to be the same.

Jasper believed it. Sword believed it. Now it was time for me to believe it.

CHAPTER SIXTEEN

T hat's right," I said. "I'm the Nightingale."

The words felt heavy, bold, as if I weren't just speaking them, but painting them up like an advertisement in great black, blocky letters you could see halfway down the street. They were words I'd resisted. That I'd been afraid of.

"I want to keep helping people," I said. "I want to change things, like my mum did. I don't know if I can. But I want to try."

I wasn't afraid of those words anymore. Or maybe I was just afraid of the person I'd be if I didn't say them. I wrapped my other hand around Sword's hilt, holding it right in front of me, my feet lifting from the floor as we floated together. I looked straight at the sword, into the mysterious gleaming words etched into its blade. "I promise, Sword. I promise I'll be the Nightingale for as long as I can. I promise I'll try to be a hero."

A jolt ran through me as I spoke. For one moment, I thought maybe I'd somehow unlocked the third power. But then we were drifting back down to the floor again, and everything was different. I really was the Nightingale. And the Crimson Knight was out there. I had become part of something so vast and huge I could barely hold it in my head. Even the way Jasper looked at me had changed. Before, it was like he'd been seeing all the ways I wasn't a proper Nightingale. But now . . . the yearning was still there, but there was something else. Pride? Awe?

I brushed a hand along the beautiful dark blue jacket and stared down at my new boots. "And, um, what about when I'm not the Nightingale?"

Jasper frowned slightly, as if the question made no sense.

"I can't go to dinner at the boardinghouse like this," I said. "Not unless you want everyone to figure out that the new Nightingale is just some girl from the Scrag."

"You were never just some girl from the Scrag, Lark," said Jasper.

"My point is that I can't just hang around like this. But I also don't want to waste time changing if there's an emergency. So I mean, it's lovely, but maybe I should just stick to something simpler."

"Oh," Jasper clapped his hands together. "No, I've already accounted for that. I used the same reconfiguration runes as the rain cloak. Except these ones should behave properly if they get wet. Just tap the cuffs together."

I gave him a sharp look. "It's not going to turn into an ascot, is it?"

"Go on, try it."

I tapped the cuffs together, bracing myself. Cloth whispered against my skin, sliding and shifting.

"See, normal street clothes," said Jasper.

I stifled a laugh. The loose trousers, long vest, and button-up shirt I now wore were certainly less eye-catching than the Nightingale costume. But they weren't *normal*. Not for me, anyways. Not for the Scrag. Sure, they weren't trimmed or gilted up, and the fabric didn't shimmer. But they were still much nicer than anything I'd ever worn. The boots had transformed into a pair of buckled shoes, and the mask had contracted to a thin band that held back my hair.

"Don't you like them?" Jasper asked, his brow crinkling. "Are they too plain? I could add some ruffles."

"No," I said. "They're the nicest things I've ever worn. And the best-fitting."

"Oh, that's a relief. I wasn't sure if I got the alterations right."

"Alterations?"

He flushed, looking away. "Well, I originally made them to fit . . . someone else."

Oh. Right. He'd planned to be the one wearing them. But there wasn't any bitterness in his expression now, only a sort of hopeful wariness.

"I love them," I said. "You're a genius, Jasper. Or should I call you Flea?"

"Please don't," he said sourly. "Or I might not tell you how to use the new aethercom I installed in the mask. I added a verbal transmitter."

"Which means . . . ?"

"We can talk through them. To help coordinate. So if there's another attack, I can tell you where to go and you don't need to waste time coming here, and you can let me know if you need anything. Like if you want to come visit."

"Visit?" I snorted. "What, like stop by for tea? Play board games?"

Jasper's blue eyes sparked eagerly. "Do you like chess? I can never get Gideon to play with me, and Gadget's not so keen on it, unless he can chew on the knights."

"I was joking."

"Oh." He looked down at the floor. "Right, plenty of better uses for your time. Mine, too."

A twinge pinched my chest. I'd hurt his feelings. Not on purpose. I thought he'd know it was a joke. Because being his friend *was* so impossible. Even more impossible than me being the Nightingale.

"I don't know the rules," I said. "But maybe you can teach me, if we ever manage to defeat the Crimson Knight. I'm not sure new clothes are going to make that much of a difference to him."

"Maybe not, but I know something else that might," said Jasper. He went to the table and flipped open one of the books, revealing a page full of mysterious symbols. "That," he said, pointing to one of them. "Do you recognize it?"

I squinted. "Isn't it the rune that was on the Crimson Knight?"

"Exactly. It's a connection rune, used to unite a number of separate elements into a cohesive unit. Like all the ephemera-boards linked to one network. I think it's what allowed the knight to be re-formed. So if you can break it—"

"He might fall apart again?" I asked hopefully.

"Exactly! It's worth trying, at least."

"That's good." I grinned. "Like I said: genius."

The book of runes reminded me of something I'd meant to ask earlier. I pointed to the runes on the blade. "So, can you read those? You know what they all mean?"

Jasper pursed his lips. "It's not really that sort of language. Not like what you and I speak. It's more like . . . numbers. Like mathematics. Or like a recipe. The symbols represent different qualities and properties—ingredients—and when you combine them in the right way, you generate effects. So, for example, if you combine the rune for 'weight' with the rune for 'reverse,' you can make something float."

"The sword told me that the runes on its blade are instructions," I said. "That they would tell me how to be the Nightingale."

"Hmm." Jasper peered at the weapon thoughtfully. "I know the one that's repeated is a rune for 'greater than,' and those are 'action' and 'strength.' And that one in the middle means the two sides of the equation are linked. So something like, 'more numerous action, more numerous strengths'? Maybe the more you use the sword, the stronger you'll become?"

I looked at Sword. "Is that it?"

The weapon gave an uncertain wiggle. Close, but not exactly right.

"I guess we'll find out."

"Right," said Jasper, drawing in a long breath. "But first, we need to face a truly intimidating challenge."

"What?"

"I need to introduce you to my brother."

"There it is," said Jasper as we flew above the palace. It was dark now, with aetherlights glittering blue in all the windows, including the same balcony doors I'd spied at yesterday. "I'd better go first," he added, once we'd landed. "Just to . . . prepare him. But don't worry. He'll love you." He pushed open the glass door and stepped into the study. I lurked outside, listening. "Gideon?"

There was a yelp of surprise. "Jasper? Great Architect, where did you come from?"

"A . . . friend flew me here," said Jasper. "I wanted you to meet her. She has some important information for you."

"A friend?" The older prince peered toward the balcony. I took a bracing breath, then marched inside.

Then froze. Rust it, I should have asked Jasper how to properly address the future king. Should I salute? Bow? "Er, greetings, Your Highness," I said, and gave something halfway in between. "I'm the Nightingale."

Gideon stared, his blond brows arching so high they nearly disappeared beneath the graceful swoop of his perfect golden hair. "Indeed you are." For a split second there was something uncomfortable in his face. Then he broke into a dazzling smile. "Hello, hello, this is an honor. Of course I've been following your recent exploits. Please, come in."

I glanced to Jasper, who nodded encouragingly. "The Nightingale has been investigating the accidents at the mines and factories," said Jasper. "And we've learned something of vital importance. Something you have to hear, Gid."

"Very well." Gideon leaned against a wide table holding a large map of Gallant and Saventry, with the river Rhee running between them. Small markers were scattered across the surface, like it was a gaming board. "Tell me."

So I told him everything, from Dark Spectacles to the Crimson Knight, with Jasper filling in any of the details I forgot. Gideon listened, eyes half-closed in concentration, making it hard to read his reaction.

"And we don't know who he's working for," I finished, "but we know they plan to have the Crimson Knight completed by your coronation. Which is why we came here, to warn you. They must be planning to try to capture you, or kill you, during the ceremony!"

Gideon's jaw tightened. After a moment, he spoke, his voice strained. "That is . . . distressing news. And was anyone else witness to this? Did anyone else see the knight?"

"No," said Jasper. "The workshop is in the middle of the Heap. Though he and the knight have probably moved somewhere else by now. He has an ally, someone he was talking to over an aethercom. But they could be planning to come for the helm at any time—it's all they need to finish the knight. He's tough enough as it is, but once he's complete . . ." Jasper trailed off, glancing worriedly in my direction. "Well, I'm sure the Nightingale can defeat him, regardless, but it would be a lot easier if we could stop them before they get that far."

"We?" repeated Gideon, with a trace of iron in his tone. "I seem to recall giving you strict orders to stick to your schooling, Jasper."

"I know, but this is more important than that. And see, I'm perfectly safe. The Nightingale kept me that way."

"Actually," I said, "your brother saved my life, Highness. He's tougher than you think. I couldn't ask for a better partner." Jasper blinked, then flashed me a smile so bright it might have been painted with aether.

"Mmm." Gideon gave Jasper a considering look. "Indeed. This evening has been full of surprises."

"So what happens now?" I said. "There can't be that many places to hide a giant metal monster. Someone must have seen him. If we put the news out on the ephemera-boards, maybe—"

"I don't think that's wise," broke in Gideon. "It would only start a panic. Clearly this is part of some greater Saventine plot to undermine my power. They probably used their agents in the so-called Aether Workers' Union to create the monster. They want the people of Lamlyle to fear artifice, to fear the very gifts that make our nation so proud and strong."

"No," I said. "That's not true. The union has nothing to do with any of this!"

"And it makes no sense for Saventry to be behind it either," said Jasper. "They hate aethercraft. They wouldn't dare rebuild the Crimson Knight. He didn't just ravage Gallant two centuries ago—he destroyed several towns on the border. It was what triggered the first Saventine war!"

Gideon was silent for a moment. Then he gave a nod. "Perhaps, but then you see why it's important that we keep the Crimson Knight's return a secret. Until we've dealt with him, it's too dangerous for the rumors to spread. Surely you see why, Jasper? You're a clever lad."

I frowned at Jasper, who had started to nod slowly. *I* didn't see. "If there's a danger like the knight out there, isn't it better to know? Besides, the coronation's two days away! We're running out of time."

"No," said Jasper. "Gideon's right. It could do more than start a panic in Gallant—it could start a war. We have to keep it a secret for now, Nightingale."

I hesitated. I still didn't like it, but I trusted Jasper. And Gideon was the crown prince. The two of them must know what was best for Gallant. So finally, reluctantly, I nodded.

"Very good," said Gideon. "I knew we could count on you, Nightingale. I will admit, I had my doubts. But I can see you are willing to do what must be done for the sake of Gallant. And have no fear, we'll still be doing *something*. I'll have the Bright Brigade secure the Heap. And the helm will be moved to a more secure location." He gave me a dazzling smile. "When there's word on the fiend's location, you'll be the first to know, Nightingale. And I trust the threat will be eliminated once and for all."

It was late by the time I crept back into the boardinghouse. All the other girls were asleep in their bunks, except for one. Sophie's empty bed mocked me, summoning up the painful memory of our fight. Where was she? My breath caught with every terrible possibility: Pinshaw had changed his mind and sent the constables after her. Or Starvenger had found out she'd been sacked and tossed her out on the street. Or she'd kept poking at the mystery of the secret aether workshop and ended up in the Heap. What if the Crimson Knight had gotten her?

I dashed downstairs. She wasn't in the washroom or the kitchen, but a faint gleam along the bottom of the basement door jolted me with relief. Of course. Whenever Sophie was upset, she threw herself into her work even harder.

Which was exactly what I found. Sophie knelt on the floor, a pot of ink beside her, painting words onto a large square of paper. It looked as if she'd pasted together some of the old ephemera proofs to make the thing. Several more placards lay nearby. I waited until she dipped the brush into the pot, then cleared my throat. She startled, but smiled when she saw me. "Lark!" Then she cocked her head, eyes narrowing as she looked me up and down. "Well?" she prompted. "Are you going to explain?"

"E-explain?" I stammered.

"The new clothes. I mean, they're lovely, of course, but they must have cost a fortune." She tsked at me. "I know this new job is paying well, but you really ought to be putting some of that coin into savings."

"Oh. Right!" I looked down at my new street clothes. "Well, you know, Mr. Jasper just wants me to be properly dressed when I, er, run errands."

She sniffed. I started to fiddle with my cuffs, then jerked my arms to my sides. The last thing I needed was to accidentally show off my *other* new outfit.

I wanted to, though. Desperately. I wanted Sophie's advice. Wanted to tell her what I'd learned about the hidden workshop and Dark Spectacles. Wanted to share the heavy weight of knowing the Crimson Knight was out there, somewhere. But how could I? Sophie had made it clear what she thought of the Nightingale. Until I could prove otherwise, I didn't dare tell her the truth. I couldn't bear to have her look at me with that same angry disgust that she'd leveled at the Nightingale.

"So," I said. "How was your day?" I stepped closer, angling

myself to read the words she was painting on the sign. NO MORE FACT. "Horrible," Sophie answered.

"It must've been a doozy, if you're campaigning *against* facts now," I teased. "I thought you loved facts."

She gave the faintest huff of a laugh as she added ORY DEATHS to the end. Keeping her gaze fixed on the sign, she said, "I got sacked by Pinshaw, thanks to that interfering vigilante Nightsoil."

Heat burned my cheeks. "You mean Nightingale?"

"I'll call her what I think of her," grumbled Sophie.

"I—I'm sure she thought she was doing the right thing."

"Intentions don't matter. Actions matter."

I stuffed all my explanations back down my throat. She was right. I'd acted without thinking. "So does this mean your investigation is totally bodged?"

"No. I'm not letting this stop me," she said fiercely. "There's too much at stake. I know Pinshaw's building a new factory. That's why there's so much more aether dust."

I bit the inside of my cheek. Pinshaw was a villain, but it was Dark Spectacles who had built the secret aether workshop. And Prince Gideon had promised to send the Bright Brigade to make sure that was all shut down and safe.

"I heard that the Nightingale shut down some sort of secret aether workshop in the Heap today," I told her. "If that was the source of all the extra aether dust, then maybe it's all right now?"

Sophie jabbed her paintbrush into the inkpot savagely.

"It's not that simple, Lark. Quotas will still go up. The factory waste will still go straight into the river. Into the water everyone in the Scrag uses every day, to wash, to drink, to clean. More and more people will start ghosting. We have to stop it."

"How?"

She gestured to her sign, and the pile of blank placards laying nearby. "With a protest!"

"You convinced the union to go along with this?"

Sophie's lips pressed tight for a moment. "Not all of them, of course. Not everyone can take the risk. But I'm sure we'll have a good crowd. I gave an excellent speech, if I do say so myself. The only problem is, I need to make about fifty more of these signs before tomorrow."

A lump clogged my throat. She reminded me so much of Mum. Proud and brave and bold. I swallowed, searching for my voice. "No, you don't."

Sophie frowned. "I don't?"

"You only need to make twenty-five." I squatted down beside her, pulled one of the blank placards closer, and grabbed one of the spare brushes. "I'll make the other half."

Sophie laughed. Then she nudged my shoulder with her own. "My hero."

We finished the last of the signs at midnight. I should have been exhausted, but it was hard to sleep, knowing that the Crimson

Knight was still out there, almost complete. My work with Sophie had helped distract me. But now, lying there in the dark, memories of my earlier battle kept slithering out of the corners of my mind, taunting me with failure and fear. Even when I did sleep, I dreamed of him. The grinding of metal. The thunder of heavy footsteps. My cries as I fell, burning.

So when I woke to the sounds of screams, I thought I must still be dreaming. Then I realized that the person screaming was Willow.

CHAPTER SEVENTEEN

I sat up groggily, blinking in the darkness, grabbing instinctively for Sword. But I didn't see any sign of danger. Only Willow, standing in the center of the dorm, crying out her sister's name.

Cora and Nora tumbled from their bunks. Below me, Sophie said, "Willow, what's wrong? Where's Blythe?"

I peered across the room to the bunk that Blythe usually slept in, over by the window, above Willow's bed. It was empty, but the blankets were rumpled.

"I heard her coughing," Willow stammered. "I asked her if she was all right, but she didn't answer. And then when I looked up in her bunk, she was gone. I—I think she's ghosting, Sophie!"

"Let's all stay calm," said Sophie. "She might have gone to the bathroom. Or down to get a drink of water. We don't want to wake Miss Starvenger, or she'll dock us all for violating curfew rules."

"Don't worry about Starvenger," said Cora. "I, er, might've slipped a batch of sleeping powder into her favorite perfume atomizer the other day."

I goggled at her. Even I had never been *that* bold. Meanwhile, Nora had already vanished out the door. She returned a moment later, signing that the bathroom was empty.

"Stay here," I whispered to Sword, before I slid down from my bunk to join the other girls, who had clustered around Willow.

"She's only been working at the factory for a year," I said. "I've never heard of anyone ghosting that quick. Had she even started flickering at all?"

"N-no," admitted Willow. "But she's been working extra shifts to try to earn the fees for the Bright Academy." Her voice was soggy and ragged with fear.

Nora put an arm around her, signing a reassurance.

"That's right," said Cora bracingly. "We'll find her. She's probably just downstairs raiding the pantry with Starvenger asleep. Let's go. We'll all make a midnight picnic of it."

Willow gave a fragile smile, but Sophie looked grim. She searched around the room, her dark eyes sharp, peering into every shadowed corner. I looked too, making a silent agreement with Sophie to remain behind as the other girls went down to check the kitchen. Sophie paced a slow circuit of the dorm room, while I went out to survey the hall.

I crept along, my entire body tensed, waiting for the shouts of relief, the cries of *We found her!* and *Come on down, there's leftover cheese pie.*

Instead, silence. Darkness.

Sophie joined me, still unsmiling. "Willow could be right. Remember what I told you about more and more workers ghosting?"

A hot wave of frustration burned through me. And what could I do about it? Nothing. Flying, ice, a magic sword that could cut through rock like butter, none of it could do a rusting thing to bring back a girl who'd ghosted.

"Maybe she's just flickering," I said. "Maybe she'll come back." But even I was having trouble believing myself.

Footsteps sounded on the stairs. The other girls returned, downcast. Willow was scrubbing at her luminous cheeks. The sight of them only made everything worse. All three of them, and Sophie, too, all faintly gleaming.

All of them in danger of flickering away.

No. That wasn't going to happen. I was the Nightingale now. There must be something I could do, some help I could find. Someone who might . . .

"I'm going to get help," I said abruptly. "Keep looking for her. She's still here, she must be. We just can't see her, or hear her. But we can get her back."

Then I ran for the dormitory and my aethercom.

❧

The knock sounded at the front door barely fifteen minutes later. I ran to answer it, breathless but not hopeless. If anyone could find a way to bring back someone who was ghosting, it was Jasper. If the situation weren't so dire, I might have laughed at myself. I'd gone from stealing from a prince to counting on him to help me in an aetheric crisis.

"Have you found her yet?" he asked as he came in, hefting a large pack that clanked and clattered.

"No," I said. "We've looked everywhere, even the roof. You don't think—"

"Blythe! Blythe!" came Willow's voice, suddenly. "She's here. Help!"

Jasper and I pelted down the hall in the direction of her cry. It sounded as if she was in the parlor. I flung the door open and charged in to find the other girls gathered there, all of them staring in horror at a frail, luminous gleam that drifted near the center of the room.

She was only barely visible, but I could make out the fall of her loose braids, the determined set of her chin. It was Blythe.

Willow stood closest to her, reaching out desperately for her sister. In the darkness, she looked almost as frail as Blythe, the faint lines of her gleaming bones visible beneath her dark skin.

"I almost had her!" Willow said. "I could feel her, just for a moment. Then I l-lost her."

"Blythe," Sophie was saying. "Can you hear us?"

The ghostly figure opened her lips. Moved them. But there was no sound. She gave a small shake of her head, seeming frustrated.

Nora stepped forward, signing something. "Hold on," Cora translated. "Don't go. We're going to bring you back."

Blythe moved her hands, the motions only barely visible, but Nora nodded, smiling eagerly. Cora snorted, translating. "She says we'd rusting well better bring her back, or she's going to haunt us forever."

"How absolutely astonishing!" said Jasper, striding forward. "So this is ghosting?"

"Yes," I said. "But I didn't bring you here to study her like a museum exhibit. I asked you to come to try to *save* her."

"Oh, right. Yes, of course. Let me take a few measurements." He began digging through his pack, pulling out various artificer tools, occasionally holding one up and fiddling with it.

"Lark," said Cora, in a very strange voice. "Who is that?" All the girls were staring at Jasper as if he were a bit of some ephemera tabloid that had just peeled itself off the wall and started walking around the room.

"Er, this is Prince Jasper, everyone. He's a genius with aethercraft, so I thought he might be able to find a way to help."

There was a moment of shocked silence, broken only by a breathless squeak from Willow.

"*Prince* Jasper?" repeated Sophie. She stepped closer, whispering, "And how exactly do you know a prince well enough to be able to call him up in the middle of the night?"

"I've been . . . working for him. My new job," I said.

Sophie frowned at me for a long moment, as if she could tell I was leaving out a very large and important part of that explanation. But before she could ask any further questions, Jasper gave a sudden "Aha!"

He had one of his tools out and was waving it through the air. Not just around Blythe's fragile shadow, but around Sophie and Cora and Nora and especially Willow.

"I see now!" he said excitedly. "The aether causes some sort of phase shift in the resonance of the corporeal form. All of them exhibit the signs to some extent, though Miss . . ." He looked up from the device at Willow.

"Willow," I said.

"Miss Willow's readings are especially unusual. They appear to be following a sinusoidal fluctuation, unlike the geometric growth of the others. It might be possible to use her as a conduit to reach Miss Blythe there."

I had barely understood half the words he said, but Sophie was nodding as if it made perfect sense. "You think Willow can reach Blythe, because she's constantly flickering herself?"

"Yes," said Jasper. "If we can create a field of resonance around Blythe, and Willow can reach her, I think we can stabilize the fluctuation."

"Great," I said. "I have no idea what you just said, but it sounded like a plan. So what do we do?"

"The rest of you stand in a circle around her. I'm not sure

she can hear us, but if she can try to focus on Willow, that would be ideal."

"On it," said Cora as Nora translated the message. Blythe nodded, reaching one barely visible hand toward Willow.

Jasper held a device in his hands that he had apparently cobbled together in the last few minutes. It looked an awful lot like two enormous harmonium trumpets attached to several dozen coils of wire. "All right, here we go. Miss Willow, try to reach her. You'll have to wait for one of your own immaterial phases. Or, what do you call them? Flickers?"

"I can do it," said Willow fiercely. She reached out, taking Cora's hand on her left. Cora, Nora, Sophie, and I linked ourselves together as well, forming a circle around Blythe.

Sophie gave me a sidelong glance as she took my hand. "You've never worked in the factory," she said. "Don't you want to just watch?"

I coughed. "You told me everyone in the Scrag is getting exposed to the waste. So I might as well help, right? Besides . . ." I hesitated, my old wariness tugging at me. But stuff it, I was done living that way. "I want to be a part of it."

She squeezed my hand. "I'm glad. I just hope this works."

"It will." I bounced on my toes, jittery with hope and fear. I'd thrown on my new coat and trousers, partly so I could have Sword with me, partly so I didn't have to meet Jasper in my nightgown. The hilt of the weapon bumped against my neck reassuringly. I had to believe this would work.

Jasper pushed something on his device, and it began to hum as sparks of aetherlight danced over the surface of the trumpets. "Go! Get her. Now!"

Willow reached out, her fingers scrabbling for Blythe's, passing through them. I gritted my teeth. Again, this time a faint catch. Willow made a noise of frustration. Then alarm. "She's drifting up!"

Willow jumped, trying to catch at Blythe. Blythe reached back, her movements frantic, desperate.

"We're losing her! You need to get her, now!" called Jasper.

"I can't reach her!" Willow cried.

Rust it. I wasn't losing Blythe. She still had too much to do. And she was going to make the best—the most *marvelrageous*—Bright cadet the world had ever seen. I reached over my shoulder for Sword's hilt. The moment I touched it, my body lightened as usual. With my other hand, I gripped Sophie tight. It had to work. It must!

The sword shivered at my touch. Sophie yelped. Then Cora. Nora gave a breathless gasp, as everyone's feet left the floor, and all of us, bound together, began to drift into the air. Willow didn't notice. She was too busy making one final snatch at the fading ghostly gleam.

Then she cried out. Not in frustration or fury. In joy. A shimmer of light filled the air, and Jasper's device gave a triumphant bleat. And then, suddenly, Blythe was back. Solid. Real. No longer fading away.

I let go of Sword, sending all of us thumping down to the carpet, where everyone fell into a tangle of hugs and tears and shouting.

"That was amazing!" Cora was saying as she practically danced around the room. "Was I imagining things, or were we flying there for a moment? That's some device you've got there, Prince Jasper," she added, beaming at him.

Blythe tugged Willow beside her and whispered something. Then she dipped a neat bow, with Willow following her lead, only slightly more wobbly. "Thank you, Highness. We are so very grateful."

Jasper flushed, ducking his head. "Well, it's the least I can do. It was all of you who had what it took to reach her. And the good news is, I think I managed to stabilize everyone for now. Provided you don't expose yourselves further, the current effects of the aether should wear off within a few weeks. Not for Miss Willow, I'm afraid, due to her early exposure, but she appears to be naturally self-regulating."

"And how exactly do you expect us to avoid further exposure?" Sophie asked, crossing her arms and giving him one of her most demanding looks. Poor Jasper. He didn't know what he was in for.

He blanched. "Oh. Well. Yes. Lark's been telling me about the issues at the factories. And the mines. I—I'm sorry that this matter hasn't been dealt with properly. But I mean to speak with my brother at once about it."

"Really?" Sophie sounded dubious.

"Really," I said, moving to stand beside Jasper. "Sophie, Jasper's a good one. He's on our side."

She arched an eyebrow at Jasper. "Hmm. I suppose there must be a few good princes in the world. I hope you really are one of them."

"I, er, try," said Jasper, entirely red in the face.

Blythe and Willow had finally broken apart. Cora had run off to the kitchen, and returned now holding a handful of chocolate bars. "Look! I broke into Starvenger's secret stash. Who wants nougat and who wants candied ginger?"

Sophie passed me a chunk, which I broke and handed half to Jasper. My feet were back on the floor, but my heart was light again. It might not be the Crimson Knight, but this was a victory I was happy to celebrate.

I did regret the celebration just a tiny bit the next morning, though. Miss Starvenger was sleeping in—no doubt thanks to Cora's tampering with her atomizer—and I had hoped to do the same. But Sophie had other plans.

"Are you sure about this?" I asked, as I stood beside her in the boardinghouse entryway, my arms full of painted protest signs. "I mean, you heard Jasper last night. He promised he was going to talk to Prince Gideon. Maybe we should hold off on the protest. You said yourself it was risky."

Sophie continued her work, dividing up the rest of the

signs into stacks. "I'm sure. I'm glad Jasper helped us last night. He saved Blythe's life. But Lark, we can't wait around for a prince to save us from everything. Besides, it's already planned. Everyone else will be there."

"Are we late?" Cora called, dashing in from the direction of the kitchen, with Nora close behind her. A moment later Blythe and Willow came pelting down the stairs as well. All of them looked breathless and eager.

"No," said Sophie. "We need to be at the rally point at noon. We have plenty of time. Mr. Caruthers is picking us up in his cart."

"You're all going?" I turned to Blythe. "You're not worried what the Bright Academy might think?"

Blythe lifted her chin. "If the Bright Academy thinks it's wrong to stand up against a villain like Pinshaw, then I don't want to be a cadet." She gave a small shake of her head. "It was horrible, Lark. Feeling like the world was just . . . fading away." She shuddered. "I'm not letting that happen to anyone else."

"Me neither," piped up Willow fiercely.

Cora winked. "I'm nowhere near that noble," she said. "I just like causing trouble."

I turned to Nora, so she could see my lips. "Nora? What about you?"

She grinned, tapping one of the placards that read PINSHAW IS POISON. She'd added her own embellishment: a cartoon of Pinshaw, black bowler hat askew as he brandished a horrible skull that seemed to be vomiting liquid aether. It was devilishly accurate, though she'd crossed out his fish eyes with large black *X*s, making it somehow even more unnerving.

She signed something that Cora translated. "I'm not wasting this masterpiece."

Rust it. They were all so . . . *heroic*. Brave and bold and bright-eyed. Just like Mum had been. A chill shuddered through me. What if Pinshaw sent flunkies to stop them? To hurt them? I could take care of myself, but could I protect all of them, too?

Sophie cocked her head at me. "You'd better not be thinking of stuffing me in a closet again, Lark. Because this is my fight. I'm not backing down."

I breathed in, felt the ice in my chest. Held the air as I looked at all of them. "All right," I said finally. "Let's go."

Along my back, Sword gave the slightest reassuring wiggle. That was right. We were both here, to keep Sophie and the others safe.

"Mr. Caruthers just arrived," called Willow, who'd been looking out the window to the street.

"Let's go," said Sophie. "Remember what to say to the constables if they try to arrest you. And don't forget your handkerchiefs. If they try to gas us, cover your mouth and nose and stay low."

Cora flung open the door as the rest of us gathered up the signs. And then Jasper's voice suddenly buzzed in my ear.

"Nightingale! We need you!"

Chapter Eighteen

*L*ark? Are you coming?" Sophie looked back at me from the door, her arms full of protest signs.

"Just a moment," I told her. "It's Prince Jasper on my aethercom." I took a step back, then whispered into my collar. "What is it? I'm kind of in the middle of something."

"So is Gideon," said Jasper's voice, faintly crackly and tinny. He sounded worried.

"What? Is it the Cri—Project Red?" I asked.

"I don't know. He just commed me, saying he and the Bright Brigade need your help. He said to meet them at the courthouse as soon as possible."

Sophie's eyes, watching me, felt heavy as lead. I cringed.

"All right," I said. "I'll be there."

"Good. Thanks, Lark. I know you'll keep my brother safe. I'm going to try to get there too, but Gid has Armsmaster Hrothsina watching me, so I don't know when I can slip away."

The com crackled off. Sophie was still staring at me. The

other girls had already gone out, taking all the signs except for the ones in my arms. Silently Sophie paced forward, holding out her arms.

"I'm sorry," I said. "I really want to come to your protest. But Jasper has . . . a job for me. It's important too. I swear."

"Right," said Sophie, her voice cool, as she took the signs from me. "Of course it is."

Then she turned away and limped across the threshold. She didn't look back.

If only my third power were to be in two places at once. But it wasn't. Instead I felt like I'd just split my heart in two, leaving half behind with Sophie and the other girls, while I carried the rest raw in my chest as Sword flew me to the courthouse. I'd made the only choice I could, though. As great a danger as the factories were, surely a monstrous metal knight was the more urgent threat.

But as I arced us down toward the wide marble steps, I saw no signs of panic. Only two dozen Bright Brigaders standing ready at attention before Crown Prince Gideon. A sleek black coach stood nearby. The low drone of its aetheric motor buzzed my skin. Unease gnawed at me.

This was *not* what I'd expected. Gideon, however, seemed delighted, flashing one of his relentlessly charming smiles as I landed. "Ah, good. Nightingale, I'm glad you could join us." He gestured to the gathered soldiers. "Move out. We need to stop them before they cause any further harm."

"Stop who?" I asked, still searching the streets around us for some sign of danger. Sword, floating beside me, spun its point in a circle as well, then gave a quizzical shiver.

"I'll explain as we travel." The prince beckoned me to the carriage, allowing me to slide inside first. Sword settled protectively across my lap as Gideon lounged on the velvet seat opposite. The driver closed the door and a moment later we were moving. I caught a glimpse out the window of the Brigaders springing into motion, their artificed boots allowing them to bound effortlessly beside us. Then Gideon touched a crystal on the door, and the windows went dark. "For security," he said.

"Oh. Sure." Sword twitched in my hand, blue gems gleaming like watchful eyes. I gripped the weapon's hilt, glad I wasn't alone, but also wishing desperately that Jasper were there. I understood Jasper's smiles, Jasper's frowns. I had no idea what the strange, sharp look in Gideon's eyes meant.

"I'm afraid that we have a situation developing," Gideon began. "One that threatens the security of our entire nation. I trust that you, Nightingale, are willing to do whatever it takes to ensure that Gallant regains her rightful place as the greatest of all nations."

I opened my mouth. It sounded like something I should

agree to, chock-full of bold words and bright ideals. And yet the gnawing feeling still chewed at me. Sophie always said that words could be weapons. That you needed to make sure you were actually *listening* to them, not just feeling them.

"You mean the Crimson Knight?"

"No," said Gideon. "The Crimson Knight is only artifice. And artifice can be controlled. The threat I'm speaking of is more dangerous than that."

The drone of the engine faded. We had reached our destination, wherever that was. I became dimly aware of a noise outside. Was it angry voices? Shouting?

"Aethercraft is the heart and soul of Gallant, Nightingale," said Gideon. "But unfortunately, there are some who fear it. Who sow doubt. And those doubts and fears are a greater threat to Gallant than any work of artifice, no matter how powerful. So. I expect the champion of Gallant to put a stop to them."

The door opened.

I gazed out onto a crowd of shouting people, many of them brandishing bold placards painted in familiar black ink.

Rust it all. Gideon wanted me to shut down Sophie's protest.

I sat frozen in my seat as the prince unfolded himself gracefully from the coach, stepping out onto the street. "Enough of this!" he called to the protesters. "I am your liege. Your soon-to-be king. And I tell you, every one of you, that if this sort of traitorous behavior continues, you'll all be arrested and punished. So come now, and give up this foolishness."

The shouting dimmed, replaced by a low, anxious rumble. I was still hidden in the coach, but I could see that the Brigaders had already formed a loose wall in front of the prince, blocking the protesters from continuing down the street. There were at least fifty, mostly miners and factory workers from the looks of it. I spotted Cora and Nora on the left flank, Blythe and Willow on the right. And Sophie, smack in the center, beside a man I recognized from the Wynchcomb Mine.

"This is not treason," Sophie proclaimed. She stood proudly, flourishing her NO MORE FACTORY DEATHS placard. "What's treason is that monster Pinshaw pumping out poison into the Scrag! What's treason is not instituting proper safety measures! What's treason is letting dozens of people ghost away for profit!"

Gideon's jaw tightened as if he were chewing on a bite of gristle. He turned to the coach and spoke to me. "You see the threat before us. That girl and her ilk are a menace." More loudly, he called out to the crowd, "This is your final chance. Walk away now, or you will be held accountable. I will order the Bright Brigade to take you into custody. And they won't be working alone."

He swept a hand toward the coach. "I call on the Nightingale, champion of Gallant, to stand beside me in this time of discontent, to support our trusted industry leaders and ensure that our factories remain open and fully functional."

For a moment, everything seemed to pause. Gideon, his blue eyes sharp and expectant. Sophie, her lips going tight. And my own heart, thrumming so loudly I might've had an aetheric motor gunning in my chest.

I knew what I believed. What Mum had taught me. What Sophie had shown me.

I burst from the coach, Sword carrying me up above the crowd. "No, Your Highness. I'm not going to do that."

The first tide of confused cries and babbling fell silent, as I floated there, high enough that everyone could see me. "You don't have all the information, Prince Gideon," I said. "The factories are dangerous. I've seen it myself. That girl over there isn't a traitor. She's a hero. They all are. They're standing up for the truth. Just because you don't want to hear it doesn't make it a lie. Please, just listen to them."

Gideon folded his arms across his broad chest, staring at me thoughtfully. He had to understand. If he did, maybe we could end this without—

"Apparently we've found another traitor," said a cool, clipped voice. Mr. Pinshaw stepped forward through the Brigaders. He must have been skulking nearby. "I told you, Highness. I fear that our fabled Nightingale is no true champion, but merely a vigilante with no respect for law and order."

I stared at him. A strange hook tugged at my mind. It wasn't an old memory, it was . . . his eyes. That was it. I searched the crowd again, looking for Nora's cartoon-decorated sign. The black *X*s over the eyes! I squinted back at Pinshaw, trying to imagine what he would look like with those pale fish eyes concealed behind dark lenses.

How had I not realized it before? Then again, no one had known it was me flying around with a raggedy black mask on my face either. Whatever the case, I recognized Pinshaw now.

"You!" I said. "It's you!" I jerked around to face Gideon, the words flooding out of me. "He's Dark Spectacles! It all makes sense now! *He* was building the secret workshop. *He's* the one trying to re-create the Crimson Knight! He must be plotting to take over Gallant, and he doesn't want the union or anyone else to get in his way!"

Startled shouts and cries of alarm broke out. Even some of the Bright Brigaders shifted uneasily. But Prince Gideon only looked disappointed. He shook his head.

"I had hoped," he said loudly, "that the Nightingale had truly returned to stand bravely at my side in defense of Gallant. Alas, it seems that this girl is a sham."

What? I stared at him, mouth open. Sword twitched its blade, mirroring my confusion.

"Mr. Pinshaw here is one of our most trusted citizens," Gideon went on, stepping sideways to stand beside the factory owner. "Gallant's future depends upon him, upon his factories. If you stand against that, Nightingale, then you truly do not deserve your title."

What? None of this made sense! Gideon knew about the

secret workshop, the Crimson Knight, everything. Why didn't he believe me?

Prince Gideon turned to the Bright Brigade. "Arrest them all. Including the false Nightingale. Use whatever force is necessary."

The blue-uniformed soldiers started to advance upon the crowd, moving to encircle them. Each of them brandished a truncheon that gleamed blue along the edge, flaring sparks.

"You can't stop us!" shouted Sophie. "The truth is going to come out, and then you'll—" She broke off, hissing as one of the Brigaders jabbed his truncheon at her. A bright flash leaped from the tip, and for a moment she was outlined in fire. She stumbled woozily.

"Sophie!" I shrieked. "Leave her alone!"

I stabbed Sword into the air. As much as I wanted to throttle Pinshaw, it was more important to get the protesters away. Except there was nowhere for them to run. The soldiers had them surrounded. A few began fighting back, growling and shouting and pushing at the line of Brigaders. I had to find them a way out. Or make one.

"Freeze!" I cried, pointing Sword at the far side of the chaotic scene.

A stream of shimmering ice flashed down, creating a wall of ice that cut off the Brigaders on the left. Another flash, and the right flank had fallen back behind a another frozen bulwark. "Go!" I shouted to the protesters. "Run!"

They did. I saw Cora and Nora dashing away, and Blythe

and Willow a moment later. The soldiers battered the ice walls, trying to stop them, but it was too late. Nearly all the protesters had escaped.

But not Sophie.

She and a handful of the unionists held the center ground. The soldiers had already charged forward. Caruthers and two others lay groaning on the pavement. As I watched, another woman fell beside them. Only Sophie was left now.

Another soldier swung his truncheon, but she ducked, then swung her placard, smacking the man across the jaw. He cursed, preparing to strike again.

"Leave her alone!" I cried as Sword and I plummeted down, landing beside Sophie. "If you lay one hand on my best friend, I'm going to jab that truncheon somewhere you really don't want it!"

He gulped and took a step back.

"Stop her!" called Gideon.

I didn't even bother glaring at him. It was Sophie I cared about. Sophie, who was watching me now with the strangest look. "Best friend?" she said softly, wonderingly.

"I'll explain everything later," I said, reaching out to clutch her hand. "I promise."

Then I jabbed Sword skyward, sending us both flying up into the air, fleeing the desolate, desperate scene.

We soared above the city aimlessly. I had no destination in mind, no plan. I'd barely gotten used to being the hero of Gallant, and now, just like that, I was a wanted criminal. And Sophie had just found out I'd been keeping an enormous secret from her.

"I'm sorry I didn't tell you before," I said as we flew. "I wanted to, but I thought it might be dangerous if you knew."

"Why would it be dangerous for me to know I'm your best friend?" she asked.

"What? No, I was talking about being the Nightingale. How I should have told you before now."

Sophie laughed. "Lark, I figured *that* out ages ago. Did you really think a scrap of fabric was going to fool me?" She made a tsking noise. "Give me some credit."

I was still unraveling the thread of our conversation. "Wait, so why did you look so surprised when I rescued you?"

"Because you finally admitted that I was your *friend*, you lunkhead."

"Oh. Wait. So then are you mad at me, or not?"

"Why would I be mad? I'm *flying*, Lark. How could I possibly be mad when I'm flying?"

She gave a wild whoop, stretching out her free arm like the wing of a bird as we swooped over a cloud. "This is *amazing*!" she crowed, slanting me a quick, dazzling smile.

Some of the tightness in my chest unlocked, and I managed to pull in a long, deep breath.

"And it's your own loss for not telling me sooner," she added, with just a trace of reproach. "I could have helped you."

"I know," I said miserably. "I'm sorry."

"It's all right, Lark. I meant what I said. I'm not mad. Think of what you can do! Is it true you can shoot beams of fire?"

"No," I said. "Not fire, just ice. But it's not really me doing the work. It's Sword."

I was starting to feel queasy, even though flying didn't usually bother me. We were above the city center now. I slipped into the open cupola of the clock tower that rose above the Royal Bank, setting us down. My feet struck the stones. I stumbled, dropping Sophie's hand, then sagged against the stone wall. The sword hovered in the air beside me, tilting worriedly as I pressed my hands to my face.

"I wish I had told you, Sophie," I said. "I've messed everything up. Pinshaw is rebuilding the Crimson Knight."

Sophie arched her brows. "The Crimson Knight? As in, the monster that turned a quarter of Gallant into the Heap?"

"Yes. You were right all along. Pinshaw had a secret factory in the Heap. That's where he was working. I didn't realize it was him until today, though. And now he's convinced Prince Gideon that *I'm* the villain. What will Jasper think?"

Sophie crossed her arms. "You're not the villain. You didn't do anything wrong, and neither did I. And if Jasper doesn't realize that, then he's as big a fool as his brother."

"But he's not," I said. "Jasper's almost as clever as you, Sophie. He's amazing with artifice. You should see what he's done. And he was the one who figured out how to wake up Sword." I gestured to the blade, who gave a sort of bow in Sophie's direction.

"Oh, right. Sorry. Sophie, this is Sword."

Sophie's eyes widened, but she gave the weapon a polite nod. "Pleased to meet you. Are you really the same sword the first Nightingale used?"

The sword tip bobbed up and down in an eager nod, then pointed at me.

"And now you work with Lark? She's your new Nightingale?"

Another nod.

I coughed. "Er, Sword, could you maybe do a swoop around the tower, keep watch in case someone comes for us?"

The sword zoomed off industriously, leaving Sophie and me alone. I lowered my voice, the words quivering slightly. "Jasper thinks Sword chose me. But Sophie, what if it was all just a big mistake?"

"What do you mean?"

I told her everything, starting with my failed robbery at the Royal Museum, the way the sword had stuck with me so persistently, everything Jasper and I had learned about the past Nightingales, and all my failures to stop the Crimson Knight.

"There's just so much I haven't done. I haven't figured out my third power. And a real Nightingale would have found a way to stop the Crimson Knight before this, wouldn't she?" I sighed. "Maybe I'm just a fluke. Just because I happened to grab the handle of a glowing sword at the right moment doesn't mean I'm really meant to be a hero. All it means is that I was scared and trying to find a way out of a rusting mess."

Sophie glanced out the open arch to where Sword was flying lazy circles around the tower. "The sword seems pretty committed to you. Don't you trust its judgment?"

I swallowed. "It's just a sword. Maybe it doesn't know any better." I felt a twinge of guilt as I spoke, but maybe it was true. Anything else might just be wishful thinking.

"I've known it less than an hour, and I can tell that thing is more than just a sword," said Sophie.

"I'm not sure why you're trying to make me feel better," I said, after a moment. "You don't even like the Nightingale."

Sophie sank down against the wall across from me. She tucked her left foot up across her right leg, wincing as she slid off the shoe. "It's not that I don't like the Nightingale." She massaged her cramped muscles, sighing. "It's just . . . one person can't fix everything. Not even if that person is the Nightingale."

"Then what's the point?" I asked. "What's the point of having a magic sword and fancy powers if I can't make things better?"

"You *are* making things better," said Sophie. "You've saved lives, Lark. That's important. It's not your fault Prince Gideon is a self-interested, nationalistic fool. You can't give up just because people aren't cheering for you now. That's not what being a hero is. We keep fighting, no matter what. Because we want to make the world a better place."

I dragged in a long breath and stared at my brave, brilliant friend. "You should have been the Nightingale," I said finally. "You're so much better at this than I am."

She grinned at me. "Maybe. But I have terrible aim. And I'd be stopping to take notes every five minutes. Anyways, just because I don't have a magic sword doesn't mean I can't be a hero too."

"You're right," I said. "Sorry. I didn't mean it that way. Only that you did just as much as I did. Maybe more. And when the soda fountain was going haywire, you were going to try to stop it, but I didn't even let you. I should have worked *with* you."

"Well, we both got credit for being dastardly traitors," she said. "Does that make you feel better?"

"Maybe a little." I managed a tiny smile as another knot slipped free in my chest. "But now what do we do? I don't want to give up, but how can I fight the Crimson Knight if everyone thinks I'm a criminal?"

"I thought Jasper was one of the good princes. And he seemed smart enough to make up his own mind."

"He hasn't answered the aethercom," I said, my voice very small.

"Maybe he's busy. You can try him again later. You need rest. And I don't know about you, but I'm starving."

"They'll be looking for us at the boardinghouse," I said. "But I think there's someone else who might help."

CHAPTER NINETEEN

hat do you say, girls?" asked Miss Dash-lilly, thrusting open the doors to the room grandly. "Will this do?"

"Whoa." I gaped at the lavish sitting room. The walls were hung with a rich satiny wallpaper striped in pale green and pink, which seemed to be the woman's favorite colors, judging by just how much of her vast apartment suite was decorated in those shades.

"There's a washroom down that hall," she said, sweeping across the room, the elegance of every gesture magnified by her vivid silk dressing gown, which hung from her plump arms in great wings so that she looked rather like a giant emerald butterfly. "And I've rung my maid to bring up a nice picnic supper. My, this is all so thrilling! And here I thought I was done with this sort of thing."

"I'm sorry," I said, feeling a twinge of guilt. "We don't want to get you in trouble."

She twiddled her fingers dismissively. "I love a nice spot

of trouble. To be honest, I've missed it. Not that I don't adore running the soda fountain, but I'm afraid it doesn't provide the same scope for my abilities as my prior work."

Sophie and I shared a look. Then Sophie asked, "Pardon me, Miss Dashlilly . . ."

"Oh, call me Dash," said our hostess, tossing herself down into a violently pink lounging chair.

"Er, Dash, is it true that you were a spy during the last war?"

Dash winked at us. "I prefer to be referred to as a 'mistress of intrigue,' but 'spy' will do in a pinch. Though it really doesn't capture the full drama of decrypting a formula for the antidote to a poison dart that caught you in the middle of rescuing a valuable asset from a Saventine prison. On horseback."

She laughed at our blank expressions. "You see, aiding a vigilante with a magic sword when she's having a minor tiff with the crown is nothing compared to that."

"I think it's more than a minor tiff," I said, nodding out the window to the ephemera-board across the street, where gleaming black letters blared out NIGHTINGALE'S BETRAYAL: SUPPOSED HERO HELPS CRIMINAL ESCAPE JUSTICE! There was even a short facsimilation of me flying away with Sophie.

Dash made a dismissive gesture. "The public hardly ever really understands true heroism. We want it to be neat, easy to package up and show off. Look at that handsome lad with his bright smile, rescuing that damsel from the dragon. But what if the handsome lad only wants to rescue her for the reward?

What if she wanted to stay with the dragon? Maybe they'd discovered a mutual love of chess and were getting on fabulously?"

The door opened just then, and a strange contraption rolled in, something like a cross between a hatstand and a bicycle, pushing a rolling tea cart in front of it. "Ah, thank you, Mary. Just leave it here. We'll serve ourselves." The hatstand-bicycle detached itself from the tea cart, bent a jerky bow toward Dash, then clattered back out the door, tugging it closed with a copper claw and leaving us alone once again.

Miss Dashlilly gestured to the tea cart, which held a platter of chicken salad sandwiches, several golden scones split and filled with cream and jam, and two enormous, frosted goblets bubbling with chocolate cream sodas. "Go on, girls. Help yourselves. You'll need sustenance if you're going to unravel this tangle. Now, where was I? Ah, the follies of heroism."

She flopped back into her chair, nibbling one of the scones. "You know, a lot of people thought I was a traitor during the war. Or, at the very least, a sellout. As far as the world could tell, I was just a fame-hungry actor, willing to perform even for the enemy."

"Didn't it bother you?" I asked. "I mean, you were risking your life for Gallant."

She shrugged. "I certainly wasn't the only one risking my life for little thanks. And at least I got to come back. Not everyone did." She looked away, her eyes fixed on a framed facsimilation on the far wall. In the short clip, Dash smiled and waved from the cockpit of what looked like an airship. Beside her sat another woman, wearing flight goggles and a shy, secret smile. Dash coughed and returned her attention to us.

"In any case, I had the last laugh. I invested my service bonus at just the right time and ended up with more money than I know what to do with. Money doesn't buy happiness, girls, but it's still nothing to sneeze at." She grinned cheekily.

"If I were rich, I'd eat this every day," I said as I devoured my third sandwich.

"You'll probably be rich too, after all this is settled," said Sophie. "Well, either that, or you'll be an exile in the northern wastes."

"Oh, thank you, that's just the sort of pep talk I needed," I said.

"You don't need a pep talk," said Sophie, polishing off the last of the scones. "You need a plan."

"A plan for what? To clear our names? To destroy the Crimson Knight? To prevent Saventry from declaring war? To stop Pinshaw poisoning the Scrag?"

"Well, if you stop the Crimson Knight, you might get the other three as a bonus, so probably best to focus on that. Hmm. Normally, as you know, I'm in favor of legislative change in the parliament, but I doubt that passing a law against Crimson Knights is going to stop this one."

"It might even be too late," I said, setting down my empty soda glass with a sad *thunk*. "Prince Gideon doesn't believe me.

He thinks Pinshaw is a pillar of society. He didn't even seem all that worried about the Crimson Knight," I added, recalling our strange conversation in the coach. "It's almost as if—"

"Crown Prince Gideon is part of the plot!" burst out Sophie.

I gaped at her, then shook my head. I didn't want it to be true. What hope did we have of thwarting this plot if the crown prince himself was behind it? And Jasper. He *idolized* Gideon. He would be devastated.

"What exactly did you hear Dark Spectacles—Pinshaw— saying on that aethercom? Did he actually say anything about an assassination?"

I thought for a long moment. "No. I guess not. Just that Project Red would be ready on the day of the coronation."

"And when you told Gideon about the knight, he said he didn't want anyone to find out."

"Yes, but that was just so no one panicked."

Sophie huffed.

I had been sitting cross-legged on the sofa beside Sophie. Now I stood and began to pace. "But . . . he's the crown prince. Why would he be helping to rebuild the Crimson Knight when he knows it's probably going to start another war?"

Sophie tapped a finger against her chin. "Maybe he *wants* another war?"

"Why would he want another war?" I asked. "Who *wants* there to be wars? People will die!"

Now Sophie looked sadly resigned. "Lots of people want

wars, Lark. People who make money off them because all the factories have to work double-time making weapons and uniforms. People who think Saventry is still a threat and that Queen Jessamine's peace accords were too generous. People who think you need to beat up everyone else around you to prove you're the best and the boldest and the bravest. But swords aren't always the answer."

"Mmm," said Dash, nodding. "Miss Sophie here has the right of it, I'm afraid."

Sword, who had been listening to the conversation, drooped sadly. I understood the feeling. A heavy weight of despair tugged at my chest. "But what can I do about it?"

"Dear girl," said Dash, "that doesn't mean there's never a time to fight back. If someone is in danger of being harmed, then you should fight back to protect them. Or yourself. But there's a difference between fighting to stop bad things from happening and fighting for your own glory, or to set one group above everyone else."

I patted Sword's hilt. "See, we're all right."

Sophie arched a brow. "For now. It's a danger, though. You have a huge amount of power, Lark, and sometimes that makes it easy to forget what you're fighting for. There's a line between making the world better, versus just making it what you want it to be."

A shiver ran through me, as if she were a witch out of a fairy tale, foretelling some grim future. But I wasn't like that now, and I never would be. "Good thing I have you around, then," I told her. "Because I know if I start going in the wrong direction, you'll let me know."

"I'll write it all over the ephemera-boards," she said, grinning.

"Right, well, first things first. If Gideon is the one behind all this, I've got to warn Jasper. And make sure the villains don't get the helm."

"Lark," Sophie said, suddenly serious. "What if he already has it? The Crimson Knight might be complete by now. And . . . and the first Nightingale died stopping him last time."

Silence.

Then Sophie and Dash both spoke at once.

"Maybe I should go—"

"I'll just need a moment to get kitted up—"

"No," I cut them both off. "I'm not risking anyone else. Besides, someone needs to spread the truth of what's going on. In case . . . Well, in case."

"I'd love to," said Sophie, "but I still don't have the connection rune to hook my ephemera press into the network. And the press is back at the boardinghouse."

"Oh! I know what the rune is!" Jasper had said it himself, that the rune on the knight's chest was a connection rune, which made something part of a larger system. I found a bit of paper and pencil to trace the rune for Sophie. "There. Start working on a new article. We'll get the press later."

Sophie eased herself to her feet, then flung her arms around me. "All right. I'll get to work now. But I expect you to come back, Lark. If things get bad, you get out. Come back, and we'll make a new plan."

"Indeed," said Dash bracingly. "Another round of chocolate sodas will get us back on track. And in the meantime, I'll track down my case of poisons. Now where did I leave that? Hmm. I do hope it's not in the kitchen."

My voice was froggy. "Thank you. Both of you."

"And you," Sophie said to Sword. "You take care of her. You hear?"

The weapon did a quick loop around our heads, blade winking brightly as if to demonstrate its complete prowess and capability.

"Right, then," said Sophie, releasing me. "I've got an article to write. And you've got a war to stop. So get to it."

Sword and I flew straight to the Royal Museum in the waning light of dusk. I'd tried the aethercom, but there had been no answer. Which meant either Jasper believed Gideon and was too angry to speak to me, or that something had gone terribly wrong. I wasn't sure which option frightened me more.

Then, just as Sword set me down on the rooftop, the speaker in my ear began to buzz. I tapped it, and a moment later Jasper's voice burst out.

"Nightingale? Are you there?"

"Jasper! Are you all right?"

"Of course, I'm fine. Where are you now?"

"On the roof of the museum. I came to warn you! Jasper, Pinshaw's the one rebuilding the Crimson Knight. And I think your brother might be helping him."

"Gideon?" Jasper's voice sounded strange. Strained. "That's hogwash."

"I don't think so. He told me the Crimson Knight was just artifice, that it wasn't something to fear. And he refused to believe me that Pinshaw is Dark Spectacles. He ordered the Bright Brigade to arrest me!"

"No, Nightingale, you're wrong. You should go," he said sharply, almost sounding panicked. A pause, as if he was sighing. Then he spoke again, the words cold and crisp. "You've already betrayed your duty, Nightingale. You might as well just go away. Gallant doesn't need you."

The air seemed to fall out of my chest. My eyes stung. I swabbed at them, dimly aware of a distant yipping. Gadget must be with Jasper, wherever he was. Then the yipping cut off suddenly.

"Jasper?" I said.

"You should go, Nightingale," his voice crackled. "Please."

The aethercom went silent.

Something was wrong. This wasn't just Jasper being angry at me. He was trying to *warn* me.

"Jasper?" I tried again, but there was no response. I looked at Sword. "We need to find out what's happened. Are you ready for this?"

The weapon flew a loop-the-loop over my head, then swooped down to smack its hilt into my open palm. I headed for the door to the stairs, but I paused on the threshold. "I don't know what's waiting down there," I told Sword. "But I'm glad you're with me. I couldn't do this without you."

The blade glinted back at me, and dimly I heard those strange, many-layered voices in my head again, whispering, *Nightingale.*

Then Sword and I plunged into the dark stairwell to face whatever waited for us below.

I crept through the halls of the Royal Museum, every nerve quivering, my palms sticky. Had it really been only six days since I'd snuck in here to steal back my future from Miss Starvenger, only to accidentally end up the Nightingale? It felt more like six months. That Lark, who had crept here in her tattered cloth mask, had been desperate. She'd thought she was alone, that the only thing that mattered was getting free of debt. That life was something you could measure and weigh, that if you kept the right balance, you could walk through it without losing any part of yourself.

But I wasn't here now to pay a debt. I was here because Jasper was in trouble and a pair of glory-hungry villains were poisoning the Scrag and risking war. Because I was the Nightingale and I had the power to do something about it. At least, that was what I kept telling myself.

If there was ever a moment for my third power to show itself, this was it. Maybe I'd burst in on Prince Gideon just as he was about to snatch up the helm, and Sword would make him fall asleep. Or melt the helm to sludge. Or turn it into a bouquet of roses. All right, probably not that last one. But *something*. Some way to end this before it went any further.

I tiptoed along the final corridor that led to the grand gallery. Carefully, slowly, silently, I edged out to peer around the pyrosaur with three horns. I couldn't see anything. The center of the hall was pitch black. Except . . . there was someone lying on the floor, not far from me, lanky limbs spread-eagled across the tiles, held in place by a rope net. Jasper!

The sword started to zoom forward, carrying me with it. "Wait!" I whispered. "It might be a trap!" The weapon halted, angling back its blade at me. "I know, but we don't need to rush in like fools," I said. I searched the shadows of the gallery. Even the high arches above. There was no sign of the Crimson Knight.

Rust it, I couldn't wait any longer. Trap or not, I had to do something. "Let's go," I told Sword, and we flew across the room. Jasper still had not moved. As we floated closer, I saw that Gadget was trapped beneath the web beside his master.

The moment the prince saw me, his eyes went wide. He

tried to speak, but a wad of cloth had been jammed into his mouth, muffling his cries. Ropes bound his arms and legs.

"Don't worry," I told him. "I'm getting you out!"

His eyes rolled left, then right, as if looking for something. Or someone. Probably a ten-foot-tall red metal someone. But his words were only a garbled *mmffffl!* I tried tugging at the strands of the net, but they wouldn't budge. They felt strange, stronger than normal rope. "Looks like we need to cut them free, Sword," I said, setting the blade against the cords that trapped Jasper's left arm. "Just be careful you don't slice— aaaah!"

The moment Sword's edge met the rope band, a jolt jabbed through me. My jaw clamped tight. My body went rigid. I couldn't move. It was as if I'd been caught by my own freeze ray.

Time slowed. I saw Jasper's blue eyes, wide with horror. I saw the rope, slashed open, revealing the thin, glimmering copper wire inside. I saw Sword twitching and turning as a sizzling light ran up and down the blade. The runes flared so bright, my eyes filled with stars. And then, abruptly, they winked out.

A hollow clang.

I blinked, trying to clear my hazy vision to see what had happened. I was free again, but my body quivered, my legs wanting to turn to jelly. All I could do was stare at the dull gray blade lying utterly motionless on the marble floor.

"Sword!" I screamed, crawling forward, trying to reach

for the weapon. My fingers brushed the hilt, but there was no answering hum. And it was heavy. *So* heavy. "Sword?" I said again, my voice fainter now, cracking on the word. Rotting rust, what had happened? "What's wrong? Why aren't you . . . awake?"

I almost said *alive*. But the weapon wasn't alive. So it couldn't possibly be dead, right? It was only stunned. Asleep. It would wake up any moment. The rope—no, *copper*—web had done this. Beneath its disguise, it was like the one that Jasper had used to trap me, back in the Heap. Jasper said it might have strange effects on aetheric objects, but last time the web had only given Sword a jolt. It hadn't damaged it permanently.

Sword would get better. It had to.

"Sword," I said. *"Please."*

"The sword won't answer you, Nightingale," said a voice from behind me.

CHAPTER TWENTY

*P*rince Gideon advanced from the shadows of the neighboring gallery. He gave me a sharp, humorless smile. "Or I should say *former* Nightingale. Because really, what are you now, without the sword? Just a silly girl in a costume."

Thumping beside him, looming over us all, came the Crimson Knight. The metal warrior was complete. The eyes of the helm were no longer empty slits. They gleamed with aether, fixed upon me as I huddled on the ground, clutching the heavy sword.

Rust it! I had to move. I shoved myself upright, onto my unsteady legs. With all my strength, I wrenched the blade up, aiming the point at the knight. "Freeze!"

But there was no rush of icy air. Only the long, low chuckle of the prince. "No more of that," he said. "But just to be safe, we'd better take away that toy."

He gestured at me. Before I could scream, a great metal hand snapped out, seizing me around the torso and yanking me into the air. I clung to Sword's hilt. *Please! Please come back! I need you!*

The massive fingers dug into my flesh. I gasped, the air crushing out of me. My fingers slid, and I lost my hold on the hilt. A distant clatter. The Crimson Knight rumbled hungrily and crouched, reaching for the fallen sword.

But Gideon had already snatched it up. "Now, now, not yet," he chided the knight. "Remember our arrangement."

I wriggled, still caught in the knight's grip. "What arrangement?"

"The Crimson Knight is going to help me ensure that Gallant returns to her place of rightful glory. And in return, I will give him what he most desires."

"So it's true. You're doing this all because you want a war."

"I don't want a *war*, little girl," said Gideon. "I want a *victory*. Not some namby-pamby peace accord like my mother agreed to. And for that, we need to complete Project Red." He turned. "Mr. Pinshaw, are we still on schedule?"

My snarl of fury came out a strangled gasp as Pinshaw stepped forward from the shadows to join the prince. "Yes, Your Majesty. The new factory will be ready tomorrow, just in time for the coronation jubilee. Once the Crimson Knight provides the necessary thermal input to initialize the systems, Project Red will be fully activated and self-sustaining."

"He looks pretty active to me," I managed to gasp out.

Pinshaw chuckled. Gideon grinned. They knew something I didn't. Something I wasn't going to like.

"Silly girl," said Gideon. "You think the Crimson Knight is the sum total of my plans? Mighty as he may be, a single artificed soldier will not ensure our return to glory. Our ambitions must reach higher than that. Project Red isn't the Crimson Knight. Project Red is my new factory. One that will revolutionize aethercraft in Gallant and move us into a new Golden Age, with me, Gideon, as its new Architect. And instead of a single Crimson Knight, I will craft hundreds. Thousands."

I stared at him, shaking my head. "You're already poisoning the Scrag," I choked out. "If you do this, even more people will die."

"Yes, more may die. But it will be for a righteous cause. It's the only way to move Gallant into the future, to ensure our security. I couldn't have you interfering with that. You've already done enough."

I craned my neck, trying to see Jasper. I could just barely glimpse him, still splayed out on the floor, bound by the web that had stolen my sword's power.

"Fine," I gasped. My head started to spin as the knight's fingers stayed tight around my chest. "You beat me. I'm no threat to you now. You can let us go."

"Oh, I don't think so. You and my dear brother still have a part to play."

"What part?" I demanded. "What are you going to do to Jasper?"

"Nothing that will permanently injure him. He *is* my brother. The only family I have left, now, thanks to Saventry."

Gideon looked toward Jasper, his blue eyes softening for just a moment. "And he's part of what inspired my plan."

Jasper gave a furious but completely garbled response. Gideon stalked over to his brother, then pulled free the gag.

"What do you mean?" Jasper sputtered. "I don't want war!"

"No, you've always been naive. Too much like Mother. But you do understand the need for Gallant to innovate. For us to reclaim the great gifts the Architect left us. Gifts like the Crimson Knight here."

"The knight is dangerous! It turned on the Architect, and it could turn on you, too, Gideon! Please, it's not worth it. You have to stop!"

Gideon tsked. "Does it look as if the Crimson Knight is about to go wild and destroy the city? No. And he will not. Because I've made him an offer he can't refuse."

"What?" I asked. "What offer?"

"I'm going to give him the two things he wants most in the world."

"Which are?"

The Crimson Knight groaned. A rasping sound came from the helm, grinding and shuddering so painfully in my ears I almost couldn't recognize the words. "Complete. Me."

"But he's already complete," said Jasper.

"Not," the monster thundered, "yet."

"I've learned some interesting facts that have been left out of our history books," said Gideon. "About why exactly the Crimson Knight went on his rampage all those years ago. You see, when the Architect created him, he wasn't meant to be simply a powerful metal warrior. The Architect was quite old by then. He knew his time was coming to an end, and he feared it. So he crafted a new body, one that could never be destroyed."

"What?" I looked at Jasper for confirmation.

Jasper was staring at the Crimson Knight. "Wait. What? Do you mean the Architect is actually inside that thing?"

"INCOMPLETE," growled the Crimson Knight.

"No," said Gideon. "The process was never finished. Perhaps the Architect had second thoughts. Or maybe someone tried to stop him. Which is why the Crimson Knight desires a new partner. Someone to merge with him, body and soul, to allow them to reach their full potential. Someone like you, brother."

"What?" I demanded.

"What?" Jasper gaped at him.

"Don't you see, Jasper? It's perfect. You and I both know you're not cut out to be a soldier. You're too soft, like Mother. But this way, you can do what you've always dreamed of: you can be the hero you always wanted to be. A champion of Gallant!" He beamed at Jasper, as if giving his brother the most wondrous gift in all the world. Then he turned to Pinshaw. "You have everything prepared?"

"Yes, Your Highness," Pinshaw said. "We'll complete the

process tomorrow, at the grand opening. Once Prince Jasper has, ahem, integrated with the knight, they should be able to activate Project Red and begin producing your new army."

"And you will be my greatest knight, Jasper," said Gideon. "You will lead them. You will crush our enemies and ensure our place as the greatest among nations!"

"Trapped inside a giant metal monster?" Jasper said. "No, Gideon. That's not what I want. I want to build things. Create! I don't need to hurl fire to serve Gallant—I can use my mind. That's what makes me strong."

"What, like giving that mutt wheels?" Gideon scoffed.

Gadget growled, then fell to gnawing and tearing at the bindings that held him beside his master.

"Jasper's worth a thousand Crimson Knights just the way he is." I beat my fists against the metal fingers that still held me aloft. "I won't let you do it!"

"Forgive me, but I don't believe you're in any position to do anything about it," said Gideon. "And in a moment, you'll be of no concern whatsoever. You'll recall I promised the Crimson Knight two things. One was a new human partner. The other was the destruction of his greatest foe. Melting down the sword will have to wait until Jasper and the knight are unified, but you we can take care of right now."

He nodded to the Crimson Knight.

The fingers around my chest tightened. I gagged, staring up into the empty gleaming eyes of the metal monster. He was choking me now, squeezing the breath from my chest. My ribs creaked painfully. I couldn't even manage the smallest gasp. My head spun. The room swirled.

Dimly, I heard something that sounded like a growl, followed by a ferocious yipping, then a crackling clap like thunder. Energy buzzed over my skin.

And then, suddenly, I was falling. Thumping down in a painful lump onto the floor. That jolt of energy . . . could it be—?

"Sword?" I gasped. But as I blinked my eyes open, I found myself staring into a pair of eager brown eyes. "Gadget?" I stammered. "Where did you come from?"

Whatever the dog had done, it had been impressive. Gideon had one arm flung up to shield his face. Pinshaw lay groaning on the ground. Even the Crimson Knight had staggered back. I remembered what Jasper had said when I first met the dog: watch out for the buildup of aetheric charge. He was like a canine version of the Bright Brigade's truncheons!

"Good boy," I said, my voice shaky. He'd given me a few precious moments. I had to put them to good use. I turned toward Jasper.

"Run, Nightingale! You've got to warn the Bright Brigade!" Jasper shouted. He was still bound beneath the net, though there was a ragged hole in it now, where Gadget had chewed himself free.

"The Bright Brigade will never trust a wanted criminal,"

Gideon snarled. He'd recovered from Gadget's electrical attack, though his blond hair now stuck out in a wild mane. It only made him look more menacing. "You're all alone," he said, softer then. "No sword. No powers. It's over, girl."

The words slammed into me, heavy as iron. Heavy as the sword I no longer had the power to lift. I'd been a mistake from the start, hadn't I? It only made sense that I'd end up with all of it stripped away. I had no magic powers. I was just a girl again.

But what had Sophie told me? *We keep fighting, no matter what. Because we want to make the world a better place.* That was what a hero was. That was what *I* was. With or without magic.

The Crimson Knight swiped at me with his massive metal hands, but I was ready this time. I'd spent half my life evading pursuit. I scooped Gadget into my arms and dodged aside.

"I'm going to get help, Jasper!" I shouted. "I promise I'll stop this!"

Then I turned and pelted toward the exit.

"So we have until tomorrow afternoon," said Sophie, her brow furrowed in concentration. We were seated at the soda fountain. Dash had taken one look at my face when I'd arrived breathless and swordless—but with an aetheric roller-dog—and ordered us all downstairs for emergency chocolate. The shop was silent and dark, closed for the night. Gadget rolled over to put his chin on my knee, and I skritched his ears as I poured out the story of my misadventures.

"I should have tried harder," I said. "I just left Jasper there! And now Gideon's going to stick him in that metal monster, then use him to start up his new factory so he can make hundreds *more* metal monsters."

"You didn't die. That's the important part. We still have a chance to stop him. We just need to take account of our resources and figure out the best way to use them. So, let's see." Sophie tapped a finger against her chin. "We've got my brain, of course. And you're a cracking good thief."

"I would be delighted to lend my assistance," said Miss Dashlilly. "Just let me know who you need me to poison. I'm also very good at distractions."

"And we have Gadget," Sophie said as the dog woofed and sparked, chasing a shadow across the floor nearby. I waited for her to add something else. A general who owed her a favor. A long-lost cousin who was conveniently the Saventine minister of defense. But she only stared into the air. I gave her a look. Sophie sighed. "You're right. It's not enough. But I know where we can get the help we need."

"Where? Gideon's right, the constables and the Bright Brigade all think we're criminals. If we go to them, they'll probably just stick us in jail."

"I'm not talking about anyone official. Come on, let's go."

"Where?"

"The boardinghouse," said Sophie. "We're going to get the other girls."

"This was so much easier when I could just fly down onto the roof," I said as Sophie and I scurried along the alley beside the town house. I paused under the small window that led to the boardinghouse kitchen. "Here, I'll give you a boost."

I laced my fingers together, kneeling under the window. Sophie braced herself against the bricks, then stepped onto my hands. She gritted her teeth as her twisted foot took all her weight, but only for a moment. I heaved as she reached for the sill and tugged herself up. After a moment of fumbling with the lash, she had it shoved open. Another moment, and she was inside.

I heard a thump. Then a muffled yelp.

"Sophie?" I whispered. "Are you all right?"

Silence. Probably she just hadn't heard me. Probably.

I backed away, then took three running steps and threw myself up to catch hold of the window. My arms strained—I'd gotten out of practice with all my flying lately—but I heaved myself up, over the sill, and inside. Scrambling down from the counter, I peered through the murky darkness of the kitchen for Sophie. "Sophie?" The lights flared, aether suddenly turning the room noon-bright. I winced, blinking. Then my stomach plunged as I saw what awaited me.

Miss Starvenger stood a few paces away against the wall

beside the trash chute. She was dressed in one of her nicest outfits, the striped plum poplin with the matching hat decorated with three fluffy ostrich feathers. In her hands was an ornate cut-glass atomizer. And at her feet lay Sophie, limp and unmoving.

"Sophie!" I shrieked. "You witch! What did you do to her?"

"Lark," she greeted me coolly. "I should have expected to find you helping this criminal, given your own predilections. But don't worry. Miss Fan is perfectly fine. She's just had a dose of my favorite perfume. It seems *someone* changed the formulation. I don't much care for it myself, but it should keep this criminal out of trouble until the constables arrive." She set the atomizer on the counter beside her with a decisive *clink*.

"Sophie's not a criminal. She's helping me rescue Prince Jasper! Let her go!"

As I started forward, Starvenger made a sour face, plucking a gold chain from her neck. "Not so fast. Unless you no longer care about your poor mother's locket." As she spoke, she thrust the necklace at the wall, shoving open the trash-chute flap. The locket dangled from her fingers, suspended over the dark abyss. "It would be a shame if I dropped it. I doubt such a delicate trinket would survive the incinerator."

My eyes clung to the glint of gold, the thing I'd been working so hard to get back. And now I was about to lose it forever, unless I let Miss Starvenger turn Sophie over to the authorities.

"Come now," Starvenger drawled. "It can't be that hard a

choice. I've seen you, Lark. I know you're willing to do what it takes to survive. So I trust you'll make the right decision. Maybe I'd even be willing to share a part of the reward."

"The reward?"

"For apprehending a wanted criminal." She tilted her lovely, glossy head, her crimson lips curving in a slow smile. "You only have to choose which you want to be. An accomplice or a hero."

It wasn't the reward that made me hesitate. That didn't matter now. It was Mum's locket. Time seemed to slow as I stared at it. Three steps and it could be mine. But I'd never make it in time. Starvenger would drop it. I knew she would. The cold certainty of it was in her eyes.

For so long, that locket had been the only link I had left to Mum. To lose it would be like losing her all over again. But my mother had fought for what she believed in. She'd stood by her friends, no matter what. If I couldn't do the same, then I had lost something a lot more valuable than gold.

I lifted my chin. "You're right," I told her. "I choose to be a hero." Then I clicked my cuffs together.

Starvenger gave a breathless gasp as my clothing transformed and the Nightingale's mask slid over my face.

Three things happened at once.

Starvenger snarled, "Say goodbye to your precious locket." I dove for the atomizer. And Sophie lashed out, kicking Starvenger in the knee.

The woman groaned, stumbling. I squeezed the atomizer

balloon, sending a cloud of sickly yellow mist into Starvenger's face. The gold chain slid from her fingers, falling down, down, down . . . and smacked into Sophie's upturned palm. Miss Starvenger toppled, thumping into a snoring, peaceful pile of striped poplin, leaving me free to kneel beside Sophie. I flung my arms around her. I guess maybe I *was* a hugging person, in the right circumstances. "Sophie, are you all right?"

"Fine, fine," she said, tapping the cotton square tied around her neck. "I remembered my handkerchief. All that preparation for the protest did some good, I suppose." Then she reached up, pressing something into my hand. "Here. This is yours."

I stared at the glinting gold locket in my palm. "You saved it," I said. "You saved my mother's locket."

"Well, you're the one who's always going on about keeping the accounts balanced. So it's only fair I got it back for you. You got me my father's books, remember?"

I held out my hand to help her upright. "I'm not worried about balancing the books anymore," I said. "I'm just glad you're all right."

"We'd better get going and wake the other—oh." Sophie cut herself off, looking past me.

I turned to see Blythe, Willow, and the twins crowded into the doorway that led out to the stairwell. I didn't know how long they'd been there, but clearly it had been long enough to give them all wide-eyed expressions of deep surprise.

"Er, hi there," I said, giving them a wave. "Anyone up for a soda? And maybe saving the world?"

CHAPTER TWENTY-ONE

"All right, does everyone know what they're doing?" I scanned the faces of the other girls and Miss Dashlilly. We were gathered in an alley not far from the Heap. It was midmorning, and the ephemera-boards were all busy with scenes from Gideon's coronation, interspersed with announcements of a grand surprise to be unveiled at the Heap within the hour.

An hour. We had an hour before Gideon and Pinshaw turned Jasper into a metal monster and completed Project Red. But if I had my way, it was Gideon who was going to get the surprise.

Cora, who had just returned from scouting the nearby streets, gave me a rakish salute. "Aye, aye, Captain Nightingale. The crowds are already starting to gather, and there's fifty-three bluecaps guarding the entrance to the Heap."

She translated Nora's report. "And one of the Brigaders said the king was on his way and should arrive soon."

"Right," I said. "Sophie, are you ready?"

Sophie was scribbling in her notebook but glanced up at my question. "Yes. Assuming your connection rune works, I'll be ready to broadcast my article over the ephemeras." She patted her ramshackle press, which we'd lugged up from the boardinghouse basement and brought along in a large picnic basket. "I'm just editing this last line."

"Good," I said. "That should cause a distraction, and hopefully help convince enough people that Gideon is lying." I turned to Miss Dashlilly and the twins. "Is the portable fountain ready? Will it do what we want?"

Miss Dashlilly nodded. "Yes. I tested it this morning." Her lips twisted faintly as she brushed a bit of something sticky off her wrist. "The twins and I will keep the Bright Brigade preoccupied. In their own little bubbles, you might say."

I smiled, though it felt weak. This whole plan was a gamble. But it had to work. It *would* work. I just had to trust that everyone could do their part, including me. I lifted my chin and gave them all a strong, confident smile. "Right. Just be sure to wait until I get Sword back from Gideon. Then Blythe and Willow and I will free Jasper while everyone is distracted."

Gadget barked.

"And Gadget will help too," I added quickly.

Blythe nodded, but her expression was severe. "You're sure Prince Jasper can wake the sword up again?"

"He did it once before," I said firmly. "He can do it again. So long as we can get to him before Gideon brings out the Crimson Knight."

"And then what?" Blythe asked. "You turn back into the Nightingale and stop the Crimson Knight, and everything's happily ever after?"

I kept my smile fixed. "That's right. But let's focus on getting Jasper free. That's the most important part. If we can prove what Gideon's up to, we won't need to stop the knight. We just need to stop the man behind it. So. Everyone ready to do that?"

Nods all around. Even Gadget gave an approving bark.

"Then let's go do this," I said.

"I see the royal carriage now," said Blythe, bobbing up on her toes to peer over the heads of the crowd gathered along the street.

She was taller than I was, so all I could see was the purple waistcoat of the large man in front of us. "We need to get closer," I said, squirming forward, trying to clear a space for Willow to follow.

Gadget yipped and trot-rolled ahead of me, his wheels sparking, making the nearest onlookers yelp and pull back. I dove after him, with Willow and Blythe right behind me, and we managed to make it to the strings of green-and-purple bunting that divided the sidewalk from the street.

Now I could see the carriage: a confection of brass drawn by two metal horses. Their eyes gleamed aether blue, and threads of smoke twisted from their brass nostrils. Ahead of them trotted an even more fantastical work of artifice.

"A mechanical lion!" Willow exclaimed.

The creature padded along the street, all shimmering gold, the lion's long mane worked from a thousand needle-fine wires. A rich purple saddle lay across the beast's back, and upon it sat Prince—no, *King* Gideon. He smiled, blond hair smoothly sculpted beneath the gold crown, blue eyes blazing as he waved to the cheering crowds. Rows of Bright Brigaders marched ahead and behind the procession.

"Do you see Jasper?" I asked, tearing my eyes from the spectacle. I had to focus on the plan, not worry about aether-powered lions.

"There's someone in the carriage," said Blythe, pointing. "See there, in the window?"

I leaned out over the bunting, trying to get a better look. Closer and closer padded the gilded lion. A band somewhere behind the carriage filled the air with music. For a long moment, the scene seemed cut from crystal, a timeless span of cheering crowds, gold and bronze and bright flags flapping, trumpets and tubas blaring triumph. My heart leaped as I caught sight of a familiar pale face, topped by a swoop of black hair. He was awake—I could see him moving. Struggling against bonds? He must be trapped inside!

The ground shook with the tread of the artificed lion. I was up in front, smashed against the barrier. There was nowhere to hide as Gideon passed by. Luckily, he'd only ever seen me in the Nightingale's costume. His blue eyes swept over the crowd. Over me. They would have moved on, dismissing me as just another onlooker, but then I clicked my cuffs together.

As my Nightingale costume skimmed over my skin, Gideon's gaze snagged, lancing into me with a sudden, fierce heat. He drew back sharply on the reins of the great gold lion as he cried out, "You!"

I vaulted over the barrier and stalked toward him. The king sneered, sliding down from his mount to meet me. He set one hand on the pommel of the sword belted to his waist. A familiar, bird-shaped hilt that glimmered with sapphires. My heart wobbled, just for a moment.

Murmurs ran through the crowd.

"The Nightingale!"

"It's her!"

"Is it true? Did she betray Gallant?"

"What should we call you now?" Gideon drawled. "Since you're no longer the Nightingale. Ah, I know. How about the Cuckoo?"

A number of the Bright Brigade had moved to encircle me. I ignored them. My job was to get that sword back. I had to trust the others to do their part.

I stepped closer, setting my fists on my hips just the way Sophie would when she was delivering a speech. "That's better than being a king who poisons his own people for the sake of progress! It's better than sacrificing your own brother for the sake of power!"

There. I'd poked the hornet's nest. Gideon snarled, seizing me and jerking me close. His blue eyes blazed with a fanatical fire. "Shut your mouth, little girl. You think just because you run around with a magic sword for a week you know anything of true heroism? Sacrifice?"

"Maybe not," I said. "But I was a pretty good thief for the two years before that, and right now, that's what really matters."

With that I brandished the sword, which I'd slid free from Gideon's sheath, then cracked it against his hand. He yelped, releasing me. I leaped back as the king opened his mouth to shout something.

I didn't have a chance to find out what it was, though, because right at that moment an enormous glimmering bubble rose up behind him, enveloping Gideon in a smooth, glassy prison. Other bubbles had already encased the nearby members of the Bright Brigade. Shouts of alarm rose from the crowds as more bubbles floated up from a small rolling cart carrying a portable brass soda fountain. I could hear Miss Dashlilly calling out, "Don't worry, it's just a minor beverage malfunction! We'll have it fixed in a jiffy!"

Inside the bubble, Gideon was beating at his sticky prison, but it refused to release him. I lifted the sword, giving him an ironic salute, then spun and raced for the carriage.

All we had to do now was get Jasper out and maybe, just maybe, we could win this thing. There was still no sign of the Crimson Knight. Or Pinshaw. I hoped that was a good thing.

I found Blythe and Gadget standing off against a handful of un-bubbled Brigaders.

"You're on the wrong side!" Blythe shouted at the Brigaders, slashing her practice saber as Gadget rolled back and forth, his wheels sparking, the sizzling charge snapping at any of the soldiers who got too close.

Willow was over at the carriage itself, scrabbling at the door. I rushed to her side. "What's wrong?"

"It's locked!" she growled. The last time I'd heard her sound so fierce was when she was chasing off a neighborhood boy who had been throwing stones at one of her cats.

"Should I try to cut it?" I asked.

"No. I have an idea." She clamped her jaw tight, as if holding her breath. Her entire body suddenly faded, winking away, as she reached out. Right *through* the door. There was a click, and suddenly Willow was solid and smiling, stepping back as the carriage door burst open and a boy with floppy black hair and intense blue eyes was clambering out of it.

"Jasper! Are you all right?"

"I'd be better if my brother wasn't trying to imprison me in a giant metal monster," he said dryly. "What's your plan?"

"We're here to stop him. I've got help," I said, nodding to Willow, and to Blythe and Gadget and the clouds of bubbles. "*Amazing* help. But we could really use the Nightingale too." I held out the dull, heavy sword. My voice broke as I said, "Can you bring it back?"

Jasper stared at the blade, then gave a short, determined nod. "Yes. But we'll need space. And time."

"Blythe and the others can give us space," I said. "But no promises on time."

Jasper gave me a crooked smile. "I'll work as fast as I can."

Things in the street had only gotten more chaotic. Everyone seemed to be pointing up at the nearby buildings, shouting. I caught a glimpse of bold black type, reading PRINCE GIDEON'S TREACHERY! Sophie's work, no doubt.

"Lay the sword there," Jasper said, gesturing to the street. As soon as I set it down, he pulled a piece of chalk from his pocket and began sketching runic symbols in a narrow oval around the sword. I risked a glance to Gideon. Several free members of the Bright Brigade had managed to reach him and were attempting to slice open his bubble prison.

"Hurry!" I said. "Gideon's nearly free."

Jasper didn't look up, didn't give any sign he'd heard me. All his attention was on his work. A heartbeat later he sat back on his heels. He whispered something under his breath, his eyes squeezing shut. Just as they had that first night in the museum, the symbols etched into the blade flared bright blue. A low hum seemed to fill the air, making my teeth ache. Then Jasper looked up at me.

"Take it."

I knelt down, my legs shaky. I started to reach out to the hilt, with its sweep of metal-wrought wings and blue gemmed eye. Then I stopped. "Anyone could be the Nightingale now," I said. "It doesn't have to be me."

Jasper blinked.

"I mean, you always meant to be the Nightingale. It was just an accident that I was the one who grabbed it first. Are you sure you don't want—"

"Yes," he said, cutting me off. Then he smiled. A wistful smile, but a certain one. "I know what I'm doing. I know what my job is, and it's not to be the champion of Gallant. That's you. I mean, if you want it. If that's what you choose."

The air felt heavy in my lungs. The moment pressed down on me with the weight of decision. It was my choice. Right there in front of me, inches from my fingertips. I could take on the mantle of the Nightingale again. It would be hard. I might be hurt. I might die. But I'd have the power to make a difference. The only question was: Did I believe I had the strength to try?

I closed my eyes for a long moment, one hand stealing up to close on the locket that hung from my neck. My mother had sacrificed everything to try to make the world a better place. How could I do any less? Besides, it wasn't all sacrifice and hard work. There was joy in it too. Satisfaction in actually doing something to make the world better.

I'd never know if I was the best person to be Nightingale. I only knew that I was going to be the best Nightingale I could be. And that was enough.

I let out my tight, waiting breath, then reached for the hilt.

Power thrummed through me. Then came a flash of brilliant light. Distant cries. And, deep in my mind, voices whispering in unison, *Welcome, Nightingale.*

Finally I felt a lightness in my hand as the sword shivered and bobbed up, quivering and awake—alive!—once more. My eyes stung as the weapon tipped toward me, blue gem glinting a rakish wink. I gave a cry of pure joy and triumph, jabbing Sword into the air, and together we rose up, floating above the street.

The Nightingale was back!

Unfortunately, so was King Gideon. He stood flanked by blue-uniformed Brigaders, across the street, just beside one of the entrances to the Heap. Blythe, Willow, and Gadget had retreated, joining Jasper below me.

"Enough!" shouted Gideon, his resonant voice carrying even over the general uproar of the chaotic crowd filling the street. "This is the first day of a new Golden Age of Gallant, and I will not allow you to spoil it, Nightingale. You are not the hero our nation needs. Not anymore."

He gestured toward the Heap. No, to the man standing beside the entrance, holding something that looked like a large aethercom. Mr. Pinshaw! The man dipped his head to the king, then pressed the device in his hand. And then . . .

The ground shuddered. It reminded me of the last time Pinshaw had summoned the Crimson Knight. Except louder. Much, *much* louder. A cloud of dust rose up, veiling everything in shadow. I swooped down to steady Jasper as the entire street quaked, jerking and heaving like rough water.

"Witness the future of Gallant!" proclaimed Gideon, as the dust settled.

I stared. Blythe gasped. Willow yelped. Gadget barked frantically.

The Heap was gone. In its place towered the new aether factory. The enormous structure had risen out of the cracked ground, a confection of copper spires and gleaming crystal domes as dazzling as Dashlilly's fountain, except that it was a thousand times bigger. Perched atop the highest tower stood a familiar, fearsome figure of red steel. Screams rose, as the crowds began to scatter, fleeing from the terrible sight.

"Crimson Knight!" called out Gideon. "Finish this! Once and for all!"

With a great bellow, the metal monster dove from the top of the factory, careering down at me.

"Go!" I shouted to Sword. "I'm not letting that metal-headed monster anywhere near Jasper. Enough is enough."

We flew straight at him. I kept my gaze fixed on the bright rune glowing on the monster's chest. That was where I needed to strike. That was the rune that would send him crashing down, dead metal once again.

But at the last moment, the knight spun away. No, *flew* away. "Rust it," I muttered. "So he can fly, too?"

Sword wiggled. "Right," I said. "I know. I just hoped it would be easy."

And in some ways, it was easy. Well, easier. I barely needed to squeeze Sword's hilt, and the weapon seemed to understand which way I wanted to go. Reunited, our bond was even stronger than it had been before.

We could do this. We had to do this. For Sophie, for Jasper, for his mum and mine.

And there it was. Our opening. We dove, every nerve taut, bending toward that single moment when sword would strike crimson steel. Faster, faster, blade bright, wind whipping my face, and then . . .

Sword smashed into the rune with a clap like thunder! A bright burst that filled my eyes with stars. I blinked and saw the Crimson Knight falling toward the street, dropping in pieces.

Clash. Crash. Thunk, crash. Thunk. Kablam! Four limbs. Torso. Helm. All struck the earth with a tremendous clatter.

Sword and I flew softly down behind the broken monster. Blythe, Willow, Jasper, Gadget, and the twins all rushed forward to greet me. There were even some cheers from what remained of the crowds. Somewhere in the distance, I heard Miss Dashlilly calling out, "Hear! Hear for the Nightingale! Who wants a free blueberry fizz in her honor?"

Even Sophie had rejoined us. She grinned at me, then up at the ephemeras still blazing her byline. "It's not managing editor," she said, "but it's a start."

"Arrest them!" bellowed Gideon, still standing boldly before the newly risen factory. "Arrest all of them!" But his orders fell empty onto the street. The Bright Brigaders who had been flanking him pulled away, muttering among themselves, occasionally pointing up to the ephemeras.

"It's over." I gestured to the remains of the shattered knight, sprawled across the street between us. "You've lost, Gideon. The Crimson Knight is gone. Project Red is over."

Gideon's mouth twisted with fury. But it wasn't the wild passion of a thwarted villain. Something snapped there, deep in the blue of his eyes, that looked more like conviction. They were strangely bright, too. Almost as blue as aether. He rolled his shoulders. Slowly, carefully, he lifted his hands to his jacket and peeled it off to stand in breeches and shirtsleeves.

And that was when I saw the connection runes. They were marked across his arms, and they were glowing. "No," said Gideon, his voice strangely resonant. "It's only just begun. I will have my army. I will have my new Golden Age."

"Gideon!" Jasper cried. "What have you done?"

More runes began to burn on Gideon's body. Literally burn, raising smoke from his shirt, eating through the fabric just below his knees, just above his heart. And one, glimmering terribly upon his brow.

"What I would have done for you, brother. This could have been yours. But since you rejected my gift, I will claim it. I will have the power of the Crimson Knight. I will ensure that Project Red lives. I will make certain that Gallant stands alone, the greatest power in the land!"

With that, he darted forward toward the fallen helm. I lunged to stop him, swinging Sword up to try to freeze him, but I was too late. The moment the king's hand touched the helm, it began to glow. A rune appeared on the metal, twin to the one on Gideon's brow. All around, the other pieces of the knight began to spark and gleam, floating into the air. It was as if they were falling, but instead of being drawn to the earth, they were drawn to Gideon. Arms, legs, torso, the great chunks of armor flew at the king, encasing him in the time it took for me to take a single, startled gasp.

Then Gideon was gone, and there was only the Crimson Knight towering over us. Jasper gave a strangled cry.

But I wasn't wasting any time. "Go!" I called to Sword, and we flew. Straight, strong, sharp at the same rune that had destroyed the knight last time, the one on its chest. Metal clashed on metal, sending me flying away like a pitiful bird bouncing off a glass window. The blow had struck true, but nothing had happened.

A low, rumbling laugh came from the knight. Gideon's laugh, but deeper, thrumming with power, edged in copper and sparking with aether. "It's going to take more than that to stop me now, little bird." And then, faster than I could even think, he lashed out. One great metal hand struck, catching me hard in the chest, sending me hurtling back.

The world was rushing air, misery, panic. Something tremendously hard smashed into my back. Sun blazed in my eyes as a crimson monster trailed smoky ribbons across a clear blue sky, flying up, up, up. Then my eyes closed, and everything went dark.

CHAPTER TWENTY-TWO

The world returned. I groaned. Pain throbbed at the back of my head, along my shoulders, and across my backside. Half of me felt like one enormous bruise.

"She's awake!" I winced at the sound. It was like someone had stuffed my skull full of nails and then shaken me violently.

"Quiet," I protested. "My head."

"What did she say?" asked a voice that sounded like Willow.

"It sounded like 'Quit while we're ahead,'" said another girl. Blythe, maybe?

A pause, then, "Nora's right, that makes no sense. We're not ahead. We just lost. Are you sure it wasn't 'Quite mad'? She might be talking about Gideon."

"QUIET," I said, blinking blearily up at a circle of worried faces. "MY. HEAD."

"Shh!" said Sophie, leaning over me. "You need to take it easy, Lark. You've got an enormous lump on the back of your head."

"I have to stop him," I said, groaning again as I shoved myself up. "Sword?"

Steel flashed eagerly as the weapon bobbed into my field of vision. I reached out with a trembling hand that seemed to have too many fingers. But the moment I gripped the blade, my world seemed to sharpen.

"Where is he?" I asked. "Where's Gideon? The last thing I remember, he was—" My words snagged as I looked up.

The gleaming new factory rose above us, a terrible, ravishing majesty of copper towers spearing the clouds. But something had changed. Now an ominous, glimmering smoke poured from the spires.

"What's going on?" I stood, trying to take stock of my surroundings.

We were still in the street. It looked as if the Bright Brigaders were moving the crowds away, directing them with sharp, urgent gestures to leave the area. Jasper was with the Brigade, but when he noticed me, he dashed over to join us.

"Nightingale! Thank the Architect you're awake!"

I grimaced. "How long was I out?"

"Five minutes," said Sophie.

"Too long."

I scowled. It was Pinshaw. He stood a few paces away, guarded by Gadget, who growled as the man lifted a hand to point at the smoke. "It's already begun. You can't stop it now."

"Can't stop what?"

"Project Red. Once the Gideon Knight has infused the

core with sufficient thermal power, the new factory will begin production."

"Production?" repeated Sophie. "You mean making hundreds of Crimson Knights? Pumping even more aether dust out into the Scrag?"

"No," I said. "That's not happening."

"You've failed, Nightingale," sneered Pinshaw. "You can't stop progress. You would be wise to—"

Gadget snarled, and a stream of sparks burst from his wheels and flew at the factory owner. Pinshaw gave a single startled yelp before toppling to the street, clutching his head woozily. Gadget trotted over, sniffing the man.

"Oh, bravo! Good doggo," Cora cheered. "Excellent work. You show him the true price of villainy."

Unfortunately, I didn't have time to enjoy the mortification of my old nemesis. I had my new enemy and his army of metal monsters to worry about. "I'd better get going," I said. "I can still stop him."

"Lark, wait," said Jasper. "You tried fighting him one-on-one already. He's too strong now. We need another plan."

"If you've got something else in mind, I'm all ears," I said.

"Er, well . . ." Jasper ran a hand through his black hair. "I'm still working on that."

"Right, which brings us back to me breaking him into tiny bits."

"How?" asked Sophie. "You hit him smack in the chest and nothing happened. Not like the first time."

"Gideon bound himself directly to the knight," Jasper said. "He created a link between his own flesh and blood and an aether-crafted construct. That sort of artifice is incredibly dangerous. And incredibly rare. In fact, there's only one other instance of it that I know of."

"What?" I said, then realized everyone was looking at me. "Oh. Right. Well, all the more reason *I* should to go after him."

"It's not that easy," said Jasper. "He's got six binding runes. I'm pretty sure the only way to unmake him now is to hit all six of them at the same exact time. It's impossible."

"I didn't say it would be easy." My voice was hard. "I know it's dangerous. I know I might not come back." This was it, wasn't it? All the other Nightingales had perished saving Gallant. I would just be one more in that tragic line.

Willow made an unhappy noise, and Blythe hugged her closer. Even Cora looked unnaturally solemn.

"I know I can't stop him," I said, more softly. "But I can slow him down. Give you time to figure out some other plan and evacuate people from the Scrag before they get dosed with even more aether dust. Try to negotiate with Saventry."

Jasper's blue eyes burned into mine. "No. There has to be another way. What about your third power?"

I gave a hollow laugh. "The third power that hasn't bothered to show up any of the other times I've been in mortal peril? I'm not counting on it. Besides, there's no power that could help strike six different . . ." The words froze on my lips. I turned to Jasper. "Remember when I asked you what the runes on Sword meant?"

"Yes," he said. "It was 'more numerous action, more numerous strengths.' Or perhaps, 'The more I am wielded, the more power I have.'"

I held Sword in front of me, staring into the blade. "It's like you said, Sophie. One person can't fix everything. But maybe *six* people can." My pulse thrummed as I stretched the blade out between us. "Sophie, put your hand on the hilt. Blythe, Cora, Nora, Willow, you too. Just make sure you're holding it. Everyone got a grip?" The other girls exchanged looks of confusion but did as I asked.

I hesitated. "It might be deadly dangerous. Are you all willing to be heroes? To help stop Gideon?"

"Of course," said Sophie, echoed by Blythe, while Nora nodded and Cora whooped and Willow asked, "Do you really think I can?"

"You can," I said. Then I closed my eyes, reaching out to those faint voices in the back of my skull, the one that had welcomed me, the one that seemed to whisper even now, though I couldn't make out the words. *This is what I need,* I told it. *Please. I don't need another power. I need this. I need help.*

I felt a shiver. Not just my wishful thinking, either, because Sophie and Blythe jumped too. Then a flash, as bright as the one that had blazed up when I first touched Sword. A ringing like festival bells in my ears. Blythe shouted. Sophie yelped.

Cora swore and Nora gasped. Willow sighed, as if waking from a wonderful dream. Something bright and sharp glittered between us. I blinked the stars from my eyes to see what it was.

I still held Sword. Its blue gems winked at me from the hilt, between the spread wings that formed the cross guard. But there were five other swords crossed over it, each of them gripped in the hand of one of the other girls. Five more gems winked up, black, white, gold, green, red. The cross guards were slightly different as well. Some of the birds worked into the metal had shorter beaks, or longer necks. Nora's looked like a swan, and Blythe's was obviously some sort of bird of prey. Sophie's sword was a raven, and Cora's a finch.

"Look!" said Willow, brandishing her blade proudly. "Mine's a hummingbird!"

I grinned at Jasper, who was watching it all with a look of deep amazement. "Still think it's impossible?"

A slow smile spread over his face. "Yes. But now I think you can actually *do* the impossible."

"There he is! Over by that cauldron," I called to Sword as we swooped above the new factory. The structure was enormous, with tall towers fencing in a vast open work floor filled with giant mallets, wide conveyor belts, and at the very center, something that looked like a column of bright red crystal. "Hurry!"

A hungry spark ran along the edge of the blade, and we sped even faster. The Gideon Knight stood directly in front of the crystal, metal hands outstretched, sending an unbroken stream of white-hot flame into it. He gleamed bright and cruel as blood, brutal and terrible. And if we didn't stop him, there were going to be a hundred more just like him.

"Freeze!" I shouted. A bolt of ice crashed down, smashing into him.

The Gideon Knight roared, staggering back. He searched the sky until his eyes found me. Then the king's voice rumbled out. "I warned you, Nightingale. You cannot stop this."

"I think I can," I called out, as I sent two more bolts of ice at him, making him do a ponderous sort of dance to evade them.

"Closer," I whispered to Sword. "We need him to follow us!" The sword waggled at me, then brought us down, flying a loop just under the knight's nose. Gideon snarled, trying to catch us, but the blow missed.

"Good," I said, "Now, up!"

But Sword was already doing another pass, this time skimming just along the knight's backside, where it paused to thwack the metal monster. Gideon launched himself into the air, rising ponderously but steadily toward us.

Sword started to dive at him, blade already frosting, but I hissed, "No, we need to stick to the plan. Remember?" The sword tilted lackadaisically as we halted midair. "I'm serious," I said. "We need to get him up into the clouds so the others can do their part!" Another tilt. "Are you jealous?" I asked. "You know you're still my favorite, Sword, right? You're the original. And you're the only one with a blue gem. And blue is the best color."

The sword perked up at this, and abruptly we were sailing up, up, up. We left the factory behind, soaring out over the open waters of the Rhee. I looked behind me to check that Gideon was following.

"I'm going to break your wings and wring your neck, you miserable girl," came a thunderous snarl. He was flying more quickly now, rising toward us, wreathed in smoke and fury.

All right then. He was definitely following.

Higher and higher we soared, into the thick tumble of woolly clouds. "Slow down a little," I said. "Good. Just enough to get him to—urk!"

With a burst of speed, Gideon had barreled up through the blanket of mist to catch me. One great metal hand clamped onto my waist and jerked me close.

"Foolish girl. You just don't seem to understand," said Gideon. "You try and try, but you can't defeat me. None of the Nightingales ever have. And you're all alone."

"No," I said. "I'm not, actually."

Color blurred at the edges of my vision. Red, gold, white, black, green.

One by one, the other girls descended from the veiling clouds. Blythe, triumphant and bold. Cora, her eyes flashing with fierce mischief. Willow, practically quivering with energy.

Nora, adding a graceful loop-the-loop around her sister as she dove into position. And Sophie, brave, determined, unconquerable, flying straight and true beside me.

Together we'd survived Starvenger. We'd saved Blythe from ghosting. And now we were going to save the world from this arrogant, power-hungry monster.

Five swords dove at five runes, even as I thrust my own beloved, trusted blade straight into the Crimson Knight's heart.

A thunderclap. Not brightness this time, but a black cloud that filled the air, my mouth, and my lungs. I could hear the others coughing. All I could do was cling to my sword, cry for it to carry us free of the stinking cloud. Eyes streaming, I held my breath, until finally a rush of clean air washed over my face. I blinked and found my five friends floating beside me, all of us in a circle, staring down as a thousand fragments of crimson steel rained down over the river, far below.

The Crimson Knight was gone. For good, this time.

"Who's on duty tonight?" called Cora. "Is it Willow?"

"Not me," said Willow, who was over by the window, teasing one of her cats with a bit of string.

"Who, then?"

Nora looked up from the couch where she was working on her geometry lesson and pointed at her sister.

Cora's face fell. "It can't be my turn. I wanted to go to

the cinema. Besides, it's been beastly quiet. Last time I was patrolling, the most exciting thing I got to do was help a woman who was locked out of her apartment. Oh, maybe Blythe will switch with me! Blythe?"

She started toward the door to the room that Blythe and Willow now shared, up in Miss Dashlilly's suite above the soda fountain. "Blythe is at a special practice with her squad tonight," said Sophie, who was busy at the table, painting posters for the next meeting of the Aether Workers' Union. Cora groaned, flopping into one of the squashy armchairs with a long-suffering sigh.

"It's good that it's quiet," I told her. I was at the table too, helping Sophie. Sword was helping as well, or at least, hovering beside me and pointing out whenever I misspelled something.

The other five swords were still a bit more sedate, content to hang in their places on the wall of the living room. Maybe that would change over time. None of us really understood what I'd done when I'd used my third power to create five more Nightingales. Or rather, five more champions. Gallant had six of us now, with the addition of the Swan, the Falcon, the Hummingbird, the Finch, and the Raven. Because the world needed more than just one hero. It needed as many as it could get.

I set down my paintbrush, taking pity on Cora. "I'll do it, Cora. You can take my shift on Thursday instead."

All the other girls had agreed when I'd asked if they were willing to be heroes, but then again, it was probably hard to say no when the fate of your country was on the line. And our lives had changed so much, in so many other ways, in the two months since we had destroyed the Crimson Knight and stopped Project Red.

We were living with Miss Dashlilly now, as her wards. We had comfortable beds, new clothes, and actual classes. Miss Starvenger's boardinghouse was only a dim, unpleasant memory. And yet, every day, we saw other people who were as desperate as we had been. Because even six heroes couldn't change an entire city overnight.

No one knew what had happened to Gideon. We'd looked but had found no body. If he'd survived the destruction of the knight, he was in hiding. And that left Jasper as heir to the throne. Of course, he was still too young to rule, but the Council of Regents seemed to actually be listening to him. He'd managed to make a few changes to the aether factories, with Sophie's advice. And there would be more ahead.

While Pinshaw awaited trial for his crimes, the management of his properties had been entrusted to the Aether Workers' Union. That included what was left of Project Red. For now, the shining new factory remained quiet. Without the power of the Crimson Knight to activate the central core, it was nothing but copper and crystal, according to Jasper. Perhaps one day it could be repurposed, but for now the focus was on refurbishing the current factories to run more cleanly and safely.

Something hummed on the table beside me. The new

aethercom Jasper had installed for our common use blinked red. I clicked it. "Jasper?" I asked. "What's wrong?"

"Oh, nothing much." He sounded breathless. "I was exploring one of the old tunnels under the palace and found a stash of old artificed metal spiders."

"That sounds amazing," Sophie interrupted, leaning over to listen in. "Are they still in good condition?"

"You could say so. In fact, they're in such good condition they're trying to kill me. So, er, could you give me a hand?"

"I'm on my way," I said.

"No fair!" Cora exclaimed. "I turn it over to you and now *you* get the bloodthirsty artificed spiders! Do you want to trade back?" she added hopefully.

I shrugged, smiling at her as I headed for the window, Sword zooming beside me. "No. This sounds like a job for the Nightingale." I hesitated on the sill, looking back. All four of the other girls were watching me with a hopeful expression.

"You know, actually, it sounds like a job for all of us. What are you waiting for?"

ACKNOWLEDGMENTS

Like Lark, I could not have accomplished this feat alone. My endless thanks to R. J. Anderson and Megan Crewe for reading early samples of this book, and for encouraging me through the challenging time in which I wrote it. And particular thanks to Melissa Caruso, who was there to read an early draft at a critical moment, and in doing so helped me find the true heart of the book.

I am so grateful to my wonderful agent, Hannah Fergesen, for unfailing encouragement and editorial insight, as well as to the entire team at kt literary for their efforts and ongoing support.

My excellent editor, Julia McCarthy, provided her wise guidance on matters ranging from the largest plot twists to the smallest choice of words. I am so fortunate to be able to benefit from her brilliance! Thank you to everyone who helped produce this book, including Rebecca Syracuse, Jeannie Ng, Marion Bordeyne, Tatyana Rosalia, Reka Simonsen, and Justin Chanda.

Thank you to my mom, Cynthia, my dad, Paul, and my brother, David, for being a shelter during the stormy summer when I was drafting this book.

And finally, I could not have written this book without the love and support of my husband, Bob.

TURN THE PAGE FOR A SNEAK PEEK AT

THE MIRRORWOOD

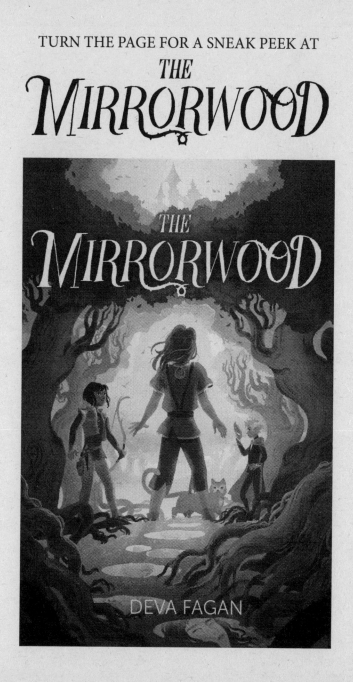

I was wearing my sister Gavotte's face on the night the blighthunters came to our cottage. All eight of us were crowded around the table, waging a fierce poetry battle to decide who would get the last slice of Da's gooseberry pie. Indigo was arguing passionately that "savage" really did rhyme with "cabbage," which is probably why none of us noticed the threat except Sonnet, who didn't care for gooseberries.

"There's someone coming down the lane." Sonnet rose from the table and went to peer through the diamond-pane window beside the door.

A spark of worry nibbled at me. Hardly anyone came all the way out to our farm. We were too close to the Mirrorwood. Our cozy cottage—a bit ramshackle with the extra rooms tacked on over the years to handle three sets of twins—lay on the farthest edge of town. If you stood in just the right spot, you could see the enormous wall of thorns bristling along the northern hills. A prickly promise, meant to bind away the magic of the blighted realm and keep it from tainting the rest of the world.

But it hadn't worked. Magic still escaped. Dribs and drabs, like the spatters of madder and saffron that flecked Mum's apron after a day working her dye pots. Fragments of raw blight that warped whatever—whomever—they touched. Twists, we called them. You might suddenly sprout wings or claws. Your skin might turn to flames or ice.

No wonder folks were scared of it. I would be too. That is, if I weren't already blighted.

For me, the greatest danger wasn't the thorns or the corrupting magic. It was being discovered by those who thought anything touched by the twists had to be destroyed: blighthunters. The crimson-coated warriors trained to fight and kill people like me. But surely there was no reason for hunters to visit our farm.

"Is it Aunt Nesta?" I asked hopefully. She was family. She knew my secret. She was safe.

"No," said Sonnet. Her shoulders were stiff, and there was a note of wary tension in her voice. "There's two of them. Riding horses."

Da and Mum exchanged a look. Mum's lips had gone tight. "Allegra," Mum said to my twin sister. "Best be ready, just in case."

Allegra groaned. "It's not my turn. Can't Fable go upstairs? It's probably just another peddler."

I started to push away from the table. "It's okay. I'll go. But if they're selling charms against the blight, buy me one," I added, trying to make a joke of it.

No one laughed. Indigo was glowering at Allegra. "Ease up, Leg. It's not Fable's fault. One extra day won't do you harm."

"Oh, I know exactly how much harm it does."

She didn't look at me, but I flinched anyway. Allegra was my twin sister, and I knew she loved me. But you can love someone and still be angry at them. Not that I blamed her, after what I'd done to her for the first five years of our lives.

Sonnet, still at the window, drew in a sharp breath. "They're wearing red coats."

No one spoke. No one moved. Hunters wore red.

"Everyone stay calm," said Mum, her voice brisk and businesslike, as if she were negotiating the price of her wool. "We'll handle it like we always do."

A chilly pit had opened in my belly. We'd had close calls with hunters before. Last summer my brother Thespian had to truss me up in a burlap sack and carry me over his shoulder, pretending I was a lumpy sack of turnips, in order to pass a hunter on the road to Aunt Nesta's. But they'd never come to our house. And I hardly ever left our family farm. The last time I'd seen anyone other than family was . . . oh. Oh no.

Last week. I'd been out gathering wild strawberries at the edge of the northern woods. The miller's son had passed by along the old hunters' trail. I'd run as soon as I saw him. But had he seen me?

More importantly, had he seen the face I was wearing?

I couldn't answer those questions. All I could do was try to be what I'd always been: Allegra's identical twin. I gulped, looking at my sister.

"Go on, then, take it." She slid closer along the bench, wearing a look of grim resignation that stabbed me in the gut. It wasn't fair. I didn't want this either. I'd give anything not to be like this.

"Sorry," I whispered, cringing at just how useless the word was, after everything I'd already done to her. Everything my blight had taken. "Sorry" would never be enough.

She only closed her eyes, bracing herself. I reached out to brush my fingers against her cheek.

That was all it took. My curse, my blight, woke hungrily. Buzzing warmth rippled up my arm, my neck, tingling across my face as skin shimmered, bone shifted, and my face reshaped itself. The wavy brown hair I'd borrowed from Gavotte lightened to Allegra's honey blond. My nose shrank, turning snub. A heartbeat later, and no one would have guessed that I was anything other than Allegra's identical twin.

Only my family knew the truth: that I was a blighted face stealer.

Allegra whimpered, gripping the edge of the table as if someone had just torn away a bit of her soul. That was how she'd described it, the one time I dared ask her how it felt. Thespian had tried to tell me it wasn't bad, like standing up too fast and getting a head rush, but I think he was just trying to make me feel better. Allegra always told the truth, even when it hurt.

I scooted back along the bench, giving her space. No one else said anything. Mum and Da had never made a fuss over my face stealing. I think they wanted to pretend it was an everyday thing, like feeding the chickens or washing the dishes. Not a curse that could have me and my entire family imprisoned, or worse.

I ran a hand over my hair. Allegra's hair. It would be fine. Hunters had never visited our house before, but we'd practiced how to handle it. Just act normal. Absolutely normal.

"They've hitched their horses at the post," said Sonnet. Mum went to wait with her by the door, while Da cleared away the dishes and Gavotte covered the last slice of pie with a napkin. Thespian sat at the end of the table, watching me out of the corner of his eye, the way our sheepdogs watched the flock.

I knotted my hands together, feeling utterly miserable. Moth sprang up onto my lap, butting his head against my fingers and purring. I cuddled him closer, his warm weight steadying me, as usual. Making it easier to breathe, to think.

Do not worry, his voice whispered in my mind. *If the hunters try to take you, I will slash out their eyes.*

"My sweet, bloodthirsty fluff," I skritched him between the ears until his purr became a deep drone.

"Oh, yes, talk to your cat," said Indigo dryly. "That'll convince the hunters there's nothing to investigate."

"Lots of people talk to their cats."

Indigo arched a brow. "But how many of the cats *talk back?*"

I ignored them. No one could hear Moth except me, in any case. And right now he was the only thing keeping me from falling into a complete panic.

Sonnet returned to the table, sliding onto the bench

beside me, her shoulder bumping mine. "Remember what I taught you, Fey? If they grab you, go for the eyes. Or the throat. Or the instep." Her hands, resting on her thighs, were clenched into tight fists. It made something sharp claw at my throat. I didn't want my family to have to do this. To risk themselves for me.

Sonnet's eyes fixed on the door. A moment later, a thump rattled the heavy oak.

Mum squared her shoulders, then reached for the handle, swinging it open. "Good evening," she said, her voice cool and calm. "How can we help you?"

"Good evening, madam," said the man on the doorstep. I couldn't see much of him, only the way his tall shadow fell over my mother. His voice was as cool and chilly as deep-buried stone. "Might my apprentice and I come in? I don't wish to trouble your family, but it would help us greatly if we could ask a few questions."

Dread shivered through me. The miller's son. He *had* seen me last week, out by the strawberry meadow.

If I'd been wearing Allegra's face—or any of my siblings', really—I'd have waved and called a hullo. There wasn't such a great difference in size between us, though Sonnet and Thespian had both shot up since they'd turned sixteen over the winter. Even so, I could still pass myself off as them, from a distance.

But that day I had been wearing my father's face. Including his long, luxurious brown beard. I was a good two feet shorter than him, so on me, it fell to my belly button. Indigo said it made me look like an overgrown gnome. So instead of waving and hulloing, I'd run, sprinting off into the woods like a startled rabbit.

I hadn't told anyone about it. The boy hadn't chased after me, so no harm done. Besides, if I told my parents, they might decide not to let me wander the wilds anymore, and I couldn't bear the thought of losing the last bit of freedom I had. It was too dangerous for me to go to town: I couldn't always control my blight, and the last thing I needed was to bump into someone at the market and accidentally steal their face. The farm, the fields, the woods, they were all I had. The only place that I could walk freely, breathe deep, feel like a normal twelve-year-old girl.

Clearly, I was mistaken.

If only I could sprint away now and lose myself in the green woods. But it was too late: Mum had already ushered the hunters inside. It would look suspicious to deny them. I sat stiffly, frozen in fear, as the two crimson-coated figures stepped into the large main room of our cottage. There were several empty chairs, but the hunters ignored them, choosing to stand before the hearth.

All the better to chase after anyone who tried to bolt.

"My name is Telmarque," said the man. He was tall and bony, with white skin and sunken black eyes that made his hollow-cheeked face look disturbingly skeletal. "And this is my apprentice, Vycorax." He nodded to the girl beside him.

She looked about my age, but the firm set of her jaw and

her intent brown eyes made her seem older. So did the sword hanging from her belt. Even the scattering of freckles across her brown cheeks didn't soften her.

Her eyes narrowed. She'd noticed me staring. I jerked my gaze away, desperately hoping she'd think I was just a curious farm girl who'd never seen a hunter up close.

"May we offer you some tea?" asked my father. "And we have walnut cakes." Da probably would have offered tea to the demon prince of the Mirrorwood if he showed up on our doorstep, he was so unfailingly polite.

But Telmarque waved aside the offer. "No. We must attend our work. The evils of the blight do not rest."

Moth settled himself more comfortably into my lap, and I fought a wild, desperate laugh at the irony of it. But there was a sting, too. I didn't think I was evil. But I hurt people. Hurt my own family, every day of every week. So maybe he was right.

Mum cleared her throat. "Then, please, let us know how we can help you be on your way."

"We've had word of a strange creature spotted in the woods near here. A young man from the village encountered it last week. A foul, hairy beast."

I stifled a huff. Da's face might be a bit hairy, but he wasn't *foul*.

The hunter continued. "Small but vicious, he said. He managed to chase it off, but it's still out there." Telmarque's lip curled, and he set one hand on the hilt of his sword as he spoke. "Have any of you seen something like this?"

He fixed each of us in turn with a skeletal stare. The air in the room seemed to have thickened, grown dim and chilly as a winter fog. We all shook our heads.

"Be very certain. We must find this beast and destroy it. We cannot afford to risk the taint spreading."

"Is that how it works?" asked Indigo, innocently arching their eyebrows. "I thought the twists from the woods caused the blight."

"Indeed," said Telmarque. "But anything blighted is tainted with the evil of the Mirrorwood and must be destroyed."

Mum shot Indigo a warning look, but they continued on, irrepressible. "Wouldn't it be better to go after the source? You seem to have plenty of sharp, pointy things. Can't you go inside the Mirrorwood and use them on the demon prince to stop this all for good?"

Silence. A weight like storm clouds settled over the room. Telmarque narrowed his eyes at Indigo. "Hunters have tried. Tried and died. The thorns refuse entry to all, as you well know. This isn't some bard's fantasy."

"Very true," said Indigo. "You're *clearly* not the princess with a heart as pure as snow."

Telmarque's jaw clenched dangerously. Indigo never could resist a sly comment. And worse, they were doing it for me. Defending me. And risking the attention of the hunters in the process.

"I saw something," I blurted out. "Yesterday."

It worked. Telmarque fixed his gaze on me, like a knife

stabbing a choice but slippery bit of meat. "What?" he demanded. "What did you see?"

"I thought it was a bear. It was over to the east, on Hay Hill." I held my breath. Please. Please let them think the foul, hairy beast was only a bear.

The apprentice Vycorax cleared her throat, straightening her shoulders before she spoke for the first time. Her voice had edges, carving out her words, claiming them. "I already searched Hay Hill, sir. There wasn't anything there."

"We'll search again," snapped Telmarque. He gave a curt nod. "Thank you for your time. If we have other questions, we will return."

The words felt like a threat, whether or not he meant them that way. Telmarque strode toward the door. "Come, Vycorax. Let us see what you missed."

The girl stiffened. She glanced at me, the furrow between her brows deepening, before hastening after the elder hunter.

Slowly, Mum closed the door behind them. We sat, not speaking, not moving, as if even a small sound might draw the hunters back. Finally Mum let out a soft sigh. "They're gone. Riding east."

Gavotte punched her twin in their shoulder. "Indigo! What were you thinking?"

Indigo crossed their arms, looking unrepentant. "I was thinking that craven ham-wit ought to stop bullying innocent people and go fight some actual evil if he's so slobbery over it."

Mum sighed. "It would've been better to say nothing at all." She flicked me a worried look.

My heart pinched. "I just wanted them to go," I said. "It'll be okay, won't it? They'll go to Hay Hill and won't find anything. Or they'll just think the boy in the woods saw the bear too."

"Ah, yes, the *bear*," said Da. "You know, I hear that bears are great fans of gooseberry pie." He nudged the last piece toward me, smiling.

But I could see the worry in his eyes. I could feel it all around me, a sticky, sickening heaviness in the air. It matched the fog of fear in my chest. This was my fault. All I'd wanted was to pick strawberries, and instead I'd brought blighthunters to the farm.

"Thanks, Da, but I'm not hungry." I scooped Moth into my arms as I stood. "Besides, Indigo had the best limerick. I'm going to bed."

"It's a clear night," Gavotte offered, watching me in that way of hers, like she could see the color of my thoughts. "You were going to show us the new constellation you found in that book of star charts you're always poring over. The Nose Picker?"

"The Rose Picker," I said, though I was pretty sure she knew the real name. She was trying to make a joke of it, to cheer me up. And I loved her for it. Loved *all* of them.

"Thanks, Gav, but I'm not in the mood for stargazing," I said, retreating up the stairs. "Good night."

My family had always bound tight, protecting me, even

letting me borrow their faces to hide my secret. To keep the red wolves away.

But they couldn't keep me safe forever. Eventually, the wolves would catch me. And if I didn't do something, they would catch my family, too.